VINES OF PROMISE AND DECEIT

A MAGE'S INFLUENCE SERIES

Seeds of Glory and Ruin

Vines of Promise and Deceit

Thorns of Hope and Betrayal

Forests of Grandeur and Malice

And set in the same world:

A MAGE'S APPRENTICE SERIES

Winds of Courage

Storms of Allegiance

Tempests of Truth

VINES OF PROMISE AND DECEIT

A MAGE'S INFLUENCE BOOK 2

MELANIE CELLIER

LUMINANT PUBLICATIONS

*For my brave and caring niece, Jasmine—
you shine bright*

HIDDEN CITY
NOMAD LANDS
KINGDOM OF CALISTA
VIRIDIAN RIVER
CALINARA
ICEBADEN RIVER
LAKE ATERRA
CADENCE'S HOUSE
HUNTING LODGE
KINGDOM OF TARTORA
CELADON RIVER
TARONA
VIRIDIAN RIVER
N
S
E
W

CHAPTER 1

CADENCE

I dropped my spoon into my soup as my nerves jangled. Something wasn't right. It took me a moment to detach my thoughts from my usual worry about my absent sister to focus on the new problem.

Whatever had caused the unsettled feeling, it wasn't immediately obvious. All around me, I felt the presence of power, as I had done ever since my seed was activated. The mages in the dining hall formed such a crowd that their abilities knotted together in a tight clump.

I stretched out further, using the new awareness that had already become second nature. In the halls and rooms of the Guild, an occasional mage was still working or had decided to skip lunch, and the blazing strength of all three affinity heads was easily identifiable in their individual suites. The members of the Triumvirate—the people's voice in Tartora's government —had their meals delivered and didn't need to frequent the Guild dining hall with everyone else.

Alongside the distant mages, servants dotted the Guild building, the faint candles of their weaker abilities moving in all directions as they fulfilled their regular duties. Their weakness might have disqualified them from a Guild apprenticeship and subsequent status as a mage, but their abilities still proved useful in daily life—as my frequent hot baths attested.

After months of monitoring the Mages' Guild for incursions by raiders, the pattern of power was a familiar background to my life—as constant as my concern for Airlie. And although I had only learned to identify the distinct feel of those closest to me, everyone in the Guild had a generally recognizable presence. Enough that none of them would have distracted me from my meal.

Which was how I knew an unknown mage of substantial power had just passed through the palace gates.

I shoved my chair back, standing abruptly. Now that I was paying attention, I realized there was more than one new arrival—several mages of strength had entered together.

My two breakfast companions stopped eating to look at me with varying levels of interest.

"Is something wrong?" Gia sounded concerned.

The crown princess still kept me company in the dining hall every day. Despite her parents' expectations, the passage of several months hadn't diminished her interest in being a normal apprentice.

And Nikolas still followed everywhere his sister led, although he regarded me now with only the faintest trace of surprise and zero concern.

"I just realized...I need to go back to my...I'll only be a minute." My words came out in a jumble, my mind barely conscious of the conversation.

Thankfully Gia accepted my confusing half-sentences with a farewell wave and a promise to meet me after her afternoon lessons. I preferred to keep my words vague and sound like a muddled fool than lie to my best friend—even though the deception was required to ensure my safety.

Within two steps of the table, Gia had faded from my mind,

however. I needed to alert the Guild to the intruders as soon as possible. And I couldn't do that directly.

My eyes met Zeke's across the hall, and I discovered he was already standing, all his attention trained on me. He must have been watching me with half an eye while he ate his own lunch. Had he somehow known to expect trouble today?

I flicked my gaze toward the doors. He nodded and started in that direction.

It was a subtle movement, but I caught Karielle watching me with shrewd, narrowed eyes. I quickly looked away, feeling a faint flush in my cheeks. Karielle had been the one to inform me that Zeke's mother was the most likely candidate to replace the elderly nomad king. When King Fenix died—assuming Zeke's mother was indeed elected in his place—Zeke would become a prince.

It had been a friendly warning, but from her perspective I had utterly ignored it. And I couldn't tell her it wasn't Zeke's good looks or charm that had kept me glued to his side all spring. Only Zeke and I knew he was my influencer—the one who had activated my seed—and therefore bound to train me.

Not that the training had been going particularly well. I pushed the thought from my mind. There were more urgent matters to worry about.

Slipping through the closest external door, I stepped into the manicured gardens that decorated the center of the horseshoe Mages' Guild. Zeke already awaited me next to a weathered gray fountain of indeterminate age. It was an established meeting place since the splash of the falling water helped obscure the quiet murmur of our voices.

"Intruders?" he asked without waiting for me to speak. "Are you sure they're not from the palace? Or a delegation from one of the other guilds?"

I groaned. "Are you ever going to let me live down that one mistake? I've had a lot more practice since then. I can tell the difference between the strong ability of a mage and the weaker one of everyone else. I can't tell you if the new arrivals are a threat, but I'm certain they're mages—unfamiliar ones."

"Where are they right now?" he asked.

I turned my attention to the Guild building, and beyond it, the palace, talking while I searched for their current position. "They came in through the front gate and were stationary for a while in the main courtyard."

"That sounds innocuous," Zeke said. "Considering that's where proper visitors would be found."

I nodded. "They're absolutely saturated with power, though. That's what makes them stand out. It's more than just their abilities, and I can't tell what it's doing. It could be some sort of concealment."

I suppressed a sigh. Surely after months of training I should be able to identify how the power was being used? But neither Zeke nor I could even confirm if it was a usual capability for a power mage, let alone how to do it.

"They're using power right now? That doesn't sound good." Zeke crouched down to place his hand on a vine that curled against the base of the fountain.

"They're moving!" I cried. "But they're not heading for the palace. They're..." I frowned, my heart rate spiking. "They're coming here."

I had expected that piece of news to warrant a response, but Zeke didn't move. Instead he stared hard into the distance, as if listening to something I couldn't hear, his expression slowly changing from concern to a sort of resigned irritation.

"What can you hear?" I asked, my pulse slowing and my sense of urgency disappearing. Whatever conversation was happening on the other end of the vine, it mustn't indicate raiders within the walls.

Zeke remained crouched there for another moment before rising smoothly to his feet. "They're not due until next week, but I shouldn't be surprised. Mother loves to catch both her allies and her opponents off guard."

"Mother?" I gaped at him. "You mean the newcomers are the nomad delegation? But they're not supposed to be here for another—"

"Five days. Yes, I know. That's Mother for you."

I shook my head, trying to assimilate the information. "I thought there was supposed to be a sizable group from three different tribes. So why are there only eight or so of them?"

Zeke's resigned expression disappeared, his sharp gaze focusing on me. "Or so? What does that mean? Can't you tell how many there are?"

I bit my lip, embarrassed he'd picked up on my hesitancy. I took a moment to count again.

"No, there are definitely eight of them. Heading this way. It's a little harder to distinguish their individual abilities with that cloud of power around them. I thought there were nine before, but I must have miscounted in my panic."

Zeke stepped close and put his hands on my shoulders, alarm in his eyes as they captured mine.

"That doesn't sound like you. Forget about the eight coming this way for now. Focus on the rest of the Guild, and even the palace. Are you sure there's no one else out of place?"

His worry rubbed off on me, setting my heart racing again. My stomach churned with the fear I might have missed something crucial. But I pushed aside the shaky feeling and drew a deep breath. Closing my eyes, I stretched out.

The familiar tapestry of power that was the Guild blossomed inside my mind. I sent my awareness racing along the vines of power, skimming over the familiar abilities that glowed inside my consciousness.

"There!" I said the word aloud, although I kept my eyes closed. "There's someone else. He's not with the others."

"That's what I was afraid of." Zeke sounded grim.

My eyes flew open, the blood draining from my face. "He's powerful, too. I don't know how I missed him."

"But you didn't miss him. That's the important thing. Where is he?" Zeke dropped his arms, his body tense, as if waiting for a word from me to go racing off.

"It's like he's hiding himself." I frowned. "But surely that's impossible—it must be coincidence."

"What do you mean hiding himself?" Zeke glanced around, as if he might find the unknown mage under a bush or lurking behind a fountain.

"He should be obvious—he's a powerful plants mage. But he's keeping himself close to other sources of power so he doesn't stand out as much."

Zeke focused in on the important point. "So he's on the move? Which direction?"

I grabbed at his arm. "You can't go after him alone!"

"You said he's a plants mage like me. I can handle him."

I shook my head at his instinctive arrogance. Given his strength, it was understandable.

"It's not just that he's powerful. I think he might not be alone."

"What do you mean?" He looked wary, finally. "You said there were nine."

I bit my lip, not wanting to make another mistake. "I did count nine initially. And I can't be sure—maybe that's all there is. But when he moved just then, for a moment he wasn't near any other source of power. I could sense him more clearly, and it was like..." I worried at my lip. "It's hard to describe. I can't exactly feel another person. I can feel a...shield of some sort?" I sighed. "Maybe that's not what it is. But it's made out of power, and it's large enough to conceal a person's ability."

"A shield of power?" He stared at me, clearly torn.

My voice dropped, uncertainty clawing at me. "There's... something wrong with it."

"With the shield?"

I shrugged helplessly. "I don't know how to describe it. It's definitely power, but it doesn't feel right." I touched my head, nearly overwhelmed by a sudden dizziness that got worse the harder I tried to focus on the strange power.

After a moment, I shook my head. "I can't explain it any better than that. But I don't think you want to go running into that shield."

The sound of voices and footsteps made us both start and look up, stepping away from each other in unison. I grimaced. Could we have looked more guilty?

"Zekiel!" The call from across the courtyard somehow managed to convey both affection and command.

Zeke gave a barely audible sigh, before calling back, "Mother!"

He started toward her at a fast stride, and I had to trot to keep up. The eight new arrivals wore long, flowing robes with varying levels of decoration. The most elaborate of them—in richly embroidered garments of deep maroon—was a tall woman with warm glowing skin and a noticeable family resemblance to Zeke.

She held her arms out in a gesture of welcome, and Zeke moved directly toward her, with me still trailing behind. Given their unexpected arrival, no Tartoran dignitaries, royals, or even mages were in attendance, although a small cluster of flustered looking people in blue and gold livery bustled around, clearly trying to herd the nomads back toward the palace.

Zeke's mother ignored them entirely, all her attention on her son. Given she had headed straight for the Guild, rather than the palace, she had clearly made him her first priority on arrival. It was a warming gesture, but Zeke didn't look particularly pleased.

"You're not supposed to be here yet," he said as soon as we were close enough for normal speech.

"Can you blame me for hurrying to see my only son?" Her rich tones bore a slight hint of amusement. "Much can be forgiven a mother who has been separated from her child."

Zeke's face suggested he didn't buy her explanation, although he closed the remaining distance between them readily enough.

I had spent months anticipating my meeting with Annora, head of Tribe Nicabar. But now that she was here, my attention was divided. Tracking the intruder—or two—who had slipped in alongside the nomads was proving difficult.

The suspicious plants mage had somehow positioned himself near Drake, Master of the Elements. And since the head of the elements affinity was with his apprentices, the cluster of strong mages created an almost solid blaze of power.

An unwelcome voice in my mind whispered that it was the perfect hiding place for another mage. But I brushed the thought aside—such a hiding place would only be necessary if the intruder knew a power mage would be tracking them. And surely that was impossible.

Zeke had reached his mother, but he didn't embrace her, instead giving a deep bow. She chuckled, reaching out her arms and pulling him close.

"I've missed you, Son," she said.

"And I've missed both you and the tribe." He bestowed his blinding smile on all eight of the nomads present.

Several of them called greetings of their own, smiles on every face, but I could see Zeke's heart wasn't in his usual charming facade. He was as distracted as I was.

I stepped closer, despite the awkwardness of intruding on such a moment, and he slipped out of his mother's embrace.

"Greetings, Tribe Nicabar." I gave a half bow, grateful for the etiquette lessons we had all been receiving in preparation for the upcoming tour. Thanks to that instruction, I knew it was appropriate to greet the head of a tribe as representative for the whole. "I believe Master Drake is on his way to welcome you."

Given his sudden flurry of movement, apprentices trailing like a constellation behind him, I assumed some palace staff member had just reached him with news of Annora's arrival.

Zeke dropped back a step, and I leaned toward him.

"I don't know how," I breathed, too quietly for the others to hear, "but the intruder is with him."

Zeke angled toward me, his brows drawing together. I flicked my eyes to the main door in the elements wing of the Guild, conscious that Annora watched us with keen interest. He swung his gaze that way in time to see the set of stately double doors burst open.

The tall figure of Drake emerged, striding into the courtyard with all the authority of his age and position. Following only steps behind was a small crowd comprised of his apprentices, other elements mages they had gathered on the way, and a number of servants in blue and gold livery.

Zeke tensed, his eyes running over the people pouring out the door, ready to spring when the intruder appeared. But after a moment, he looked back at me with confusion in his eyes. There was no one out of place.

I frowned, equally bewildered. "He's there! But I don't..." I trailed off, concentrating. The milling crowd made it hard to match the view before my eyes with my sense of the many abilities.

One of the men in blue and gold took a step in our direction, and I clutched Zeke's arm.

"That's him!" I hissed. "He's dressed as a servant!"

Zeke didn't hesitate. The man's eyes came up to meet mine, and he broke into a sprint. But Zeke moved equally quickly.

They collided in the center of the courtyard, long before the man could reach either me or the nomad delegation. Zeke tackled him around the middle, sending them both crashing to the ground.

The intruder—who couldn't possibly be a servant with an ability that blazed that brightly—swore loudly. Chaos erupted around us as several people in the crowd screamed.

Some fled back to the building while others rushed toward the two plants mages struggling in the dirt. Already vines had sprung from the earth, wrapping around one and then the other as they fought for supremacy.

Drake, who had almost reached the nomads, turned back to identify the source of the commotion. At the same moment, Annora stepped forward, anger and determination making her even more formidable.

Neither of them spoke, but a strong wind sprang up, rushing toward the combatants, while simultaneously, a single, thick vine sprouted from the ground and lashed toward the intruder. The wind was Drake's, so the vine must belong to Annora. Clearly Zeke's mother was also a plants mage.

The intruder shouted, somehow slipping out of the grip of the clinging vine. With one desperate spin, he turned them both, thrusting Zeke into the brunt of the wind, so that Zeke's body created a small windbreak for his attacker.

Once again, the intruder's eyes met mine across the distance. The determination in his had been replaced with resignation as he thrust a dramatic hand toward us.

Only a single deep rumble gave warning before the ground beneath us split, sending Annora, Drake, and me tumbling down into the newly formed chasm.

CHAPTER 2

CADENCE

"Cadence!" Zeke screamed my name as I fell.

My stomach dropped, my mind scrambling to function as my body began to tumble. All around me power flared. Reaching out for it was as easy as breathing. But how could I use it to break our fall?

For a horrible half-second, my mind went blank. Then my instincts kicked in, fueled by months of study with Zeke. The details around me came into focus, and I sucked in a shuddering breath.

Invisible lines, like a network of roots, spread through the earth, thrusting it apart as the chasm cracked open deeper and deeper. A different root system—one that glowed with the similar light of a second plants mage—attempted to bring the earth back together. Annora was fighting to wrest back control of the ground. And all around us, noticeably different from the roots of plants mage power, bright vines of elements power snaked through the chasm, gathering air around each of us to slow our fall.

I didn't need to work out how to use the power on the world around me. Far more experienced mages were already doing it. All I had to do was help them.

I seized the power in the first root network and yanked it away from the earth beneath us. Thrusting it toward the power of Drake and Annora, I shaped it to mimic theirs, strengthening their efforts.

The earth creaked and groaned, the crack no longer growing beneath us. For half a breath, my feet brushed against the bottom of the chasm, and then Drake's newly strengthened bubble of air sent me soaring upward.

Racing at our heels, the earth closed again, Annora's power now bolstered by that of the intruder instead of fighting against it. But as we neared the surface, our progress slowed. The intruder had withdrawn from the battle which meant I was no longer receiving a stream of new power to augment the efforts of the other two.

We continued to rise, however, a gentle cushion of air propelling me the final distance and depositing me in a crushed garden bed. A last rumble from the earth sounded as the ground closed back together, leaving only a jagged line of disturbed dirt to show where the chasm had been.

I gulped, dropping slowly to my knees and then to all fours as I took deep, gasping breaths.

"Cadence?" Zeke knelt beside me. "Are you all right?"

I nodded wordlessly, fighting against my heaving stomach. When it settled, I glanced up at him, nodding again in response to the half worried, half proud look on his face.

At first Zeke had struggled with teaching me. Without any idea how power mages were supposed to function, he had been at a loss when I couldn't understand how to use the power I so easily gathered. For a while, we had been forced to focus on my most basic ability—sensing the people around me and the vines and roots of power that sprang from them. It had been an important first lesson given my secret role surveilling the Guild.

But eventually it occurred to me that I didn't need to work out how to shape the power myself if I used someone else as a guide. In the weeks since then, I had spent many hours practicing the trick with Zeke. He had performed every type of feat he could think of while I augmented his efforts using leftover power I could seize from around the Guild. It didn't matter what he did—as long as I could follow his pattern, I could mimic it.

Unfortunately I had yet to manage any of the feats on my own, but at least I was able to harness my power for something useful. With my help, he had performed acts he could never have managed on his own due to the limits of his strength. I was like a second pair of arms coming in to help him move his bed—except the amount of leftover power in the Guild made me more akin to the strongest weightlifter ever known. While Zeke seemed sure there must be a limit to my strength, we had yet to find it.

But this had been my first attempt to suck away power as another mage expended it, instead of merely skimming up their leftovers. It had been surprisingly easy, although that might have been due to the intensity of my need. Most people could perform unexpected prodigies when their life depended on it.

I glanced across at Annora and Drake and winced. If their appearance was anything to go by, I must look completely disheveled. But they, at least, were upright and calling commands. Groaning, I forced myself onto my feet.

Zeke put a steadying hand under my elbow.

"Did it work?" he whispered. "Did you help them?"

When he had shouted my name as we fell, it probably sounded like concern to everyone else. I just hoped his mother had been too occupied to notice and didn't resent that his first thought was apparently for me. She had no way of knowing he had actually been shouting for me to remember my training.

I nodded. "Thank goodness Drake and your mother were there. Helping them was easy, thanks to all our practice."

"See!" He grinned broadly. "I told you it was a useful skill."

His mother caught his eye, her brow lowering at his inappropriate response to the moment.

He let me go and hurried over to join her. I once again trailed behind, wondering why everything felt so sore when I had never actually hit anything. Apparently I had tensed every muscle I possessed on the way down.

"You did an impressive job identifying the threat, Zekiel," she said, a note in her voice I couldn't read. "And I'm told you've been guarding the entire Guild! Clearly your time here has been well spent. I never dreamed you were capable of such feats."

Zeke stiffened slightly. But although he didn't look in my direction, his mother's eyes flicked briefly to me before returning to her son. My heart, barely recovered, began to race again, but her next words had nothing to do with me.

"It would have been nice if you'd managed to hold on to our attacker, however." She said the words mildly, despite the criticism. "It appears he's escaped."

Zeke grimaced. "I was only distracted for a moment, but it was long enough for him to slip out of my grasp. He bolted immediately, and since half the Academy took off after him, I stayed to see if you needed help." He gave her a cheeky look. "Surely a son can be forgiven for worrying about his mother."

"His mother. Yes." She raised an eyebrow, but her expression softened, and after a moment she sighed. "I suppose you can hardly be blamed in the circumstances. We must hope those who pursued him have been successful."

"What have you done to my garden, Annora?" The sharp voice made us all spin toward the wing on the opposite side of the courtyard.

A short woman with unlined golden skin but gray in her sleek, black hair stood behind us. She eyed the visible line in the dirt and the crushed garden with disfavor.

Annora, however, grinned broadly. "Master Augusta! It's a pleasure to see you again after so long."

The Master of Plants, head of the plants affinity at the Tartoran Mages' Guild, continued to eye her for a moment before a smile spread across her face.

"You were always a troublemaker, Annora. But then my breathless apprentices inform me this was not your doing."

"No indeed, Augusta." Drake frowned across the ruined garden, half his attention still on the gates, as if he was considering going after the team of people who had pursued our attacker. "Annora was the one to seal the chasm."

Augusta's brows drew together. "Chasm?"

"It went deep," Zeke said to his influencing mage in a concerned voice. "Far deeper than should have been possible."

His mother nodded. "For a moment even I struggled to counteract his efforts." She inclined her head toward the Master of the Elements. "And I'll admit to being grateful Drake was present to cushion our fall. Although I soon gained mastery over the chasm itself, I was glad not to have to worry about catching myself as well."

Zeke's brows drew together, his eyes flying to mine. I shrugged slightly, still hanging back, not wanting to draw anyone's attention.

"How could he be so powerful?" Zeke asked, and I understood his unspoken thoughts.

Annora was a plants mage of great strength. Even before I met her and sensed her power, I had known she must be—due to both the strength of her son and her position as head of a tribe of great renown. And yet she had struggled at first to match the strength of our attacker. She thought she had subsequently mastered him with ease, but she didn't know of my assistance. Zeke, however, did.

"It is impossible," Augusta said flatly. "The raiders cannot possess a mage of such strength."

"Beside the General," Drake said, a look I couldn't read passing between the two masters.

I frowned. On the night of the raiders' full-scale attack on the Guild—the night my sister disappeared—there had been a mage present of enough strength to smell people on the air. Considering Airlie had been hailed as the first mage with such an ability in two generations, I didn't share their certainty of the weakness of the raiders. But it didn't seem like the moment to insert myself in the conversation.

And perhaps it had been the General himself who had searched for us that night. Smelling the air was an elements ability, and he was an elements mage.

"Clearly what happened was not impossible," Annora said briskly. "I can assure you none of us imagined the ground opening beneath our feet."

Her glance encompassed both Drake and myself, and I froze at the keenness of her gaze as it rested on me. Her eyes moved on within a second, but I was left with the uneasy impression that I hadn't been avoiding notice after all. Like her son before her, Zeke's mother was far too inclined to see me.

Given the timing of Airlie's disappearance, and the protective role she had agreed to take on, only Evermund's influence kept her from being labeled a traitor—and me along with her by association. He housed and fed me and, in return, I tried not to cause trouble by drawing too much attention to myself. The powerful mages of the Guild didn't need reminding of my unwelcome presence.

A clamor of voices at the Guild gates sent Drake hurrying away from us. He met the mixed group of guards and mages part way across the courtyard, their conversation too low for us to overhear. But there was no mistaking the thunderous look growing on his face or the absence of a prisoner in their midst.

Annora's delegation closed protectively around her, leaving Zeke free to sidle up to me.

"He *was* powerful, wasn't he? It wasn't some trick? There weren't other raiders concealed somewhere helping him, or..."

"Unfortunately, no. He was at least as powerful as your mother."

"And what about me?" he asked, trying to sound casual. "Am I more or less powerful than her?"

I rolled my eyes. "It's not that exact. You're both powerful mages, that's all I can tell you."

"Really, Cadence?" He gave me a woebegone look. "You couldn't have had pity on my ego and claimed the glow of my power might be a little stronger?"

I gave him a small shove. "Hardly. The last thing you need is a bigger ego."

He chuckled, and my eyes involuntarily flicked to his mother. When I caught her looking in our direction, I took the smallest step away from him. His gaze followed mine, the humor dropping from his face.

But before any of us could respond further, Drake reached us, the pursuers clustered around him.

"He escaped," he announced, anger in his voice and on his face.

Augusta raised a forbidding eyebrow, her gaze seeming to land on every single person in the crowd around Drake.

"How is that possible?" she asked in a cold voice.

"I won't have you blaming any of my people." A guard captain I recognized pushed to the front of the group, the guards in the crowd moving immediately toward him as if he offered shelter. "I've just spoken to the most senior guard who was part of the pursuit, and they couldn't have foreseen what happened."

"And what exactly did happen?" Annora asked, cutting in before anyone could protest.

"They chased him as far as the river, intending to trap him there," Captain Huxley said, meeting her gaze steadily. "It's an established procedure. My people are trained not to provoke fights with mages around crowds of civilians. And with the

Viridian running alongside the city, it provides a convenient barrier for all but elements mages. Given your attacker had already shown himself to be a plants mage, the elements mages among my people expected the water to be a tool in their favor."

"Expected?" Annora asked. "I take it events did not transpire as hoped."

"They did not." Captain Huxley's voice stayed steady, no note of apology or hint of weakness creeping in. "But they couldn't have foreseen it, as I said."

An elements mage of medium strength stepped forward from the growing crowd, directing his comments toward the head of his affinity.

"I've certainly never seen a plants mage do the like."

Another stepped forward to join him. "Or an elements mage, if we're honest."

Drake frowned, his brows drawing closer and closer together.

"Would it be too much to ask that you illuminate the rest of us as to exactly what happened?" Annora asked in a commanding tone. "I would like to know the fate of the man who attempted to assassinate me the moment I arrived in Tarona."

I flinched slightly, but only Zeke beside me seemed to notice, and he stayed silent. The two mages did likewise, both of them looking to Captain Huxley, relief on their faces when he resumed the story on their behalf.

"By all accounts, upon reaching the river, the intruder stepped into a small vessel he must have concealed there previously. As soon as he did so, it was whisked away—upriver—at impossible speeds. By the time any of them even realized what was happening, he was long gone."

"The boat moved upriver at high speed?" Augusta looked between the two elements mages with lowered brows.

When they both nodded, she looked to Drake. "He can't have reversed the flow of the river. Even if he had been an elements mage, such a feat would require too much strength. Even you could not accomplish it. But a tight stream of air, perhaps? An elements mage might do the job in such a way, but I thought he had a plants affinity?"

Drake frowned. "Only a plants mage could have opened the earth the way he did. So a jet of air like you describe is out of the question. Although air is one of our specialties, I don't think anyone in my affinity could call a flow of sufficient strength so quickly—or hold it with such sustained force. The Viridian flows strongly at this time of year."

"While he couldn't have changed the flow of the entire river, what about a narrow stretch of water, just on the surface?" one of the elements mages suggested, clearly caught up in the academic question. "That would require far less strength."

Drake frowned, his eyes narrowing as he looked between Annora and Augusta. "It is a question my affinity will consider further. Clearly this man was a plants mage cross elements, so it is possible there is some twist to his ability we have not yet encountered." His gaze flicked to Captain Huxley. "There is always an element of unpredictability when someone comes under an influence other than their own affinity."

Although his tone and look suggested the captain was somehow to blame for not foreseeing and planning for the unexpected, Huxley's manner remained implacable.

Annora broke the tension, inclining her head in agreement with Drake's words. "I, myself, have found great value from having my plants seed activated by a healing mage. I find being plants cross healing gives me a range of flexibility I would not otherwise have achieved. But it seems in this case such flexibility was used against us. We must be more wary in the future."

Drake rumbled his agreement, while Augusta's brows drew tightly together. The two of them exchanged a look as Captain Huxley stepped forward with a respectful bow toward Annora.

"May I suggest we move toward the palace?" he said. "I'm sure King Marius will be eager to welcome you to his kingdom. And we cannot delay informing him of this attack—along with the remaining Triumvirate member, of course. Extra defenses will naturally be..." His voice trailed away as he moved out of earshot, the nomads and the two masters accompanying him.

I sent my extra sense ahead of them, identifying Colton—the Master of Healing and third member of the Triumvirate, alongside Drake and Augusta—in the palace with both the king and Evermund. They had likely gathered to welcome the unexpectedly early contingent of nomads, not yet aware of the attack.

As the three most powerful mages in the kingdom, the Triumvirate not only led the Mages' Guild but also represented all the guilds. The king did not have authority to govern without their input, and Evermund—the Royal Mage—stood as liaison between them. All of them would be expected to greet a visitor with as much status as Annora.

Some of the mages followed behind them, while the rest of the crowd slowly spread across the courtyard. Zeke, however, stayed put, watching me with searching eyes.

"You look worried. Do you think he'll be back? He can hardly sneak up on you, of all people. In fact, if you hadn't been here, he might have succeeded in his aim."

"And what was his aim?" I asked in a small voice, distracted for a moment from my concerned thoughts.

Zeke glanced around us, lowering his voice. "You don't think he was here to assassinate my mother? He certainly went straight for her. The raiders can't like the idea of a new alliance between the nomads and the Tartorans. They're sheltering in the fallen kingdom, and Calista has more borders with the nomads than Tartora. An alliance would help King Marius in his determination to see an end to the raiders."

I grimaced, trying not to sound nervous. "I hope that's what everyone else saw."

Zeke frowned. "What do you mean?"

"He was looking straight at me, Zeke," I whispered. "I think he was coming for me, not your mother. If she was his target, he could have struck before she was surrounded by a guild full of mages. He slipped into the palace alongside her delegation, remember?"

Zeke's eyes widened. "Do you think he only made a move because you detected him? Perhaps he hoped to catch you when you were alone and abduct you like they did to Airlie."

A surge of warmth toward Zeke gripped me. He must be one of the only inhabitants of the Guild who would reference Airlie's abduction as fact. Although they didn't say so outright —at least not to me or to Evermund—most of the mages believed she had absconded by choice. After one of the guards reported seeing a girl in a blue gown leaving the palace grounds part way through the festivities in company with a handsome young man, everyone decided Airlie had been sick of the demands put upon her due to her incredible strength and had chosen an easier life.

"He was hiding," I whispered, voicing my real concern.

"In the servants' livery, you mean?" Zeke ran a hand along his jaw. "I wonder how he sourced it? I suppose it can be done in the city easily enough."

I shook my head. "No, he was hiding from me."

"From you?" Zeke stared at me.

"Remember what I said by the fountain? All his movements were designed to keep him hidden from a power mage. He could have walked through the palace gates at any time, but he waited for the arrival of the nomads because it gave him a chance to enter alongside other unknown mages of significant strength. If he had come in alone, I would have sensed him immediately. But alongside the delegation, I almost missed him. I would have missed him if you hadn't made me double check."

I took a deep breath. "They definitely know about my ability, Zeke. That's why they're coming for me." I gulped. "And they're not going to stop, are they? How many other powerful mages can they possibly have?"

"Surely not many." His brows creased. "I just wish we knew how they got the one—even if it was his cross ability that gave him the edge."

"But it wasn't."

The lines on Zeke's face deepened. "What do you mean?"

"That man was definitely a straight plants mage. I have no idea how he disappeared up that river, but he wasn't plants cross elements. I couldn't say anything earlier because how would I explain to the others how I knew?"

Zeke shook his head. "But that makes no sense. Even being cross elements, his escape was already inexplicable. If what you're saying is true..."

"It is," I said firmly. "I'm sure of it. Living at the Guild, I have plenty of experience sensing all variations of abilities. I can easily tell a mage with a straight ability compared to one who is cross-influenced. You know that."

For a moment we stared at each other wordlessly. Slowly, the concern in Zeke's eyes grew.

"What then? Did he have help?" His eyes widened. "Wait! You said there was someone else with him—someone shielded. So, were they the one to help him escape—or are they still here?"

CHAPTER 3
CADENCE

"Cadence! Zeke!" Gia's call made us both start and turn toward the door that gave access to the apprentice section.

Wedged between the elements and healing wings, it was small and unadorned, located on the far side of the courtyard. We waited as our friend raced toward us, Nikolas on her heels.

"Is it true?" She came to a halt in front of us, her eyes round and her face flushed with excitement. "Are the nomads here early? Was there an attack?"

"Don't sound so hopeful." Zeke looked amused.

Could the twins see the strain behind his humor? I hoped not.

"How could Gia resist excitement of any variety?" Nikolas asked in a long-suffering voice.

His sister just rolled her eyes, not letting his attitude depress her suppressed energy. "Are you both all right? Someone said Zeke detected the intruder and fought him off."

I groaned. "Why am I not surprised that's the story already circulating? Next people will be saying Zeke single-handedly closed the chasm and chased him to the river as well."

"The chasm? So it's true that he split the ground?" Her expression changed, growing thoughtful and concerned.

"The raiders shouldn't have a plants mage that powerful," Nikolas said grimly. "Where did they get him?"

"Get him?" I stared between them. "You think the General kidnapped a mage from Tartora? Or the nomads, perhaps?"

"It wouldn't be the first time, would it?" Zeke gave me a significant look.

"I haven't heard any reports of missing mages." Gia frowned. "But the raiders have been taking people from some of the border villages. We'd heard stories from before you came to the Guild, but after Airlie was taken, Evermund pushed for a full investigation. Father has only just received confirmation."

Horror washed over me. "That's awful! But surely our attacker couldn't have been abducted. Why would he be working for them in that case? Unless..."

I stopped talking, dire possibilities filling my mind. Perhaps the raiders had some way to force compliance—or even brainwash their abductees.

What was happening to Airlie right now?

"Airlie is strong," Zeke said, seeming to read my mind. "And I don't just mean her ability. From the few weeks I knew her, it was clear she's mentally tough as well. She's not going to start working for the raiders."

I smiled weakly, appreciating his reassurance while also feeling guilty for the twang of irritation that shot through me at his compliment about Airlie. What kind of person could feel resentment toward a sister who might be dead, for all I knew? But somehow it still hurt to be reminded that she was so memorable, while I had become adept at fading into the background.

"If the nomads are here already, where's your mother?" Nikolas asked Zeke, pulling me out of my moment of unpleasant introspection.

"They're not all here," he replied. "Only my mother and some of the delegation from our tribe. Captain Huxley escorted them to the palace. I'm sure your parents have been alerted to their arrival by now and were waiting to greet them."

"Of course they're at the palace." Nikolas gave Gia an irritated look. "I told you we should have gone straight there. We were supposed to be part of the group greeting the nomads."

She glared at him. "How could I go rushing off to the palace to meet dignitaries when my best friends have just been involved in a life and death struggle with a violent attacker?"

Nikolas didn't look impressed with her argument. "Well, now you've seen they're both fine. We need to go."

"Will you come with us?" Gia looked at Zeke. "Your mother must be eager to spend time with you if she came straight to the Guild."

"So it would appear. Although I notice there's no sign of her now." He hesitated, glancing at me.

"You all go," I said quickly. "I've got enough to do here."

Zeke lingered, looking at me with a torn expression. I could tell he wanted to go with them to find out more information—Zeke always liked to know everything that was going on. But he also didn't want to leave me.

"Really, I'll be fine." I gave him a shove in Gia and Nikolas's direction. "I'll be safely locked in my room avoiding getting caught up in raider assassination attempts."

Gia shuddered, seeming to accept my words at face value, and Zeke relaxed slightly. Had he been picturing me wandering around the Guild, poking my nose into cupboards? As my influencing mage—and therefore trainer—he, of all people, should know that wasn't necessary. I had built up my range enough to complete a sweep of the grounds from any location within the walls.

But as I allowed my friends to escort me to my room—the one that had once belonged to Airlie—a brief wave of dizziness hit me. I paused halfway across the courtyard, looking back. It was gone as quickly as it had come, and the instinct to search for it pulled at me.

I reached out, hunting for anything out of place. An elusive shadow flitted across my awareness, something unfamiliar and tainted. Just brushing against it provoked a queasy feeling. Could it be some strange power lingering from the recent battle?

I hesitated, wanting to investigate further, but the sensation had faded. I couldn't even be sure what direction it had come from.

"Cadence?" Gia had also stopped, looking back at me inquisitively. "Is everything all right?"

I shook myself and hurried to join her. Whatever I had felt, it was gone now. And if it was true the raiders were after me— and one of them might have remained behind—then it would be inexcusably foolish of me to wander around alone, attempting to seek them out.

"I can stay," Zeke whispered as I hesitated in my doorway.

I shook my head. He hadn't seen his mother in over a year. He should be with her now. And it would certainly look strange to the royal family if he chose to stay with me instead.

"I won't leave this room until you get back," I promised. "But you should go."

He looked reluctant still, making me wonder again at the complicated dynamics I had glimpsed between him and his mother. He had always spoken of her with affection, so there must be real love between them on some level.

"Go!" I pushed him out of the doorway, and he relented with a final warning look, following the twins down the path toward the closest palace entrance.

I stayed in the door long enough to catch his backward glance in my direction before firmly shutting it behind me and turning the lock. The door that connected the room to Evermund's suite had been permanently secured before I moved in, so there were no remaining entrances. Evermund had even asked a plants master to reinforce both of them for me, thinking I might be nervous about staying there alone after the attack and my sister's disappearance. But his effort, though kind, had provided little in the way of reassurance. The battle had only made me confident that a determined mage could still access the room.

I didn't feel fear, though. I collapsed onto the bed while I considered the unexpected thrill that shivered down my spine. After all these months of waiting and fearing, the raiders had come. If they had succeeded in abducting me, would they have taken me to Airlie? I couldn't deny the thought had a small, furtive appeal. I had never been apart from my sister before, and her absence gaped inside me like a jagged hole.

I sat up abruptly, shaking off the thought. Airlie had always protected me, and now it was my turn to protect her. I needed to stay free and rescue her, not get myself captured as well. And the first step in that goal was locating the missing raider.

But two hours later I collapsed down again in defeat. No matter how much I concentrated, I could detect only the faintest wisps of a power that felt alien and wrong. Maybe there had never been a second mage at all. Maybe what I had felt had been some sort of object. It seemed impossible—inanimate objects didn't hold or store power, although some could be manipulated by it. But I had already seen the impossible when the raiders used neutralizers—large, seed-like objects that could bind a person's ability. Such a thing must somehow possess a power of its own, however unnatural that seemed.

I shivered at the thought of being so bound. Now that my ability had been activated, I could barely remember what life had been like without it. My memories of before seemed muffled—as if I had been missing a sense as central as sight or hearing. I had no desire to ever encounter a neutralizer again.

But if there was a powerful object hidden in the Guild grounds, I needed to find it. I couldn't imagine where it might be, however. And if the raider had indeed been carrying something like a neutralizer, why hadn't he used it?

I sighed, not moving from my comfortable position, sprawled on the bed. As always, I had more questions than answers. I regarded the ceiling of the room, ignoring the elegant furnishings around me. Had Airlie felt this weight of responsibility when she lay in this bed? Had she felt the heaviness of knowing others relied on her to keep them safe?

I wanted nothing more than to leave the Guild behind and go searching for my sister. But what good could I do her on my own when I had no leads on where she might be found? I had a better chance of eventually helping her by staying with Evermund—one of the most powerful mages alive and the only other person still actively trying to find her. He must have a sense of responsibility as strong as Airlie's to continue the search for an apprentice who had only been under his tutelage a matter of weeks before disappearing completely.

And even if I had a lead, how could I abandon the Guild when I was the one monitoring for intruders? That raider could have been after Annora—or Gia or Nikolas. Or even Zeke. I couldn't be certain I was the only target—it wouldn't have been the first time the raiders tried to combine an abduction and assassination. And to make matters worse, the whole Guild believed Zeke was the one keeping them safe with his network of vines—despite his inability to teach any of the other plants mages how to replicate his supposed feat.

I had overheard Karielle and Bryce discussing the matter several weeks ago. Zeke's trick of eavesdropping using a vine network had been developed by Tribe Nicabar, and from the sound of it, Master Augusta and her apprentices believed he was in trouble with his tribe for revealing their secret. They thought he was acting on instructions from his mother to withhold the information necessary to expand the trick to allow full surveillance.

Karielle had managed to connect to a nearby vine and use it to listen to sounds happening elsewhere on the vine's network. But she was nowhere near being able to surveil the whole Guild. And while Master Augusta wasn't overtly admitting any failure on her own part, her apprentices believed she'd had no more success than them. Of course, neither had Zeke in actuality, but he couldn't tell any of them that.

The thought gave me pause. It must be hard to have your influencing mage and all your fellow apprentices believe you were intentionally misleading them. But Zeke was doing it for my sake, to keep my secret. And he had been protecting me when he revealed his tribe's secret as well. Of course he had also been in danger, along with the twins, but I couldn't help wondering uneasily if the reveal was behind some of the tension between him and his mother.

I worried at my bottom lip. How quickly everything had changed. I had gotten too used to the quiet months following the attack, and I'd let myself believe the raiders were no longer after me now that they had Airlie.

But now, just as Zeke's mother arrived to disrupt everything, I discovered the raiders had merely been biding their time, waiting for the right opportunity to infiltrate the Guild. They must think me a formidable opponent if they believed it necessary to go to such lengths. They were wrong, though. With no experienced power mage to guide me, I was still a long way from unlocking the true potential of my ability.

A knock on the door sent me bolting upright. I hurried over to peer out the window, despite recognizing the feel of the presence outside. It was only her familiarity that had made me overlook her approach, but my last hour had left me sufficiently jumpy that I wasn't taking any chances. As soon as I confirmed Gia was alone, I shook my head and opened the door.

"What are you doing here? Shouldn't you be at the palace with your family? Evermund hasn't returned yet, so the formalities must still be ongoing."

She breezed into the room. "Nikolas stayed behind. He can represent us both."

I looked at her doubtfully. "You're the heir, not your brother. Somehow I suspect they want you."

She shrugged, her expression turning mulish. "They agreed to give me two years as Apprentice Gia, and I'm holding them to it. I did my duty and greeted the new arrivals. They don't need me for everything else."

I hesitated, wondering if I should say something. But after a moment, I shrugged and let it go. Gia was usually friendly and approachable, despite her rank, but she had a tendency to clam up on this topic. Plus I disliked siding with Nikolas over Gia in anything, just on principle.

In the privacy of my mind, I couldn't help agreeing with him on this matter, though. While I deeply appreciated Gia's overtures of friendship toward me, it didn't seem possible to just stop being a royal for two years without ramifications. What would happen when Gia one day took the throne, and the Guild was being run by Karielle and Bryce and the others? Would she regret pushing them to ignore her rank and treat her like one of them?

I pushed the thought aside. I had enough worries for right now without borrowing ones from decades in the future.

A deep bell sounded, not as loud as in the apprentice section of the Guild, but still clear.

"Oh good!" Gia jumped to her feet. "I was hoping I was back in time to eat."

She slipped her arm through mine and tugged me out of the room, leading me across the courtyard.

"Are the nomads offended by the attack?" I asked. "Annora doesn't blame your parents, does she?"

"She seems remarkably relaxed about it, actually. Given how often she referenced Zeke's contribution, she seems to have taken it as an opportunity to showcase her son's skills." Gia laughed, but I couldn't dredge up even a chuckle.

Whatever she was saying now, in the moment Annora hadn't seemed at all convinced Zeke was responsible for identifying the intruder. So what did she think had really happened? Had Zeke told her about me?

The question of what he had told his tribe was one that had occupied my mind for some time. But for some reason I couldn't bring myself to ask Zeke directly. Part of me was afraid of the answer, and part of me just didn't want to deal with the issue. As long as he said nothing, I could proceed as if no one knew but him.

But despite my desire to avoid the matter, the arrival of his mother made it impossible not to acknowledge the questions clamoring at the edges of my brain. Was it possible I was part of the reason the tribes had decided on this unprecedented delegation? Even thinking the idea felt presumptuous, but I couldn't shake the memory of the timing. Zeke had activated me, and the very next thing, the tribes had announced they were coming.

Was it just a coincidence? Or was Annora—potential future queen of the nomads—here to examine me? And, if so, what had she made of the events of the afternoon? Was she mentioning her son's role to the Tartoran royals because she did believe it had been his effort, after all? Or was she trying to flush out anyone else who might know the truth? Or perhaps she was even trying to help us cover up my involvement?

It was too confusing. Without more information, I couldn't come to any reasonable conclusion.

Something niggled at my mind, distracting me enough that I stumbled. Gia jerked to a stop, helping me regain my balance.

"What is it?" she asked.

I paused, my head cocked as I tried to identify the intrusion. But the faint hint of strange power that had brushed against me was gone, the momentary dizziness dissipating almost as soon as it appeared. And though I pushed my senses wide—concentrating as I hadn't earlier—I could feel no further trace of it in any of the Guild buildings or in the gardens.

I shook my head. "Never mind, it's nothing. I just stumbled."

Gia gave me a strange look before squeezing my arm. "You've had a trying day. We shouldn't have left you alone."

I smiled weakly, hoping I looked grateful and not scared. But as we continued on, I couldn't help glancing back. The garden and courtyard appeared just as they always did, although the sections where we had wreaked destruction shone with new layers of leftover power. Clearly some plants mages had used the afternoon to erase the signs of our misadventure.

So why had I felt the strange, twisted power again after finding no trace of it when searching from my room? As Gia towed me into the building, I glanced back for a final time. If the feeling had come from an object, then it must be well hidden somewhere near.

I drew in a steadying breath. I didn't like the idea that a raider might have managed to conceal themselves well enough to stay behind. But the possibility of a neutralizer on Guild grounds wasn't much more appealing, either.

I tried to consider the matter dispassionately but came up short of answers. Surely nobody would stash such an item in a bush. So where was it?

CHAPTER 4

CADENCE

Zeke didn't reappear until lunch the next day. And since Gia and Nikolas were kept away by royal duties, I was left to study alone in the library all morning. I could only assume they were together, occupied with the newly arrived nomads.

It made sense Zeke would be involved in whatever formalities were underway, and it might mean a lot of solitary days for me in the lead up to the tour. I was used to having his company for at least some of each morning, an arrangement that had been formalized when he received permission to tutor me as practice for his first real apprentice.

Evermund had agreed to the suggestion readily, relieved to have such an easy option for keeping me occupied. But I still didn't know why Augusta had consented to release Zeke for those hours. Like the other two Triumvirate members, she usually worked the promising mages under her influence harder than the rest of the Guild apprentices—the cost of receiving such a prestigious placement. Zeke always brushed the matter off, leaving me to wonder if the concession could be attributed to his strength and skill or to his unusual status as a high-ranking nomad.

It was even possible Augusta's concession had been for Evermund's sake, not Zeke's. The Royal Mage considered himself responsible for me, but he had many official duties and might have requested his fellow master assist with keeping me occupied. I certainly wasn't offended if so. What Augusta might not know was that he preferred to spend his limited free time in the search for Airlie—an activity I fully supported. I spent my own free time on the same goal, although I had fewer avenues to pursue than Evermund.

Dwelling glumly on my lack of success with helping Airlie, I walked back toward the dining hall for lunch, still alone. I only made it halfway, however, before I had to grasp a wall to stay upright—hit again by a lightning fast wave of dizziness. It was gone almost before I registered it was there, but my mind pursued it anyway, my efforts focused not on my own balance, but on trying to grasp hold of the elusive sensation. After a moment, I straightened, disappointed. Once again it was gone.

"Cadence! There you are." Zeke hailed me from further down the corridor. As he neared, his expression grew concerned. "What's wrong?"

I shrugged. "Maybe something, maybe nothing." I glanced around, lowering my voice. "I never managed to track down a second raider. Maybe they never existed. But I keep feeling... traces."

"Traces?" He frowned. "Of that strange power you felt?"

I nodded. "It gives me the strangest feeling—like I've brushed against something unhealthy. I've been wondering if our attacker could have left an object behind. Something like a neutralizer, perhaps. But if it is an object, I don't know why I would sense it in the courtyard one day and the corridor the next."

Zeke hesitated. "You can't sense anything more now?"

"No." I sighed. "It's gone again."

"Let's get some food into you, then." He gently prodded me

down the corridor, keeping pace as we reached the double doors.

"This really isn't necessary," I said, as he put a hand under my elbow and guided me to an empty table. "I'm fine."

"What isn't necessary?" Gia asked, appearing behind Zeke with a full tray.

I shot a swift glance at Zeke, but he took her arrival in stride.

"Cadence is feeling a little light-headed. We need to get some food into her."

"Again?" Gia put her tray on the table and pushed it toward me. "Here, have this. I'll get another one."

"Please allow me," Zeke said smoothly, although his brows had drawn together at her initial comment. "I'll bring back food for both of us."

Gia accepted the offer, sliding into the seat next to me with a ready smile and a stream of complaints about her morning.

"It's not as if they needed me there for any of it," she huffed. "They didn't even want me, other than for show. I can just imagine how they would have responded if I'd started giving out opinions."

"I'm sure they'll be interested in your perspective once you're a qualified mage," I offered, unsure what else to say.

"Maybe," Nik grunted as he took the seat on Gia's other side. "Or maybe they'll want her to silently attend meetings for the next thirty to forty years, waiting for her turn to come."

I shot him a glare as Gia's expression turned slightly sick. Anybody would think he was trying to goad her into doing something outrageous.

"I'm sure that's not the case," I said with totally unfounded confidence before curiosity compelled me to add, "Were they discussing the raider attack? What are they going to do?"

"A census." Gia rolled her eyes, snatching a fork off the tray Zeke deftly slid in front of her and scooping up a mouthful of mashed potato. "The most boring possible response to something as provocative as an attack."

"A census?" I looked from her to Nikolas to Zeke. "What kind of census?"

"They want to know where all the kingdom's mages are," Zeke said. "To find out if any are missing. Mother's assured him the rogue mage can't have come from the nomads. There's no way the General could have abducted any powerful mages from among the tribes without word getting out. Tribes are more akin to extended families, and any of them would call on the king for assistance in defending themselves against such an outrage. And he, in turn, would call on the other tribes. So we would all hear of it."

I nodded, although rumor suggested old King Fenix wasn't capable of anything much these days. But no doubt his tribe would act for him, if needed. Each generation, one tribe was elected to guard the nomads' single fixed city—giving up their roving ways in exchange for dominion over all nomad tribes for the span of their leader's life. And apparently uniting the tribes to protect themselves against external threats was included among the ruling tribe's responsibilities.

"So Father fears the General has somehow managed to abduct Tartoran mages," Nikolas finished. "The Mages' Guild has authority over all mages, but they don't actually require all of them to live here at the Guild. Many mages are spread across the kingdom, and some have little contact with the Guild after they graduate from their apprenticeships. As long as they don't cause trouble, they're left alone. Which might turn out to have been a mistake."

"Considering the mages serve all sorts of useful purposes across the kingdom—from healing our people to preserving our crops—it's hardly a mistake," Gia said. "Hopefully the census will determine if any of them have gone missing along with the abducted villagers."

"So they definitely think the raiders have multiple powerful mages?" I asked with a sinking feeling. "Is it so impossible they have just one or two who've come from among their own number?"

"Yes, it is," Nikolas said dismissively. "We would know if they had bloodlines of such power—beside the General himself, of course. For generations now, anyone born with a strong seed has been sent to the Guild—or to one of its far-flung mages, at least—for an apprenticeship. It means the only people with strong abilities are mages, further ensuring that only their apprentices—who automatically become Guild mages in turn—can have strong abilities in the next generation. There just aren't people wandering around out there with powerful abilities—unless they're accredited Guild mages, of course."

"Except the General." I played with my potatoes, too distracted to eat.

Why did everyone dismiss his existence? If he could have a strong ability outside of the Guild system, why couldn't others?

"Well, there's always an exception," Nikolas said shortly.

I glanced at Gia, but she just shrugged while Zeke looked almost as confused as I was. I sighed. Clearly Nikolas wasn't going to engage on the question further.

I changed topic. "Are they moving the tour forward?"

Given the preferred lifestyle of the nomads, King Marius and Queen Celestine planned a tour around the kingdom for the duration of their stay, rather than expecting them to remain within Tarona's walls.

"No," Gia said around a mouthful. "There are more members of Tribe Nicabar to arrive still, as well as the delegations from Tribes Callen and Patrin."

"So it's definitely happening?" I asked. "Members of the ruling tribe are actually leaving the hidden city to come to Tartora?"

Zeke nodded. "Mother confirmed it. Tribe Patrin knows its rule is coming to an end—King Fenix can't possibly last much longer—and they're seeking to position themselves for the future. They'll want to leverage their current status to its fullest while they still have it."

"Even so, it's significant," I said. "I know there have been nomad delegations in Tartora in the distant past because I looked up the records myself. But I don't think any of them included members of the ruling tribe."

"Thus why we've all been studying nomad culture for the last months," Nikolas said. "Father will be furious if anyone coming on the tour disgraces the kingdom through ignorance."

"So they'll all be here in four days as planned?" I asked. "And we leave on the tour in five?"

I couldn't help a small thrill of excitement when Gia nodded. I'd been counting down to the tour for what felt like forever. Finally Evermund and I were going to have the chance to take our search further afield. He'd been looking for signs of Airlie everywhere his official business took him, but I knew I would have better luck than him—he couldn't sense her the way I could. If I could only get close enough to bring her into range, there was nowhere the raiders could hide her from me.

"I'm afraid we're not going to be around much." Zeke gave me an apologetic look.

I glanced at Gia who looked a little sour but didn't dispute his words. With foreign delegations involved, she couldn't fully embrace her Apprentice Gia persona for the next few months, no matter how much she tried to pretend otherwise.

"I don't think I'll have time for the library myself," I said. "Every mage included in the tour has been having their apprentices prepare for them, so I've offered my help to Evermund. I'm the closest thing he's got to one with Airlie missing."

Gia placed her hand over mine, giving my fingers a quick squeeze. "Evermund has asked everyone going on the tour to keep an eye out for any sign of her. I'm certain we'll find something."

I nodded, smiling my thanks and trying not to let my mind stray back to the search for Airlie. There was too much to do here at the Guild first. Once we were safely underway, I could commit my full attention to finding my sister.

The four of us parted with equal expressions of abstraction, all absorbed in thinking about the upcoming tour, no doubt. But on my way toward my room, I glanced through the windows into Evermund's suite. The sight that greeted me made me halt and shake my head. Pulling the door open, I joined him in the enormous sitting room.

"Are you trying to make my life difficult?" I asked with a laugh.

"What?" he said in a distracted tone before glancing my way. "Oh, Cadence, it's you. I don't suppose you've seen my book on tidal forces along the southern coast?" He looked down at the books gripped in each hand, as if hoping one of them might suddenly turn into the missing volume.

When I didn't reply he looked up, a grin spreading across his face at my expression. "No? Fair enough. It's just that we'll be traveling along the coast during the tour, and I thought—" He cut himself off. "Never mind that."

His dismayed expression as he looked around at the mess of books on the floor made it appear as if he was only noticing it for the first time. "Are you sure you're willing to pack for me? I realize I'm not helping the task. I can always ask for some servants to be assigned the job instead."

The note of uncertainty in his voice at the mention of enlisting servants made me shake my head briskly. I owed a lot to Evermund for taking me in after Airlie's disappearance, and packing his disorganized possessions was the least I could do.

"Do you have a list of the books you want to take?" I asked.

"A list?" He winced. "That would be a good idea, wouldn't it?"

"Let's make one now." I rummaged through the mess of the room, emerging with a piece of parchment and a pen. Sitting at the table in the window corner, I looked at him expectantly. "I'm sure you have a mental list, at least. You name them, and I'll jot them down. I expect I'll locate them all in the process of cleaning up this mess."

He winced again. "I always thought I didn't have time for an apprentice, but now I'm starting to think it's quite the other way around."

I rolled my eyes, refraining from pointing out that he didn't do any actual teaching as the law would require if I was truly his apprentice. What he needed was a personal secretary. I was glad he didn't have one, though. I appreciated the opportunity to be useful in some way during my stay with him.

It was the role Airlie would have filled if she was still here, and doing it made me feel close to her.

Or better than her—because you're here and she's not, a nasty voice in my mind said. *For once* you're *the helpful sister.*

I frowned and pushed the tip of the pen down harder, nearly puncturing the page. That was old resentments talking. I wanted nothing more than for my sister to be home safe and ready to take back the role that belonged to her. And not just as Evermund's apprentice—I looked forward to handing back responsibility for monitoring the Guild to her as well.

Maybe then I could get a good night's sleep.

My hand stilled, the scratch of the pen quieting. How could I think about anything but the danger Airlie might be in right now? Was this how she had always felt? As if the crushing weight of her responsibility for me robbed her of the ability to breathe freely?

My words from the ball repeated through my mind as they had all too often in the last months. I had spoken in thoughtless anger when I told her I would be better off without her around. I hadn't really meant it, and I'd assumed she would know that —at least once we both cooled down.

But was it possible she had taken me seriously? Aloud, I'd been steadfastly refusing to even consider the possibility Airlie might have left by choice. But in the darkest depths of my mind, I worried that maybe she had. She would never have left because of a handsome face, but perhaps she'd been driven away by me—the sister she had spent her whole life trying to protect.

Was it my fault the Guild had been left unprotected that night?

I took a deep breath and forced my hand to continue writing. It didn't matter what I had said at the dance. I had never been the one holding Airlie responsible for anything—she was the one who held herself to such an unflagging standard. And no outburst of hurt or temper by me had ever changed that.

She hadn't left by choice. I was sure of it.

Mostly.

CHAPTER 5
CADENCE

The list of books Evermund considered essential for a tour through the kingdom turned out to be astonishingly long, and it took me several days to track them all down. I eventually located the missing book on ocean tides under my own bed.

"Yes!" I cried as I slithered backward across the plush green carpet, only to bump my head on the edge of the wooden frame.

"Ow!" I rubbed at the sore spot as I emerged to find Zeke in the doorway, watching me with a bemused expression.

"Under the bed is a favored reading location is it?" he asked.

I laughed. "This isn't my book. It's one of Evermund's that's been missing."

"And you thought of looking for it under your bed? That's admirable dedication to the search."

I grimaced. "I'd looked absolutely everywhere else in the entire suite. And then I remembered that before Airlie moved in here, Evermund used this room as a study—a very messy study. And the servants brought her bed in before they finished moving all his books out. So I thought it was worth a look," I concluded, on a triumphant note.

"Very impressive deduction," Zeke said approvingly. "I'm glad you haven't been bored in my absence."

I bristled. "It might not be the most important task, but at least it gives me something to do."

Zeke shook his head. "I didn't mean it like that. You're far from unimportant, Cadie. You're the one monitoring the safety of everyone in the Guild. They might not know it, but I haven't forgotten."

I turned away slightly to gather some things from my bedside table, hiding the rising flush in my cheeks. After months of studying together, he called me Cadie regularly now, with the ease of frequent interaction between us. But I still hadn't entirely mastered my reaction to him. It didn't matter how many times my sensible mind reminded my heart that Zeke's attentiveness to me almost certainly had to do with his particular interest in power mages. After a lifetime spent in Airlie's shadow, I couldn't help responding to his concentrated attention.

"We rarely see any of you Triumvirate apprentices at meal times," I said once I had mastered myself enough to turn back around. "The whole Guild is abuzz with preparations for the tour. I can only imagine the palace is even worse."

"It is. You can't move without tripping over someone rushing in the opposite direction. I'll be glad when the whole thing's done."

I bit my lip, not meeting his eye as we strolled out into the garden together. Zeke's two year apprenticeship to the head of the Tartoran plants affinity would finish during the tour. He would graduate and then return to his tribe with his mother. He might look forward to the end of the tour, but I was dreading it.

Months ago he had suggested I might accompany him to the nomad kingdom after his graduation, but he hadn't mentioned it since, and I hadn't brought it up either. If we hadn't found Airlie by then, I couldn't abandon the search. And if we had found her...

My thoughts sputtered and died. I spent so much time thinking about finding my sister, I rarely considered what might come next. She would still be Evermund's apprentice for well over a year. I couldn't find her only to immediately leave her again. But how would Zeke react if I told him that?

And what about your own future? a small voice asked in the back of my mind. *Power mages are well understood among Tribe Nicabar. They might be the only ones who can help you master your ability.*

I pushed the thought aside. Zeke might be my friend, but Tribe Nicabar owed me nothing. If they welcomed me in, something would be expected in return, and I wasn't ready to make that kind of commitment.

"Even the apprentices who aren't going seem busy," I said to fill the awkward gap in the conversation. "Master Colton is remaining behind to run the Guild, but Bryce and the others have been as scarce as the rest of you."

"Apparently Colton has assigned them to help Hayes—since he's the one representing the healing affinity on the tour."

"Oh, right. That makes sense since he doesn't have apprentices of his own."

"A good thing, too," Zeke said with a rueful grin. "If seconds weren't barred from having apprentices, no one would ever take on the role."

"Can you imagine if they did?" I shook my head.

The promising proficients who undertook terms as seconds to the affinity heads already had enough on their plates without apprentices of their own. As well as standing in for the heads in their absences and completing much of their administrative work, they also conducted a majority of their apprentices' training for them.

It was one of the less subtle ways in which the Mages' Guild stretched the requirements imposed generations ago by the crown. Mages who activated someone committed to personally housing and training the new apprentice. It kept strong mages from growing too rich and influential, but it was a significant inconvenience now that strong mages were in short supply, and the kingdom needed them to activate all promising candidates. So classes weren't allowed, but no one took issue with the apprentices of the affinity heads being trained as a group by their influencer's second.

"Bryce has been green with envy," Zeke said cheerfully. "He and the rest of Colton's apprentices keep complaining about how they have to do all the work but are going to miss out on all the fun."

I scrunched up my nose. "Is it going to be fun, though? The work isn't about to stop. We'll be traveling constantly, always setting up and packing up camp. And you know Masters Drake and Augusta aren't going to do any of that work for themselves. And Evermund will likely be kept too busy to do anything himself either."

Zeke grinned down at me. "You'll see. Travel has its own rewards to make up for the extra effort. Always a new vista and new experiences. There's nothing like the adventures that arise while you're traveling."

I gave him a skeptical look but didn't respond. He had grown up with that lifestyle, so he probably felt bored and stifled after two years at the Guild. But for me, the months here hadn't yet dulled the novelty of living somewhere so large and bustling.

"I've no doubt that once we're gone, Bryce will enjoy ruling the roost back here, at least," I said instead. "Not only will the rest of the Triumvirate apprentices be gone, but many of the senior mages as well..."

My words trailed off as I froze, closing my eyes against a wave of nausea.

"Cadie?" Zeke gripped my arm, but I ignored him, pushing away all distractions.

Grasping at the sensation of wrongness that produced the ill feeling, I propelled my senses outward, trying to track down its source. My awareness raced through the nearby sections of the building.

But I found nothing out of the ordinary. And before I could seek further, it was gone.

I let out a huff of frustration.

"You felt it again?" Zeke's eyes darted around the courtyard.

I nodded. "But it disappeared before I could pinpoint it, just like the other times. I don't understand where it could be coming from."

"Never mind."

I could tell Zeke's reassurances were shallow, masking his own unease, but I didn't have any words of comfort to give him.

"I don't like leaving the Guild when there might be someone—or something—here." I resumed walking toward the apprentice entrance, but slowly now.

"You've scanned the whole building time and time again," Zeke pointed out. "What else can you possibly do? The entire royal family as well as most of the Triumvirate—not to mention you—will be on the tour. That's where you're needed."

"Yes, of course." But I bit my lip, still not happy about the situation.

We wove between two rows of wagons which had been wheeled into the courtyard the day before. Already most of them were filled with a vast array of items, with several of the wagon trays covered in sheets of lashed down canvas. The food would be loaded last, but anything else—clothes, tents, cooking supplies, spare parts, tools, bedding—was being sorted and stowed now.

Evermund had packed his own clothes—two packs to my one, given the formal garments he would need—and all three bags had been collected by a harried looking servant the day before. The servants were all working even harder than the apprentices, and those staying behind must be looking forward to our departure. Although many of them were to accompany the tour, of course—either riding ahead to prepare each new campsite in preparation for the main tour group, or else following in a second collection of wagons at the rear of the cavalcade.

The main palace courtyard had been left clear of vehicles, ready for the imminent arrival of the remaining delegation members, but every other spare spot around the building was stuffed full of more wagons. And the ones I had seen were already crammed with the items needed by the party from the palace. The entire undertaking was enormous and demonstrated how seriously King Marius took this opportunity to connect with the nomads.

The complicated logistics of the operation could have been a nightmare for me, given my efforts to monitor all movement around the palace and Guild. But thankfully the people pouring in and out of the palace grounds bringing supplies for the tour came almost entirely from other guilds. Most guilds had a handful of mages assigned as liaisons, but they didn't do menial tasks such as delivering goods. And as long as the people coming and going through the gate had only weak abilities, I could easily relegate them to the back of my mind.

When the delegation members arrived, however, they stood out. This time I was prepared for it and didn't panic. Instead I monitored from afar as my friends joined them, along with a constellation of blazing power from the senior members of the palace and Guild.

As well as my friends, Annora was also instantly recognizable thanks to the number of times I had tracked her from afar in the last few days. I hadn't mentioned to Zeke how often my thoughts—and my ability along with them—dwelt on his mother. I wasn't sure if it would offend him that my friendship with him wasn't enough to make me trust his tribe.

The milling group of distant mages lingered in the main courtyard before making their way to the palace's formal dining hall. Knowing they would be there for some time, I forced my mind back to the task of packing Evermund's letter writing kit. But I hadn't made much headway when a hurried knock sounded on the internal door of the suite.

I raced over to pull the door open, confused as to why Karielle would be searching for me. She stepped into the room as soon as the way was clear, looking around with a rushed glance before turning back to me.

"Where's Evermund? I don't suppose he's with Master Augusta?"

"Is she missing?" I asked, bemused.

Karielle groaned. "We haven't seen her since before she went to greet the delegation, and Adabella is insisting she needs to consult her on a matter of urgency."

Karielle's tone suggested she wasn't equally convinced the matter was urgent, but as Augusta's second, Adabella possessed the same authority over Augusta's apprentices as the Master of Plants herself. But Adabella had only been newly assigned to the position and was clearly nervous about being left behind at the Guild to oversee the plants affinity in Augusta's absence.

I was about to say they'd all stayed to have the evening meal at the palace when Karielle spoke again.

"She's not in the palace dining hall, but neither is Evermund, so I thought you must know where they are." She gave me a pleading look.

I bit my lip, glad I hadn't spoken. I'd developed a reputation among the apprentices for always knowing where Evermund could be found, although none of them knew the real reason why. If I'd blurted out my assumption that he was with the diners, I might have found it difficult to backtrack with his actual location.

A moment's sweep of the Guild located Evermund, along with Augusta.

"I believe the Triumvirate are all meeting in Master Colton's suite," I told her. "Along with Evermund. Last minute preparations for our departure tomorrow, I imagine."

"Oh, thank goodness," Karielle exclaimed. "I have enough to do tonight without trekking all over the Guild knocking on doors. Thanks, Cadence."

She began outlining her list of last minute tasks, and I stepped out into the hall with her while she talked. When we reached the first corner, she stopped herself with a rueful twist of her lips.

"Listen to me, chattering on when you must have a list of your own just as long. At least I have Blake to share the load with, even if Zeke and Nikolas haven't been much help. We've hardly seen them lately."

I laughed off her concern. "Evermund isn't a demanding master. My biggest challenge was finding all the books he wanted to take."

"Books?" Karielle shook her head. "Not exactly helpful luggage for a tour. Thank goodness we're not responsible for transporting everything. Although I don't think Master Augusta packed a single volume. She's taking a full wagon's worth of seeds, though."

"Seeds?"

"It's been a long time since she left Tarona. Once word got out that she'd be leaving the capital, plants mages all around the kingdom started putting in requests for her time, expertise, and any unusual seed requests." She rolled her eyes. "The kingdom will be a wonder of greenery by the time we make it back to the Guild."

"That's a good use of the tour, though," I said, refraining

from adding that it seemed like a better use of time than the politics Evermund was always immersed in.

Karielle's demeanor changed, a hint of excitement creeping in. "I'm actually looking forward to it—although it's easy to forget that in the middle of all this last minute work. I was fortunate to win a position as a Triumvirate apprentice to start with, but this is a totally unique opportunity. I'm hoping to learn a lot." She stopped herself short again. "I can think about all that once we're on the road. Thanks again for the help, Cadence!"

She waved at me as she took off down the corridor at a half-run. I watched her go with a bewildered shake of my head. When I'd first met Karielle, I wouldn't have dreamed the sophisticated apprentice ever dashed through the halls—or that she'd come to me for help with anything.

I sent my ability ahead of her, checking the masters were all still in Colton's suite. Reassured on their location, I turned back to Evermund's suite.

Distracted by the rest of the Guild behind me, I didn't pay any attention to the empty room in front of me as I stepped back through the door.

A wave of something familiar, and yet twisted enough to feel wrong, washed over me, stronger than I'd ever felt it before. My stomach roiled, writhing and spinning so rapidly that I faltered, dropping to my knees as I fought to keep from losing my last meal all over the fancy carpet.

With an effort, I looked up, straight into the eyes of an older woman I didn't recognize. She wore simple clothes, nothing like the garb of a Guild mage or the livery of a servant. And her face blazed with determination.

The room wasn't empty, after all.

CHAPTER 6

CADENCE

I gasped, the shock driving back the wave of nausea enough that I managed to stagger to my feet. I opened my mouth to scream for help, but the woman held up both hands in a placating gesture.

"Wait! Please! I'm not here to hurt you."

I let my breath out in a huff, surprised. My eyes narrowed as I gave her a closer look. I would have guessed her to be middle-aged, rather than elderly, but her face was lined and drawn, her skin gray and her eyes tired behind the determination. She didn't look as if she could overpower a kitten let alone a person.

"Who are you?" I asked warily.

Her shoulders slumped slightly, as if relieved to be past the first hurdle.

"I'm Dara."

"And you're with the raiders." I didn't say it like a question, although nothing in her manner or appearance fit with the previous raiders I'd encountered.

She hesitated for a moment before nodding. "But I'm not like Lawson. I just want to talk to you."

I raised my eyebrows. "Lawson? Is he the plants mage I *met* a few days ago?" My sarcastic emphasis made her wince.

"I told them that was a bad idea." She sighed. "At least the General agreed I could come as a backup plan of sorts. I would have preferred to try words first and force second, rather than the other way around, but..."

"So you've been here since this Lawson attacked me?"

I leaned slightly forward despite myself. After so many days puzzling over the matter, I couldn't walk away from an opportunity to get some answers.

She nodded slowly. "I..." She paused and gave me a considering look. "I helped him sneak in. I'm sorry about what he did. He was supposed to abduct you, not put your life in danger." She frowned, a flash of anger crossing her face.

"So you were behind the shield?" I stopped abruptly, a sliver of excitement taking hold as a possibility occurred to me.

Reaching out with my ability, I tried to probe at hers. I'd never needed to search for someone's ability before, it was as obvious a feature as their hair color or height. But the writhing, twisting sensation that surrounded her like a shroud shielded any sense of her ability.

I would have to push past the sensation to discover her affinity, but attempting to do so made me gasp and pull back. Direct contact with the strange power around her was too much on top of the nausea her presence already evoked.

"You get used to it eventually," she said in a kind tone. "You just have to protect yourself from the nausea. Find the core of your ability, and then coax it out larger. Imagine that instead of a ball at your center, it's a shell around your entire body."

I stared at her, and she nodded encouragingly. Another wave of the nausea made my knees tremble, so despite my uncertainty, I reached for my own ability.

I never noticed it unless I was paying particular attention—in the same way I didn't have a constant conscious awareness of my arms and legs. But when I tried, I could sense it just like I sensed everyone else's.

Zeke never talked about it in my training—which made sense since he couldn't feel his own ability the way I could. He drew on it instinctively, an integrated part of him like his brain or his muscles. And so I had largely ignored mine as well. When I tried to use my ability, I reached outward for the power that lingered in the air, ground, and building around me.

But now I reached inward instead. Focusing my attention on the ball that blazed at my center, I imagined it thinning and stretching. It responded slowly at first and then faster. When I pictured it as a shell over my skin, like Dara had described, I blinked and it was done.

I gasped. The nausea was gone, cut off instantly. Nervous, I reached for Dara, the remaining tension leaching out of me when my ability responded like normal.

Freed from the ill effects of whatever surrounded her, I examined it more closely. I could still tell something was wrong with the power that swirled around her, but it no longer affected me physically. And now that I was examining it more closely, I could see it wasn't really a shield. There were gaps, and with a little care, I could reach her without disturbing it.

As soon as I did, I let out a second gasp. Looking up, our eyes locked.

"You have a power ability," I whispered.

Some part of me had suspected it from the moment I realized a second person might be with Lawson, hidden behind a shield of power. But it had seemed impossible, a fanciful wish to find someone else like me.

And yet, here she was. And within minutes of meeting her, she had already taught me something I hadn't worked out on my own.

"What's wrong with you?" I asked, and then flushed at my awkward choice of words. "I mean this..." I waved vaguely in her direction, not sure how to label the strange power that surrounded her. "It doesn't feel right. You had a shield of power when you first arrived, but it wasn't like this. It was normal power. Was it hiding this?"

She hesitated. "You know, I suppose, that there's a corruption in Calista?"

I frowned. "You mean the protections that have rendered it barren and unlivable?"

Thanks to Zeke, I now knew they weren't really protections at all, but I didn't know what else to label them.

"Some people call them that. But they're more of a curse than a protection." Dara swayed slightly, and I wondered if I should get her a chair. Any concern about her as a potential threat had been entirely swallowed up by the discovery of someone else who shared my ability.

"But we're not in Calista," I said. "The protections, or curse, or whatever you want to call it, are contained by the border."

Dara's lips twisted. "They're getting worse. Haven't you noticed? The border isn't enough to stop them anymore."

"So you do live across the border?" I asked, my gaze fixed on her. "You and the other raiders?"

She frowned and didn't immediately answer. But she must have decided the information was hardly a secret because she eventually gave a slow nod.

"Some of it clung to me when I traveled here. I would have pushed it away, sent it back, but..." Her words trailed off, her breathing growing labored.

"Is that why the borders are failing?" Anger colored my voice. "The raiders have been harrying the border regions and even the capital more and more frequently. Are you all dragging this tainted power across every time you come? No wonder it's destabilizing everything!"

My brows pulled together, and I opened my mouth to ask more questions about their location, but her face softened, and a hint of pride entered her expression.

"You're so beautiful, Cadie. And the General says you're

powerful. Just like your father hoped. He would have been so proud of you."

I drew back, more shocked than if she'd suddenly slapped me.

"My father? What do you know of my father?"

"You don't recognize me?" she asked softly. "Even a little bit?"

"Recognize you?" I looked more closely at her face, trying to see past the lines of fatigue. A vague sense of familiarity stirred, but I couldn't be sure if it was real or if I was willing it into existence in response to her suggestion.

Could she be one of the abducted villagers from near the border? I'd interacted with women of her age in our various trading visits, but none of them had made much of an impression.

I bit my lip and then shrugged. "Maybe? Why? Should I know you?"

She sighed, sounding disappointed. "I suppose you were too young. I think you were only four the last time Quirin and I brought our son, Renley, to visit you." She grimaced. "It didn't go too well. Quirin and your father argued, and then..." She sighed again. "Your parents did have some friends, you know. But sadly your mother died soon after that visit, and clearly your father never mentioned us."

I shut my gaping mouth as I struggled to comprehend her words. My parents had once had friends who would visit our remote home? How had I not remembered that?

A moment later, my astonishment was replaced with a resentful resignation. Of course Father had never mentioned them. He had controlled everything about our lives, and Dara and Quirin had clearly challenged that—if the fighting and their subsequent banishment was any indication. Even Dara's power affinity interfered with the secrets he wanted to keep from me.

My jaw clenched.

"Don't be too hard on him," Dara said softly, seeming to recognize and understand my emotions. "He was a stubborn old man, but he was in a difficult position. Even Quirin acknowledged that after he calmed down."

"You knew my mother?" I asked, ignoring her comments on my father. I wasn't prepared to talk about him with a complete stranger. "I wish I had more memories of her."

"She was a wonderful woman," Dara said. "And she loved you very much—you and your sister, both. You were her whole world." She paused, as if something else lay beneath her words, but after a moment she just shook her head.

At the mention of Airlie, I sucked in my breath, realization flooding me.

"Airlie is older than me! Did she remember you?" Anger filled me, making my limbs tremble. "Did you go to her as an old friend and lure her away? If you visited our house while our parents were alive, she probably trusted you! And you delivered her straight to the raiders, didn't you!?"

Something twisted in Dara's face, but it was gone in a flash.

"We were trying to help," she said, a pleading note in her voice. "We didn't want anything to happen to either of you. When we heard about the first two attacks, and the plans for a third one, we asked to come along. We were hoping to get to both of you and make sure you were out of harm's way. My son is just the same age as her, and if anything happened to him, I would—"

I leaned forward, suppressing the tension that made me want to leap at her and shake her until she told me everything.

"You abducted my sister!"

Dara winced. "We invited her to visit us, yes. Just like I'm here to invite you."

I gaped at her. "You think I'd just walk off with you after you took my sister!"

"If you come with me, you can be with her again. And we can help you, Cadence. Our settlement is full of those who share your affinity, like I do. We can teach you how to use it."

I gaped at her. A whole settlement of people with power abilities? How was that possible? For the briefest moment, I was tempted. But the thought of what Airlie would say if I turned up there with Dara made me stiffen.

"Airlie was tricked, but I'm not walking into your trap with my eyes open. How do I even know my sister is still alive? What have you done with her? Is she safe, at least?"

Dara drew herself up. "Of course she's safe. We wouldn't let anyone hurt her."

I looked her up and down coolly, raising an eyebrow. I didn't have to say anything to convey my doubt that she possessed such protective capacity. Just my expression was enough to bring some color back to her pallid cheeks.

"She was angry and upset from the dance," Dara said with a little more spirit. "She came out to get some fresh air and was delighted to see a familiar face and to reconnect with old friends who would listen to her troubles. I think she relished the chance to get away."

I stiffened, pulling myself up to my full height. I'd never been tall, but I felt substantial beside Dara's withered frame.

"Don't you dare," I said with fire. "Don't you dare try to say it was my fault she left! Airlie would never abandon me."

"Your fault?" Dara looked genuinely surprised. "No, of course not. I didn't mean to suggest...She didn't like being pushed into activating the prince and princess when she'd only just been activated herself. She was worried, I think, and weighed down with too much responsibility for someone so young." She shook her head, looking motherly.

I deflated somewhat. Did that mean Airlie hadn't told them about our fight? Guilt clawed its way up my throat. She might have been too loyal to mention it, but would she have trusted them so quickly and gone with them so readily if she hadn't been upset at my words? If I hadn't driven her away, she would have been safe inside the ball.

"You say Airlie is safe with the raiders," I said, steering myself back onto firmer ground. "But don't pretend she's there by choice. My sister would never stay away for so long—and without even sending word."

A faint click sounded behind me, and I eased my position slightly so that I blocked more of Dara's view of the door. She seemed far too absorbed in the conversation to even notice our surroundings as she clasped her hands together, closing her eyes and gripping until her fingers whitened. When she opened them, all the remaining animation had left her face.

"Yes, it's true," she said quietly. "Airlie is a prisoner of the raiders. They've bound her ability with a neutralizer to keep her from escaping. But I swear she hasn't been harmed."

"That is extremely fortunate for you," an icy voice said from behind me, making Dara start violently. Evermund stepped around me to confront the frail woman. "I don't take kindly to having my apprentice abducted."

Dara shrank back from him, her eyes widening.

"I...I don't..."

I stepped forward and placed a restraining hand on Evermund's arm. I didn't want him frightening her into insensibility.

"Her name is Dara, and she's an old friend of my parents."

"Your parents were part of the raiders?" Sutton asked, pushing around to stand on Evermund's other side.

Evermund's arm muscles tensed, and I pulled back, looking toward Dara in shock. I hadn't even considered that aspect of the situation.

But she was shaking her head vigorously. "No, they had no interest. Quirin and I tried to convince them, but..."

"And now the General is trying to *convince* Airlie?" Evermund asked in a dangerous tone.

"Of course he is. She's one of us."

I looked sideways at Evermund's face, but he showed no reaction.

Sutton, however, spoke. "Calistan, you mean?" He looked from Dara to me. "Airlie and Cadence are Calistan?"

"No." Evermund said the word with a note of finality. "They're Tartoran. May I remind you that Airlie is apprentice to the Tartoran Royal Mage?" He looked sternly at Sutton, something passing between the two men that I couldn't read.

"You can't claim them," Dara said defiantly. "Not when Cadence is—"

"Where have you been all this time?" I asked loudly, cutting her off. I tried to keep my expression calm, despite my racing heart rate. "You said you helped Lawson sneak into the Guild, but that was days ago. Where have you been hiding?"

With the two men present, I couldn't mention the times I'd felt a hint of her presence, but I wanted to know how she'd slipped away from me on every occasion. And I wanted even more to stop her blurting out any hint of my affinity.

Dara blinked several times, as if struggling to absorb the change of topic.

"Lawson is a plants mage," she said at last. "He opened the ground so I had access to the underground tunnels. The ones that you hid in during the attack."

"You've been hiding here for days?" Sutton asked in outraged tones.

I tuned him out, considering her words. No wonder I had felt her most often while crossing the courtyard, and no wonder my subsequent searches of the buildings had turned up nothing. I had never even thought of the tunnels, given their entrance had been collapsed during the attack on the night of the ball.

"So you confirm that Airlie was abducted by the raiders and is being held by them against her will," Evermund said in a hard tone.

Reluctantly Dara nodded.

Evermund turned to Sutton. "You witnessed the confession."

His eyes traveled to me, and a grin spread across his face, although it carried more danger than humor.

"Now we have proof," he said. "No one can deny the truth after this."

A rush of emotions threatened to overwhelm me, piling on top of the confused swirl already muddying my mind. We could conduct a proper search now, with resources and official support. I glanced out the window, but it was already getting dark. Was it too late to leave today?

"We have more than that," Sutton said, nothing in his satisfied tone indicating the skepticism with which he had previously viewed Airlie's disappearance. "This woman must know where the raiders are based."

Dara took an alarmed step backward, looking to me as if she thought I might shield her. I didn't budge. I wanted to know where they were more than anyone.

Evermund, however, showed no trace of enthusiasm at Sutton's words.

"It's a good point," he said slowly. "Why would the General allow you to come when you must know a lot of information he doesn't want falling into our hands? And why did you wait so long to reveal yourself? Cadence has been alone in this suite many times since this Lawson's attack."

They were good questions, and Dara seemed intimidated by them, trembling so hard she could barely stand. I took a step closer, sucking in a breath as I properly examined her. Her eyes were wide and unfocused, not even looking at Evermund, and the last flecks of color had faded from her cheeks.

I leaped forward just in time to get an arm around her back before her legs gave way. I wasn't strong enough to catch her completely, but we sank to the ground together, my support allowing her to drop slowly.

Once we were all the way down, I gently lowered her head to the floor, arranging her flat on her back. I stayed kneeling beside her as Evermund joined me.

My breath came fast. "What's wrong with her?"

He picked up her limp wrist, closing his eyes for several seconds before opening them to look at her face. After a moment, he glanced up at Sutton who stood watching us with an open mouth.

"She's still breathing, but barely," he said. "I'm the wrong affinity to tell you any more than that."

Sutton nodded once. "I'll go for Colton." He rushed out the door before I'd processed his words.

"Is she that bad?" I asked Evermund, my voice wavering.

Despite the anger I felt toward Dara for helping abduct Airlie, she was a link toward both my past and my affinity that I wasn't ready to lose. And she hadn't told us anything yet about where Airlie could be found.

She stirred slightly, her eyes fluttering open. "It's too late," she said weakly. Her eyes found mine. "Surely you can...see it."

The pause told me she didn't mean *see* with my eyes. I reached out with my ability, blanching as hers flickered, growing weaker by the moment. And it hadn't been strong to begin with. If I hadn't been so excited by her affinity, I would have realized immediately that she wasn't strong enough to ever be chosen as a mage. But that weakness was different from what I felt now.

Now she was barely clinging to life. I suspected if I had the capacity to monitor her other vital systems, they would be failing just as fast.

I pulled away, horror clogging my throat. Freed from the

physical symptoms of the strange, sick power that swirled around her, I had been ignoring its presence. But I focused on it now. While I wasn't paying attention, it had become a maelstrom, writhing at a faster and faster rate.

As I watched, her eyes closed, her frame seeming to shrink in on itself. I turned a horrified face to Evermund, who bent over her frowning.

"Is she...?" I could barely get out the question.

"She's only unconscious—for now."

I stood. "Hayes's room is closer than Colton's. I'll run and see if he's there."

I didn't wait for Evermund to respond, dashing through the door and down the corridor as fast as I could run. Mages and servants walked the hall, hurrying in all directions on last minute tour errands. I ignored them, pushing past anyone in my direct path.

I careened around a corner into the apprentice section which was wedged between the elements and healing wings. I only made it three steps, however, before I collided full tilt with a solid figure.

"Cadence?" Zeke grabbed me by my upper arms, keeping me from falling. "What's going on?"

"Hayes!" I cried. "I need Hayes. Quickly!"

He didn't question me further, taking my hand and pulling me around another corner.

"He just left the dining hall. This way."

I caught sight of a familiar figure, walking slowly away from us.

"Hayes!" I shouted.

He spun around, jogging toward us once he caught sight of my face.

"We need you. She's dying," I gasped out.

Hayes also didn't waste time with unnecessary questions. "Which way?"

I started running again, back in the direction I'd come from, both of them trailing behind me.

"Evermund's suite," I gasped out between breaths. "One of the raiders. She knows where Airlie is, but..." I couldn't bring myself to say it. We were so close to the answers I'd been searching for, but I could feel them slipping away.

I increased my pace, the others matching me.

The door was still open from my precipitate departure, so we barreled straight through. But as soon as I saw the two people inside the suite, I pulled up short, Hayes nearly running into me.

Across the room, I met Evermund's eyes.

"She's gone." He sounded weary and defeated.

I wanted to deny it, but I could feel the awful truth for myself. Her ability no longer burned inside her, and even the strange, twisted power that had clung to her was gone. Faint traces lingered on the air in all directions, as if it had dissipated on her death. But already they were fading and would likely soon be gone. We were too late.

"This is why," Evermund said. "The General let her come because he knew she was dying. She revived briefly, although she refused to answer my questions. All she would say is that she promised to stay away from you until she knew the end was near. That's why she came out of hiding tonight."

"So she didn't tell you where to find Airlie?" I asked, unable to stop myself from asking, although his words and demeanor had already told me the truth.

"I'm sorry, Cadence," he said heavily. "We got nothing."

CHAPTER 7
AIRLIE

I stood on the tallest rise in the encampment and pretended to survey the stunted landscape beyond the log walls, as I did every morning. The briefest glance showed it looked as it always did—barren, dusty ground with the occasional stunted or misformed tree. In a couple of places a few of them clustered together, but other than that, only the rise and fall of the surrounding hill country broke up the view.

No animals were in sight, but in the far distance I could catch the slightest glint of sun on water. I had grown up near the eastern edge of the vast Lake Aterra, but this was the closest I had come to its western shore.

The majority of my focus, however, was on the space within the walls. From the corner of my eyes, I scanned the wooden buildings, the canvas tents that housed the more recent arrivals, and the general comings and goings. The one gate stayed firmly closed—as it always did—and no possible avenue of escape presented itself.

I sighed and started the walk down the gentle slope toward a small house on the western side of the unnamed settlement. I had wondered at its lack of name at first, but those who first established it had considered it a temporary haven, and those who followed needed no name for the only location in their world.

As usual, eyes followed me. Some of the residents continued about their daily business without reference to my passing, but all of the General's warriors made a point of stopping and watching me until I passed into range of the next person. It was a message I had long since received—I was always being watched.

I slipped inside the door of my temporary home, some of the tension within my muscles easing. It was always a relief to get away from the constant surveillance. And contrary to my initial expectation, I had grown comfortable with Dara and Quirin in the weeks since my capture.

But when I looked around the room, there was no sign of either of them. I frowned. Dara was always here at this time of day. I had expected her to be waiting for me, no word of censure on her lips although I was late to help with the day's food preparation.

At first, after their betrayal, I had stayed in my room, refusing to speak to them. They showed patience with my surliness, offering me no violence and delivering meals at regular intervals, but it was the inactivity that got to me in the end. That and the realization that I was more likely to effect an escape if I was free to roam the camp.

I emerged with a begrudging acceptance of my new housemates that was mostly feigned. But somehow, over the weeks that followed, it became real. Out in the camp I was watched by hostile eyes, but with my father's old friends I felt almost safe.

It wasn't entirely an illusion, either. Since venturing out into the wider world of the raider camp, I had learned it was thanks to their intervention that I had received a room in their house. Without them speaking up for me, I might have spent these weeks in the open pen the raiders used as a makeshift prison.

"Dara?" I called, looking around the room.

It wasn't large enough to hide her, containing only a simple wooden table and chairs and a small kitchen. My brows lowered as I examined the space. Dara should have been back.

I had slipped out of the house early, but the buzz around camp had all been focused on the late evening return of the most recent resupply trip. Dara didn't usually go with them—it was the first time she had done so since my arrival—and I had actually been looking forward to seeing her again.

In her absence, Quirin had turned silent enough to count as surly, and I hadn't caught so much as a glimpse of their son, Renley. Not that I missed Renley's company.

I had come to accept that Dara and Quirin had acted out of a misguided desire to protect the daughter of their old friend. Not so their son, however. The old playmate I had greeted with shock and excitement outside the ball had been a deception. Renley had participated in my abduction out of loyalty to the General, not consideration for me, and he was dedicated in his pursuit of a position among the General's warriors.

Dara argued that I was being too hard on him. She pointed out that he had given up his room for me, moving into a barracks-style dormitory that housed single males. But she was blind to his obvious delight at the necessity. Now he could spend his time with the people he wished to emulate.

My frown deepened as I registered that nothing in the room had been touched from the night before. But the door to Dara and Quirin's bedroom was closed, so perhaps she was still sleeping after her late arrival.

I moved into the kitchen and began to rummage among the basic supplies kept there. I hadn't opened anything, however, when the front door opened again. I looked up eagerly, only for the smile to drop from my face.

"Oh, it's you."

Renley regarded me with a hooded expression I couldn't read. "Who were you expecting?"

"I haven't seen your mother since the supply team got back. She would normally be here this time of day."

His brows lowered. "My mother?"

I stared at him, thrown off by his obvious confusion. After an awkward moment, he cleared his throat. Something in his manner and voice seemed less haughty than usual, as if his constant assurance of the superiority of his cause had been temporarily superseded by some other emotion.

"You really haven't heard?" he asked.

I shook my head, impatient. "Heard what? Where's Dara?"

He drew himself up. "She's gone."

"Gone?" I continued to stare at him. "What does that mean?" I drew in a quick breath. "Surely she can't have been killed on the supply mission? I thought they were just hunting this time?"

"Not killed." He hesitated, glancing at the firmly closed door of his parents' bedroom before shrugging and continuing. "She's dying. She has been for some time. I thought she would have told you, given you two are so close."

A hint of resentment crept into his voice, and for the first time I wondered if he had minded giving up his bedroom, after all. But his words were too shocking for me to give much thought to such minor issues.

"Dying?" I shook my head. "Dara's seemed increasingly weak lately, but she never...Why did she go on the trip, then? She should have stayed home to rest!"

"Resting wouldn't have helped. She was too far gone for that. And she cared about you, even if you refuse to accept that all of us Calistans are equally victims, and the General is just trying to reclaim what's ours. She gave up her final days—days she could have spent with her family—to bring you your family."

"What?" I felt the blood draining from my face. "What are you talking about?"

"She went to fetch your sister."

He sounded almost smug as he said it, as if despite framing it as a positive, he knew the news would be unwelcome. Clearly he resented Dara's care for me.

"Dara is dying, but she's gone back to Tarona to try to abduct Cadence?" I said the words slowly, as if a slow pace would make them intelligible. "That makes no sense."

"Do you think I would lie about my mother's death?"

I looked up quickly, examining his face. For all my dislike of Renley, the emotion I read there was real. He was putting on a face of bravado to hide actual grief.

A churning, painful sensation erupted in my stomach, growing into a storm of grief, fear, and anger that engulfed me. Storming over to their bedroom door, I thrust it open. But there was no sign of anyone, the neat bed looking unused.

I spun around and marched across to the door. When Renley didn't move out of my way, I pushed past him and outside. He trailed behind me, so I threw a question over my shoulder.

"Where's Quirin?"

After a moment's silence, he pointed toward the back of the camp. I picked up my pace, running toward the camp's small graveyard. If Quirin was there, then everything Renley said must be true.

I came to a sudden stop at the sight of the older man kneeling in the dry ground beside a small stone marker. He looked up at my approach, his face streaked with tears, and I read Dara's name etched into the stone.

"It's happened," he said in a roughened voice. "I can feel she's gone."

"I..." Now that I was here, I didn't know how to begin.

"Renley just told me…" I looked over my shoulder at Renley who had just caught up. "You said she went after Cadence."

"She did," Quirin said, looking back toward the stone marker. "When she heard Lawson was being sent to the Guild, she convinced the General to let her go, too. He needed someone with a power affinity to accompany Lawson, so he agreed." His face twisted. "Better to send a dying woman than risk one of the few with a power ability who are loyal to him."

"And you let her go?"

He laughed, a mirthless sound. "I never let Dara do anything in her life. We were partners in everything, and I couldn't deny her wish in this." He looked into my eyes for the first time. "It saddened her to see you so despondent. She thought you needed your family with you."

My anger, punctured by the weight of sorrow that hung over Quirin, swelled again.

"If Cadence has been hurt, I'll—"

I cut myself off, infuriated by the empty threat. I had only known what it was like to be powerful for a few short weeks after my activation, but it had been enough to make the loss of my ability now hard to endure. I plucked at the neutralizer strapped to my waist, an absentminded gesture I had developed during my captivity. I had only tried to remove it once—a futile effort that had brought the General's warriors swarming—but I had dreamed many times about doing so. When I did finally get loose, I was going to bring this whole settlement down.

"Where is she?" I asked instead. "I insist on being taken to my sister."

"She's not here," Renley said impatiently from behind me. "I told you. My mother went to get her."

I looked between the gravestone and Quirin, my anger overtaken by confusion.

"Her body isn't here," Quirin said quietly. "I just wanted

something to mark her passing. We sacrificed the chance for a final goodbye when she chose to go after Cadie."

"Don't call her that," I snapped, regretting the words almost immediately. Whatever he had done to me, I was talking to a man who was already utterly broken.

He cleared his throat. "Cadence, then. She and Lawson broke off from the hunting party and will have continued on to Tarona. The General only permitted Dara to carry out her plan because she was on the verge of death. It would have been too risky, otherwise."

"How very convenient for him," I said, scorn dripping from every word. "Because the life of a good woman is nothing compared to the General keeping all his precious secrets."

Quirin glanced up at me, and I stumbled back a half step, speared by the intensity of the fire in his eyes. But a second later the emotion was shuttered, the gaze that moved on to his son holding nothing but grief.

Interesting. Quirin agreed with me, but he was hiding it from Renley. Maybe I wasn't the only one who saw that his son was in thrall to the General.

"Lawson will be bringing Cadence back on his own," Renley said. "They haven't arrived yet."

I blinked, hope blossoming again. We didn't know anything for sure, then.

But when I opened my mouth to ask another question, Renley grabbed me roughly by the arm and towed me away. I would have protested if I hadn't caught a glimpse of Quirin. He had turned back to Dara's marker again, his shoulders shaking, and our presence apparently forgotten.

As soon as we were out of range of Quirin, I yanked my arm free and glared at Renley.

"Cadence is tougher than any of you suspect. She'll find a way to avoid capture."

"We captured you, didn't we?"

"I was tricked," I hissed through gritted teeth. "But Cadence is too young to remember any of you. She won't be so easily fooled."

"Won't she?" He raised an eyebrow. "Maybe not, but then maybe she'll come by choice. Maybe she wants to be reunited with you."

I froze. Surely Cadence wouldn't willingly walk into the trap just because of me. No, she was smarter than that.

"Why do you care so much, anyway?" Renley asked impatiently. "You were always trying to avoid her so she wouldn't ruin our games. You found her annoying."

"I was six!" I glared at him. "If you had any siblings you'd understand. Of course I found her annoying when we were both children. But she's also my best friend."

Renley shrugged, as if such matters were beneath him.

"Why does the General want Cadence so urgently anyway," I muttered. "Cadence's seed hasn't even been activated yet. She's only just turned seventeen, and there was no one to activate her but me."

"Are you sure about that?" Renley gave me a superior look. "Only the presence of a power mage drove off the General the night we took you. So, unless there's some other power mage hanging around the Guild..."

I gaped at him, unable to think of anything to say.

His satisfaction grew. "Why do you think we've waited so long to try again? A more cautious approach is needed with a power mage in play."

"But how is that possible? Who...?" I shook my head.

I'd had weeks to adjust to the shocking revelation that a fourth affinity existed and that Cadence had a power seed. It had explained a lot of the things our father always refused to talk about. But in all those weeks, no one had mentioned their belief that Cadence had already been activated.

I quickly pulled myself together. "If that's true, then Lawson has no chance. Your precious General wouldn't want Cadence so badly if her ability wasn't strong. It's not as if he doesn't already have access to plenty of people with a weak power ability—that describes almost every one of the original inhabitants here."

"Don't underestimate us," Renley said with narrowed eyes, although I knew his own power seed had yet to be activated. "Lawson wouldn't be able to succeed without the help of one of us—even if we aren't as strong as your precious sister. You'll see. Combined they'll succeed. Mother will have used her ability to help Lawson get in, and then been ready as back up if his initial efforts failed. If Cadence really is too powerful for Lawson to capture, then Mother will have found a way to convince her it's in her—and your—best interest for her to come willingly. They had a designated meeting place for her to send Cadence to meet up with Lawson and everything. If his attack went wrong, all he has to do is wait for her there. I have no doubt Lawson and your sister will show up here at any moment."

My hands clenched into fists, and I considered launching myself at Renley. But that was another thing I had tried once only. The General might have given in to Quirin's persuasion to let me wander the camp at will, but he wasn't letting me get away with anything that might presage an escape attempt.

Instead I took several deep breaths. "I don't believe Lawson is strong enough to do anything of the kind. You're the one who'll see. He won't come back at all. If Cadence doesn't take him down herself, someone else at the Guild will. Evermund wouldn't just sit by and let her be taken."

Despite having only known him for a short time, my faith in Evermund was absolute. In all my dealings with him, he had demonstrated that he took his responsibilities seriously. He wouldn't leave a young, vulnerable girl to fend for herself.

A clamor arose near the gates, like a crowd gathering to greet someone. Renley flashed me a triumphant look.

"That will be them now."

He took off running, and I dashed after him. We were soon ducking and weaving around others, all moving in the same direction. Renley got close enough to see the gates first, swinging back to me with a huge grin on his face. My heart seized.

"It's Lawson," he said as I reached his side. "Just like I said."

I jumped up, trying to see over the people in front of me. One of them moved, disappearing back into the crowd, their curiosity apparently satisfied, and I pushed forward into their place.

Lawson, a plants mage with whom I'd had almost no contact, stood just inside the gates, his expression closed off. He certainly didn't look like a triumphant conqueror. I waited several breaths, scanning in every direction before training my eyes on the gate behind him. When it started to slowly swing shut, I turned back to Renley, buoyed by relief.

"You may be right that he escaped, but I was right about my sister. She isn't here."

He scowled at me, and my heart pinched. In my excitement at Cadence's escape, I had forgotten she wasn't the only one absent from Lawson's side. The mission had failed, but Dara was gone, just like they'd known she would be.

How had she spent her final moments? The last of my elation dissipated, and my anger toward Renley grew slippery and hard to cling to.

I couldn't even blame him for the hard, bitter look he directed at me. As indoctrinated as he was, he couldn't put the blame where it truly lay—at the feet of his idol.

"Don't look so delighted," he said through his teeth. "You thought your beloved Guild could easily dispose of one mage, but Lawson just waltzed in and out again without a scratch.

He's more powerful than you understand—and one day I will be too!"

I rolled my eyes. Quirin and Dara had power abilities, but Dara had told me weeks ago that their seeds were too weak for them to have ever qualified as mages. And their son's seed had been assessed as a similar strength. All of the original inhabitants were the same.

Renley might choose to delay his activation so he could hold on to a childish dream, but it didn't change reality. He would never be a powerful mage.

My dismissal infuriated him, and he stepped close, towering over me, although there was less than a year between us.

"You think you're so clever, Airlie, but there are plenty of things you don't understand. These setbacks are only minor. The General will prevail, and those of us who support him will receive the abilities we truly deserve."

When I didn't look convinced by his fantasy, his voice lowered. "And don't think your sister is free. The General is always two steps ahead, ready to try something else whenever one opportunity fails. And this time he won't be waiting weeks for the next chance."

I frowned, worry gripping me for the first time since seeing Lawson's solo return.

"What does that mean? What is the General planning?"

This time Renley was the one to roll his eyes, stepping away from me. "You don't think I'd tell you that, surely? Just be ready to welcome your sister to Calista. And maybe once she arrives, you'll finally see that the General is right, and we are the future of this kingdom."

CHAPTER 8
CADENCE

Hayes walked slowly over and knelt beside Dara. Placing his hands on her arms for a moment, he closed his eyes. For several long seconds, no one said anything.

He opened them again with a heavy sigh, looking down at Dara before gently closing her eyes. When he stood, his face was somber and drawn.

"I don't think it would have mattered if I'd gotten here quicker. Her condition is unfamiliar to me, but I've never seen such deteriorated organs. To be honest, I'm surprised she lasted so long." He frowned. "I don't know how to classify her ailment, but something in her body was very wrong."

I swallowed, unnerved by the confusion on his face. Hayes was the Master of Healing's second. Everyone spoke of him as the most likely candidate to take Colton's place one day—once he had achieved his mastery and Colton was ready to step down. What had happened to Dara that Hayes had never encountered it before?

I worried at my lip. Could I trust her assertions that Airlie was safe? Looking down at the still body, I tried to make sense of my emotions. Was I sad at her death? Should I be?

She had been one of the raiders and by her own admission, instrumental in Airlie's abduction. But she had also been friends with my mother. She had spoken my name with the warmth and pride of a mother herself, and I couldn't deny that it had affected me. Somewhere, beneath my anger and confusion, sorrow pricked.

Hurrying footsteps made us all turn toward the door in time to see Sutton lead Colton in.

"Oh, Hayes, you're already here," Sutton said before catching sight of Dara and falling silent.

Hayes looked to the head of his affinity. "I was too late to attempt any assistance, but I'd be interested in your assessment regardless. I couldn't determine what ailed her."

Colton raised both eyebrows at this admission. "That certainly surprises me."

He dropped to one knee beside Dara's body with surprising agility given his age. Unlike Hayes, he looked into the distance instead of closing his eyes, but when his focus returned to us, he wore the same frown Hayes had worn, and he had no more answers for us.

"It's certainly a strange matter." He looked at Evermund. "And you say this woman was a raider? You didn't do this to her?"

He shook his head. "We were only talking when she collapsed. Although Cadence was here before I arrived." He glanced at me. "Sutton fetched me after seeing the two of you through the window and growing suspicious."

"She made no attempt to attack me," I said. "And I certainly didn't do anything to her. All we did was talk."

"She claimed she was already dying before she arrived in Tartora." Evermund looked down at her. "She seemed to know the end was very near."

"Is it possible the raiders did this to her?" Sutton asked, unease in his voice.

Everyone silently regarded each other as we considered this unnerving possibility.

"Why would they do that to one of their own?" I asked.

Sutton shrugged. "Who can say? The General doesn't seem like the sort to quibble at using his own people for experimentation if it came to that."

I paled. If Dara hadn't been able to protect herself from him, then she definitely hadn't possessed the authority to keep Airlie safe.

Colton cleared his throat. "If the raiders have some new weapon or ability that can affect a person in such a way, that is of great concern. As is this woman's infiltration of the Guild." He glanced at Zeke. "You didn't hear her coming?"

Zeke's eyes flicked sideways to me for the barest second before he shrugged. "Nothing definitive. I had a hunch the raider mage might not have been alone, but after all these days with no sign of anyone else, I thought I must have imagined it."

Colton's hand landed heavily on his shoulder. "Next time, report any suspicions, no matter how small, young man. We can't afford any more attacks while we have the delegations with us."

Zeke nodded, carefully not looking in my direction again.

I bit my lip. Should we have told someone? But what would we have told them?

At least Dara hadn't turned out to be a danger to anyone. But if we'd found her earlier, could I have convinced her to tell me where to find Airlie? She had been sympathetic enough that it might have been possible. Perhaps Colton and Hayes could even have helped her.

Tears welled in my eyes. I'd made a mistake—one with real consequences.

"You couldn't have known," Zeke whispered in my ear.

I looked up, hoping my gratitude showed in my face. The other four were still clustered around Dara, absorbed in a conversation about how to proceed. But of course Zeke had seen me and understood my emotions.

"If only I'd thought to look underground," I murmured back.

He shook his head. "Everyone's been distracted with the tour. You can't blame yourself. And none of us are responsible for whatever it is that happened to her." His eyes wandered toward her body, fresh concern filling his voice. "Maybe no one is responsible for it. She was a power mage, wasn't she? That's how she hid from you?"

"Not a mage, but we shared an affinity." I kept my voice low, even though the others in the room weren't paying us any attention.

"What if..." He let the words trail off, as if he didn't want to speak the rest of the sentence aloud.

I considered his words, trying to work out what had him so worried. As soon as I guessed the direction of his thoughts, my stomach clamped and twisted.

"You think this might have happened because of her affinity?" I asked. "Like a condition that's unique to us? Is that possible?"

He shrugged. "I've never heard of anything like it, and I can't imagine why you would suffer different illnesses from the rest of us. But how else can there be a condition neither Hayes nor Colton have ever encountered?" He growled. "I wish I could get a proper look at those books in the forbidden section of the library. There must be more practical tomes in there that would mention such a thing if it exists."

"I would settle for something that actually explains how to use my ability." I glanced at the others, but they were still involved in their own conversation. "We only spoke for a matter of minutes, but she taught me something new. I might be stronger than she ever was, but she actually knew how to use her ability. If only I had someone—" I cut myself off as I realized how my lamentation might be received.

Sure enough, Zeke grimaced. "I know. I'm sorry. I wish I could be more help. I didn't expect your affinity to work so differently from the other three." He ran a frustrated hand through his hair.

"Actually, I might have an idea about that. From what Dara showed me." I groaned. "But I don't have time to think about that now. We just got proof about Airlie's abduction. She needs to be my focus now."

"Airlie?" Zeke gave me a strange look. "I don't think—"

I held up a hand, cutting him off. "Don't tell me I need to focus on myself, or that I can help her better in the long run by learning more about my ability. I've been telling myself that for months, but this is different. If I have a chance to go after her, I have to take it."

"I—" Zeke frowned, glancing toward Evermund before shrugging and letting the matter drop.

I gazed out the window again. Some light still lingered thanks to the start of summer, but how long would it take to gather forces and supplies? Too long, probably.

Evermund approached, breaking my focus. "Master Colton is going to take charge of Dara's body. He and Hayes would like a chance to study the condition that killed her more closely."

I nodded, only half listening.

"I'm going to speak to the king," he continued, capturing my full attention.

"Good." I nodded. "We've wasted enough time."

Zeke looked at me sideways before directing his words at Evermund. "Do you mind if I come?"

Evermund's brows rose, but after a moment's hesitation, he nodded his assent. Zeke looked back to me.

"You don't mind being left alone, Cadence?"

I assured them I didn't just as two servants stepped through the door carrying a stretcher. They were clearly used to working with Colton because they barely broke stride at the discovery that Dara had already died, moving with detached efficiency as they lifted her body onto the stretcher.

Within moments everyone had left the suite, going their separate ways while I stood alone, tears in my eyes. She might have been a raider, but I had sensed kindness in Dara, and she deserved a better send off than this.

Where was her husband now? Was he already mourning her?

I returned to my interrupted packing with mechanical movements. Only once I'd finished loading the last of Evermund's office supplies did I look down at the bag and give myself a mental shake. I was wasting my time. These were items for the tour, not for a rescue mission. We wouldn't be taking them with us.

With dismay, I remembered that our bags of clothes were already removed. Most likely they had been loaded into a wagon already—probably into the most inaccessible spot, given how such things always seemed to go.

I winced. Hopefully whichever servants were assigned the task of retrieving them wouldn't be too resentful about the matter.

Without anything to keep my hands busy, I soon found myself pacing up and down the suite. My mind whirled in circles, trying to settle on the practical matters needed for such a journey but instead leaping from thought to thought without latching on to anything.

It seemed forever, but finally the door opened again. I burst into speech without waiting for Evermund to step fully inside.

"I'm ready to leave immediately. We'll just need to have someone retrieve—" I broke off as I absorbed his face and manner. I had never seen him look so thunderous.

"What happened?" I faltered.

"There will be no rescue mission."

"What?" I stared at him, trying to absorb his words. "The king won't send any guards with us? We have to go on our own?"

Evermund's eyes sparked. "We are not even released for that. My uncle accepts that Airlie has been abducted and is being held against her will, but he cannot spare anyone with the tour about to begin. Not even me."

"Oh." I sank down onto the closest chair, all the anticipation draining out of me. "I suppose especially not you. You're one of the strongest mages in the kingdom."

My earlier thoughts seemed foolish now. We were in the aftermath of a fresh attack with multiple foreign delegations present, and we were due to leave on the tour tomorrow. Of course the king wouldn't agree to send out a group of mages and soldiers on a separate mission.

I looked up at Evermund. I had never heard him refer to the king using their family connection before or heard him speak of his monarch with such rebellious anger. But when he felt my eyes on him, his mouth twisted into an apologetic grimace.

"I'm sorry, Cadence. I know the timing is bad, but I thought I had a chance of convincing him. If we had your sister back, it would be a strong extra layer of protection on the tour. But..." He sighed, slumping into a chair himself. "He said if we had specific information on her location, he might have considered it, but as it is..."

Disappointment churned inside my stomach alongside embarrassment at my naivety. But I had to acknowledge the king's point.

"If only Dara had told us where they are." I sighed.

"He's on edge because of the strength of that mage who attacked us."

"She said his name is Lawson," I reminded him, inconsequentially.

"Lawson, then. We still don't understand how the General got his hands on such a powerful mage. The census has been completed, and no one of particular strength is missing from Tartora. Not from any affinity."

"He must be a raider, then," I said.

"He must." Evermund looked more uneasy than that fact seemed to warrant. "And, given that, King Marius is on edge. We don't know if another attack is coming."

I opened my mouth, only to close it again. Since I was the primary target of their attacks, it might help the tour if I was to leave in search of Airlie. But I was never going to convince Evermund of that, let alone the king—not without revealing my true affinity. And if I did that, they were more likely to lock me up than let me go chasing after the General.

I sighed. I might have confirmation that the raiders had taken Airlie, but all the old impediments still applied. I would be unlikely to find her—let alone rescue her—on my own.

"Gia said you asked everyone to look for signs of Airlie during the tour," I said after a long heavy pause. "Maybe now they actually will."

Evermund ran a weary hand down his face. "Yes, perhaps they will. At least I've regained some credibility from this."

I gave him a sideways look. How much had his position been damaged by his support of Airlie? It was just like with Zeke. Both of them had accepted undeserved blows to their reputation in support of Airlie and me.

Pushing aside my own crushing disappointment, I stood up and managed to paste on a small smile.

"Surely we'll find some hint as to the raiders' location during the tour. And we're leaving tomorrow, so perhaps the delay of our rescue mission isn't any great blow after all."

Evermund's return smile looked equally feigned, but at least we were both trying.

"We're supposed to gather early in the morning," he said,

"but don't worry if you sleep in. Whatever their stated intentions, half the court, three foreign delegations, and half the Mages' Guild will not be leaving at the crack of dawn."

My smile grew a little more real. "That's a certainty. Even with just Airlie and me, we never left for our supply-gathering trips at our intended time. Of course, it was always me that was the hold up, and it used to drive Airlie crazy."

"Sleep as late as you want, and you won't need to worry about being the delay this time, I promise you," Evermund said with a smile that was half-amused, half-frustrated.

Taking the hint, I said goodnight and hurried outside to my room. For all the joking, I was far more worried about getting to sleep at all than sleeping late.

CHAPTER 9

CADENCE

As it turned out, both predictions ended up coming true. After spending much of the night tossing and turning, my thoughts a helpless muddle of the upcoming tour, Airlie's predicament, and confused sorrow over Dara's death, I finally fell asleep and slept long past my normal waking hour.

Despite the permission given me by the Royal Mage himself, I responded to my lateness with mild panic. Throwing myself out of bed, I stuffed my final travel items into the small bag I intended to carry with me. I lingered over my books, running my fingers over my mother's old favorite. But a moment later I shook my head and sprinted out the door without it.

I wasn't a senior official, and I couldn't justify taking heavy and unnecessary baggage on the tour. As it was, I was fortunate no one had paid enough attention to me to ask why I was going at all. Evermund's responsibility to keep me housed and fed as a dependent of his apprentice could easily have been met by leaving me behind at the Guild.

As I stepped into the courtyard garden, my heart nearly stopped. It was empty. All the wagons had already gone.

A moment later, my breathing resumed, as I remembered

the tour guests were starting on barges on the river. We would float downstream during the day but moor the barges each night. Since the boats didn't have enough space to house so many important guests overnight, the wagons would travel the river road alongside us, setting up a camp ahead of us each evening. No doubt they had actually left at the nominated time.

I was racking my brain, trying to remember if I was supposed to head straight for the river or muster somewhere in the Guild first, when Evermund strode out the door to his sitting room.

"Ah, there you are, Cadence." He grinned at me. "You'll be shocked to hear that, despite the late hour, no one has yet left for the river. I saved you some breakfast."

I smiled back, relieved, and accepted the two rolls he held out, wrapped in a napkin.

"Thanks!" I pulled one free and tore it in half. "Where should I be now?"

He grimaced. "I'm obligated to travel with the royal party and the delegates. But I'm sure you'll enjoy the journey more with your friends." At a curious look from me, he added, "I believe my troublesome young cousins have insisted on spending as much time away from their parents as possible."

My smile grew as I hurried through my impromptu meal. The journey might actually be fun if I could spend it with Gia.

"In fact, here come the apprentices now." Evermund glanced toward the apprentice door where a stream of people was emerging into the courtyard, heading for the open gates. "I'll leave you to join them. Please do make it onto one of the barges. I would hate to have to leave the tour on the first day to come back and find you."

"Don't worry. I'll be there," I assured him, before catching sight of Gia and dashing off with a belated wave.

I heard the soft sound of a chuckle before plunging into the noise of the apprentice group. From the faces around me, it looked like those proficients fortunate enough to have been chosen for the tour were part of the group, probably having been given the task of keeping an eye on the apprentices.

"Cadence!" Gia shouted my name, running over to latch on to my arm. "I thought I was going to have to tip you out of bed myself."

"Lacking your sense, we've been gathered in the dining hall since just after dawn, as instructed," Nikolas said in a sour voice.

I tried to hide my amusement for his sake. "Evermund predicted we would be late to start and told me not to rush."

"It's nice for some." Nikolas sent a poisonous glare in Gia's direction, but she ignored him completely.

"I've always wanted to go on a river trip," she said. "I used to plead with my parents to take us when we were younger."

"Shockingly, they refused." Nikolas looked in my direction. "I imagine they weighed the risk of Gia ending up in the river at about fifty-fifty and decided to forbid the whole thing. If you think she's bad now..."

I snorted. "Promise me you won't end up in the river this time, Gia. I don't fancy performing a heroic rescue."

Gia laughed. "With this many elements mages around? You wouldn't have to lift a finger. Exactly like I explained to our parents all those times. If I had tumbled in, a little wetting wouldn't have hurt me."

"Perhaps they thought it would be a bad look for the monarchy," Nikolas said. "Back then they hadn't accepted that their oldest child is an uncontainable hoyden."

"Goodness!" I slipped my arm through Gia's. "Lack of sleep makes you cranky, Nikolas."

Gia chuckled. "Haven't you noticed? He's always cranky. It's part of his charm."

She blew a kiss at her brother, who rolled his eyes. But I noticed his expression lightened somewhat. Even sleep deprived, it was hard not to absorb the air of excitement all around us.

The group surged out through the gate, spilling into the city. Many of the residents of Tarona awaited us, lining the streets in a merry throng. They were here to see their monarchs and the foreign delegations, but they still cheered and waved at the sight of the group of mages. The atmosphere of holiday excitement had gripped more than just the Guild.

Gia and I waved back as Zeke and Bryce appeared beside us.

"Have you come to see us off?" I asked Bryce, noting the wide grin on his face.

He shook his head. "Master Colton decided at the last minute to send one of us along to assist Hayes. I'm the oldest, so the task fell to me."

Zeke clapped him on the shoulder, reminding me that the two were peers and that it wasn't just Bryce who would soon be completing his apprenticeship. I pushed away the uncomfortable thought, focusing instead on my pleasure at seeing Zeke. Last time I talked to him, he hadn't been sure if his mother would insist he travel with his tribe, or if Augusta would win the day with her insistence that he had yet to complete his apprenticeship and was therefore under her authority for the tour.

"It's good to see you here," I said. "This is starting to actually look like fun."

He laughed. "Only you were ever in doubt about that." When Bryce said something to the twins, he leaned a little closer and spoke in a quieter voice. "I think Mother only requested my presence with her so that she could count it as a concession when she later relinquished her claim." He rolled his eyes.

"Regardless of the reason, I'm glad she did relinquish it," I said. "It will make it a lot easier for us to sneak in some training than if you'd been with your tribe."

"Actually, about that—" he began, but Gia pointed out a collection of cute children, waving frantically, and I turned to her, happy to cut off the conversation. I wasn't ready for Zeke to suggest I spend time with his tribe.

We spent the rest of the short walk waving and calling greetings to the crowd. The Guild and palace were located near the eastern edge of the city, so it wasn't long before we reached the river. The water stood in place of the city wall on this side, allowing direct access to the docks for loading and unloading cargo.

The usual hustle and hum of dockworkers had been replaced with bustling servants in blue and gold livery, hurrying on and off what looked like an endless row of royal barges. I stopped in my tracks to gape at them.

"Is the entire palace coming?"

Gia laughed and shook her head. "The whole kingdom doesn't have enough barges for that. Plus we'll be sleeping in tents and riding once we reach the coast. Only those able and willing to manage the trip were considered for inclusion."

The wide, low vessels had a rectangular shape, only the pointed prows giving them the somewhat rounded look I associated with boats. A low cabin took up most of the large deck, leaving only a broad walkway all the way around the edge, with a little extra space at the prow and stern.

One of the proficients at the head of the group began gesturing and calling instructions, leading the apprentices toward the barge at the back of the line. But when we tried to follow, a second proficient stopped us. Ignoring Gia's mutinous look, he directed her toward the front barge which gleamed with fresh paint in the royal shade of purple.

For a moment I thought she meant to ignore him, but after a brief hesitation she complied. When I tried to disentangle my arm from hers, however, she held on tight. I glanced helplessly back at Zeke only to find he and Bryce remained with Nikolas. After a moment of consideration, I relaxed.

While travel with the entire royal family wouldn't be my first choice, at least Evermund would be there as well, so I wouldn't be completely out of place. Especially if I wasn't the only non-royal apprentice in attendance.

Gia scowled as we waited our turn to file over the broad plank that gave access to the deck. Nikolas directed a reproving look at her, edging around us to take the lead.

"Pretending to be apprentices doesn't change the truth."

Her scowl deepened, but she turned it toward the ground, refusing to engage.

He shrugged and looked at me. "The apprentices are in the last barge. No one is going to put the crown princess in such an exposed position."

I raised my eyebrows. "Are they expecting trouble, then?"

He shrugged. "After three attacks within the Guild itself? They would be fools not to." He strode onto the boat.

I winced, trying not to imagine what form the attack might take as Gia dropped my arm and prodded me onto the plank. But when I stepped up onto the wood, all other thoughts were wiped out by a sick feeling in my stomach.

I froze, only moving again when Gia prodded me once more from behind. The sudden nausea had been all too familiar— although it was usually far more debilitating. I stepped onto the deck, moving out of the way so Gia could join me and then following in her wake, paying little attention to my surroundings.

Dara was dead. I couldn't be sensing her now. Could it be a faint trace of the power that had once clung to her?

I frowned as we reached the stern. The sensation still lingered, stronger than the wisps I had felt after Dara's passing.

I probed inward, remembering her words, and realized with surprise that my ability was still shaped into a shell around me.

I hadn't given it any further thought after the tragic turn of the evening, but apparently it didn't require any conscious effort to hold its shape.

Tentatively, I directed my ability back into its old ball. Immediately a wave of nausea, stronger than anything I'd felt in the Guild, hit me. I grabbed at the ship's rail to keep my knees from buckling.

"Cadence?" Gia asked. "You look sick."

Her voice was a distant buzzing, my mind unable to focus on her words past the effort to keep the contents of my stomach in place. The boat rocked slightly in the swift moving current, and I lost the battle.

Grabbing the rail with both hands, I leaned over the side and was sick into the water below. Even when the full contents of my breakfast had been expelled, I kept retching until my brain kicked back in, and I instructed my ability to re-form the protective shell.

I waited a moment as the nausea subsided before raising my head weakly to find the other four watching me with identical expressions of horror.

Nikolas chuckled. "We haven't even left the dock yet. This is going to be a long trip for you."

My eyes narrowed, but I didn't have the time or energy to be offended by his amusement. I had far bigger problems than if my nausea had been caused by seasickness as he assumed.

"I'll get you some water," Gia said, goaded into motion by her brother's heartlessness.

She dropped onto a knee to rummage in the pack she had dumped on the deck. Bryce, on the other hand, murmured an incomprehensible excuse and slipped away. From the queasy look on his face, I suspected he didn't want to be around anything that might tip him toward sickness himself.

Zeke, however, stepped forward and surprised me by sweeping my hair up and away from my face. He held it patiently while I searched my pockets for a tie to hold it in place. As soon as I had it secured, he let his hands drop, but he didn't step back.

"Are you all right?" The furrow on his brow was so deep, I was caught by a momentary, foolish urge to put a fingertip into it.

"Here!" Gia thrust a water skin at me, and I used it to clean my face and wash out my mouth.

I handed it back to her with murmured thanks, but my focus was on Zeke.

"We have to get back to shore!" It was a struggle to keep my voice low.

His frown returned. "It wasn't travel sickness, then?"

I glanced at the others. Nikolas had turned to look over the railing on the other side, toward the dock, and Gia was busy replacing the contents of her bag which she had thrown out in her haste to find the water skin.

I adjusted the protective layer of my ability, making the smallest crack so I could test what was on the other side. As soon as I opened it, I slammed it back into place, cutting off the roiling sickness waiting on the other side. If anything, it had grown stronger.

I grabbed Zeke's arm with both hands, my nails digging in as my anxiety rose.

"We have to get everyone off the boats!"

"Slow down," he murmured. "Why? What happened?"

I swallowed, trying to separate my thoughts from the urgency that was more physical reaction than logic.

"It's the same feeling that lingered around Dara—like tainted power. She said it was whatever power destroyed Calista—the so-called protections. But whatever is here now is much stronger than what clung to her."

Zeke's eyes widened, and I remembered we hadn't had a proper chance to debrief my meeting with Dara.

"Could this be coming from the raiders?" he asked with alarm.

"Maybe. Dara basically told me they've been dragging this tainted power into Tartora with them every time they cross the border. That's why the border regions have started having trouble with it. But it doesn't really matter if they've sent it intentionally or not—either way it isn't good. And a boat seems like a vulnerable place to be."

Zeke looked back over his shoulder. "The royals have arrived, along with my mother. They're boarding right now."

"We have to stop them!"

"Any suggestions how?" Zeke looked down at me, his mouth twisted.

"There has to be a way." I tried to think despite the unbalanced feeling that was now leaching through my shield. "Colton! Colton said if you had so much as a hunch, you should report it."

Zeke frowned. "Colton stayed behind, remember? And I'm separated from my vine network now. How would I explain it?" He hesitated. "Unless you want to tell them the truth?"

I froze. Could I do that? My eyes found Gia, who had been called over by Nikolas, perhaps to watch their parents board. I would love to tell her the truth. But telling Apprentice Gia meant giving the information to Crown Princess Morgiana—and through her, the royal family.

King Marius's grandfather had attempted to massacre every person with my affinity—down to the last baby. I couldn't tell him the truth when I hadn't even found Airlie yet.

"No, we can't tell them. We have to find another way."

Our barge lurched as men on the dock unlooped the enormous ropes lashing us in place. Panic rose up in me. We were launching.

"What about the raiders themselves?" Zeke asked, his voice an echo of my own dismay. "Can you sense them along the

bank at all? If you can pinpoint them, I could say I saw something out there."

I grasped onto the idea, sending out my awareness to sweep
along the far side of the bank. The barge rocked as the men on
the dock used stout sticks to push it away from shore and into
the current, but I fought to keep my focus.

After a moment, I looked back at Zeke. "There's no one
anywhere near."

I turned toward the dock. It was harder to search on this
side, given the mass of people, but it didn't take long to determine no one among them had unusual strength or a power
affinity of any level.

I looked helplessly back at Zeke. "I can't find any sign of
raiders."

He frowned doubtfully. "What about that strange power
you felt? Is it decreasing? Maybe we're moving away from it?"

This time I was more cautious as I manipulated my ability,
leaving the smallest of openings for me to sample the environment around me. I immediately closed it, however, shaking my
head so hard my brain hurt.

"It's getting worse."

Zeke hesitated, clearly torn. "It didn't hurt anyone at the
Guild. Are you sure it's a danger?"

I glared at him. "Didn't hurt anyone? Dara died!"

"Sorry." He grimaced. "But we don't know what killed her.
It wasn't as if the power was attacking her." He glanced at me
sharply. "Was it?"

Reluctantly I conceded that it hadn't seemed to interact
with her at all. But I couldn't accept the idea that it was safe to
ignore what I felt now.

"I wish you could feel it for yourself," I whispered. "It feels
so...wrong. Twisted and warped. It keeps writhing, and..." I
broke off, pulling away from the memory before it became vivid
enough to send me back to the side of the barge.

I gestured toward the rail. "Just a moment of its full force made me violently sick. If I wasn't protecting myself right now, I'd still be retching even though there's nothing left to come up."

A curious gleam leaped into Zeke's eyes. "You're protecting yourself? How?"

I shook my head. "We can talk about that later. For now, what are we going to do?"

I gazed over the stern of the barge, watching the row of vessels now bobbing in the current behind us. The apprentices in the final boat might still be waiting their turn to launch, but most of the barges were afloat now. I shivered. They looked so vulnerable on the water.

Zeke turned toward the prow, hesitating. "I'll just have to tell them there's a danger and think of how to explain it later."

I nodded, understanding his reluctance but unable to come up with a better plan. Before he could leave, however, we were hit by a surge of the twisted power so strong that I felt it through my protective casing.

CHAPTER 10

CADENCE

The world around us turned upside down.

Water erupted into the air on all sides, spray flying in every direction. The boat lurched, tipping one way and then another, as impossible gusts buffeted it from both sides and the river beneath it heaved and surged.

Screams and shouts echoed around us as we tipped dangerously. I stumbled, losing my footing and sliding hard against the rail. I started to overbalance, my momentum tipping me over the top when another body slammed into me, sandwiching me between him and the boat and anchoring me in the process.

"Sorry!" Zeke gasped, regaining his feet and gripping the rail solidly in both hands with me protected between his arms.

He established his grip just in time. The boat lurched in the other direction, and we both would have slid all the way across the deck without his hold.

When the boat tipped back again, settling flat in the water with a jarring thud, a long green rope appeared. The vine flung itself across the expanse of river from the far bank, latching on to the rail and wrapping itself around like the tentacle of a giant octopus. A second one appeared, but this time it landed on Zeke, winding around his arm.

He shouted but held his grip, saving us as the boat lurched again, tipping backward this time as the wave hit the front of the barge.

"Much more of this, and we'll sink," Zeke shouted in my ear, struggling to be heard above the rush of the wind and the slap of the unnatural waves against the wood.

Gasping from the spray that kept hitting my face, I twisted within the circle of his arms, trying to see over his shoulder to check if Gia was safe. But at Zeke's shout of pain, I spun back around.

"My arm!" he cried, and my eyes flew to the vine in time to see it turn to ash and blow away, leaving behind a red welt as if it had burned him in the process.

Still he held on, determination masking the pain on his face. "What sort of attack is this?" he asked.

The wood at the stern of the boat sprouted, green life appearing from the aged wood only to rip itself free and fall into the churning water below. It was as if the entire world had assumed the roiling, writhing wrongness that had turned my stomach.

Realization gripped me. This was what that tainted power looked like in action, throwing itself against the natural world without order or purpose. Was this sort of mindless, chaotic attack what the border villages had been enduring?

Reaching out with my awareness, I searched for the power, grateful for the protective casing that allowed me to do it without discomfort. I found it everywhere.

A vine made of tainted power lashed toward two figures on the opposite side of the stern. I called a warning to the twins, but my cry was lost in the explosion of water as the power hit the surface of the river just beside the boat. Both of them were thoroughly drenched, but when the water receded, they remained behind, grimly clinging to the rail.

Gia's face was scrunched in concentration, roots of power sinking below her, through the hull of the boat and into the water as she fought to calm the stretch of river directly below us. But she had only been activated by Master Drake a matter of weeks ago, and her skill was little match for the fury of the attacking power. No sooner did she calm the water than it was hit with a fresh vine of twisted power. I could only imagine the same process was underway with elements mages up and down the river. Without their efforts, we would no doubt have flipped already.

"We should tie ourselves on," Nikolas shouted over the wind.

Gia nodded but didn't move, her attention on her battle with the river. His eyes latched on to a coil of rope looped over a hook near the stern. Letting go of the rail, he lurched toward it just as I sensed the tainted power that clung to it.

"Stop!" I screamed at full volume, but the howling wind tore my words away.

Nikolas reached for it, his fingers making contact. Immediately the tainted power leaped to him, and a cracking sound carried through a brief lull in the wind.

He screamed—a sound of pure pain—as one of his fingers visibly flattened, crushed by an invisible force. He snatched his hand back, but it was too late. The power clung to him.

He screamed again as the next finger was crushed, and Gia abandoned her efforts, rushing toward her brother instead. Now I was screaming as well, fighting against Zeke's hold as I tried to get to them. If Gia touched Nikolas, the power might spread to her.

With the boat still throwing us this way and that, I couldn't untangle myself from Zeke fast enough. Instead I reached out with my ability.

It fought me, repelled by the tainted power instead of drawn to it like it was to normal power. But my fear gave me strength, and I forced my ability to obey my direction. Seizing the tainted power, I was immediately hit by the full force of the nausea. It ripped through me as if my protective shell didn't exist.

I gritted my teeth, letting Zeke support the majority of my weight as I concentrated all my energy on wrestling with the tainted power. We fought back and forth, as I tried to tame the wrongness. It bucked the restraint, and I felt my grip slipping.

The wind died for a moment between gusts, and I caught Nikolas's pained groan. Fresh determination filled me as the boat rose up on yet another wave.

Fighting the strange power wasn't working. Instead I gave up the struggle, restraining my instinctive urge to smooth the power back to normalcy. Embracing the wrongness, I let it wash over me, changing my own ability to match its turmoil instead of the other way around.

My knees gave out as my stomach rebelled, the nausea now racing through every part of me. My eyes watered, and I could barely see, bile rising in my throat. I was limp within Zeke's arms as my physical body rejected the unnatural twisting of my ability.

But the tainted power no longer fought me or attempted to repel my ability. It had gone docile beneath my command, recognizing my authority in a way it hadn't earlier.

I still didn't know what I could safely do with it, however. I had no pattern to follow like the ones provided by Annora and Drake when the chasm opened beneath us. And even if I'd learned how to shape it myself, I didn't know if the tainted power had the capacity to follow any normal pattern.

For now, the best I could do was get it away from the barges and the river. I looked toward the eastern bank. Forest started only a short distance from the water, the trees in this section clustered too thickly to allow for buildings among them. Further north, as well as downstream, towns had been built on patches of cleared land, but here there was nothing but trees.

Somewhere, from what seemed like far away, Zeke was calling my name. But I knew if I broke concentration for even a moment, the illness boiling inside me would become unbearable, and I would cease to function. Only the overwhelming focus on my task was keeping me sane.

I threw the tainted power I had gathered off the rope and Nikolas's hand toward the forest, driving it far into the trees. In the distance, the screech of disturbed birds sounded, and I urged them onward. Hopefully whatever damage the power did to the trees would be enough to scare off any animals lingering in the area.

Once all the power had streamed away, my changed ability reached happily for the next closest vine of tainted power. Across the water a distant scream sounded, and I threw away my hesitation. Grabbing at the closest chunk of power, I hurled it toward the trees as well.

As soon as it was gone, I grabbed for the next vine, and then the next one. I kept going and going, reaching further and further away until I could reach no more. A distant jangle of tainted power upstream called to me, but I couldn't reach far enough to grasp it. And since it was beyond reach of the people I could sense on the line of barges, it was safe to leave it be.

Although the final barge must carry people who felt familiar to me, it was hard to identify them. Their abilities now repelled me, as the tainted power had once done. For a moment I lingered, caught up in the curiosity of it, and then someone shook me roughly, returning my focus to my own body.

As soon as the mental distraction ended, I retched violently, my whole body spasming. I thought it was Zeke who held me, but I couldn't be sure, couldn't even care.

My body, no longer silenced, screamed its defiance of the

change to my ability. I shuddered, feeling traces of the tainted power clinging to me, as it had done to Dara. What had she said? If she was stronger, she would have sent it back, pushed it away.

I mustered the faltering remnants of my strength and thrust the lingering power over the side of the rail. It dissipated into the water below, too weak to cause any harm against the might of a river.

Slumping back against the deck, I took a shuddering breath. But while the nausea had eased, my insides still clanged, my head resounding like a giant bell. Something was still wrong.

With horror, I realized that my own ability remained twisted and attuned to the tainted power. Even now, I could feel the distant echoes of it in the forest, calling to me.

I tried to push it away, but there was nothing to push. No power remained near me, just my own ability, writhing in my chest. A scream built inside me, but I tamped it down, the need for secrecy too deeply ingrained to let it out.

But I wouldn't be able to hold it in for long. I had to do something. I tried to reach for the normal power that coated the boat, remnants from every mage in the small flotilla working to keep it afloat. But now my ability pushed away from the power, trying to slide around it instead of grasping hold.

I groaned, dredging up more willpower and forcing myself to latch on to it. It fought against my ability, but I dove into the sensation of it, like I had done in reverse with the tainted power.

With a deep sigh of relief, I felt my ability swap back to its normal state. I kept my eyes closed for a moment, just feeling the rhythm of my breaths as they moved my chest up and down. The boat rocked slightly, but nothing like the violent pitching of earlier. Instead we floated gently downstream, as we had before the onslaught of the tainted power.

But calls and hurrying feet around me made me open my

eyes. Zeke's face hovered over me, a look of concern etched on his features. When I gave a weak smile, he sat back on his heels, giving his own sigh of relief.

"Are you all right?" A healing mage I vaguely recognized appeared over his shoulder.

I pushed myself up to a sitting position and nodded.

"Just feeling unwell." I grimaced. "I was sick even before we left dock."

The woman winced. "That can't have been a good experience for anyone with seasickness."

"I don't think it was a good experience for any of us," Zeke said. "How is the rest of the barge faring?"

"Some bumps and bruises, and a couple of broken limbs," she said. "Everyone inside has been healed already, though. We got to you last because we didn't realize there was anyone back here. You're lucky you didn't get washed away."

"I would have been without Zeke to keep me steady. His arm was injured, though."

The healing mage turned to him with a businesslike look, although she kept talking as she placed her hand just above the blackened skin.

"As soon as the boat stopped pitching, we did a head count and realized the prince and princess were missing. Thankfully they're fine. And you will be, too." She paused a moment before pulling her hand away from his smooth, undamaged arm. "There you go. All better."

"We were lucky to get through with nothing worse," Zeke said, his gaze focused on Gia and Nikolas.

Hayes stood next to the prince, who was flexing the fingers of his injured hand experimentally. I could no longer see any sign of damage to the two fingers that had been crushed, and Nikolas was even smiling slightly.

His uninjured arm was wrapped around his sister's shoulders, tucking her in against his side in the most tender gesture I had yet seen from the pair. From the subsiding shudders that still racked her frame, I suspected she had been crying on his behalf.

"I'm glad Hayes is on board," I said, and both the other two nodded.

"His Majesty may decide he wants Master Drake stationed on this barge in future as well," the healing mage said. "Although I'm sure the apprentices were glad to have him with them on this occasion. Whatever that was, it came from upstream, and as the last barge, they would have been first hit."

I glanced across the water, although there were too many barges between us to get a good look at the one that carried the apprentices. The healing mage ambled away in response to a signal from Hayes, and I looked at Zeke.

"Don't worry," I said, wanting to remove the concern from his eyes. "There were mages spread across all the barges, and their efforts were enough to keep anyone from going overboard. I would have noticed if anyone was in the water. It was a smart idea to put Drake in the last barge. Given Calista is upstream, it placed him in the first line of defense."

"But would the elements mages have been enough to keep everyone safe if you weren't here?" he asked. "It was you who drove off the attack, wasn't it?"

"If it even was an attack," I countered. "Where are the attackers, if so? There's still no one anywhere near us."

Zeke's eyes narrowed. "Whether the raiders directed it downriver from afar, or were lurking nearby, hoping to leap in when the barges capsized, is irrelevant. There's no way the timing was a coincidence. And stop trying to distract me. It was you who sent the power away, correct?"

I nodded. "But it was the elements mages on all the boats who kept us from sinking. It would have been over long before I could help if it wasn't for their efforts." I frowned, considering the matter. "If I hadn't sent it away, the tainted power would have run out eventually. But I have no idea if we had enough mages present to hold out that long."

"Tainted power?" Zeke stared at me.

I shrugged. "I have to call it something. It's what I felt earlier on the river and before that on Dara. It's power, but warped and directionless—just attacking everything without purpose. If this is what's lurking in the fallen kingdom, I can understand why no one lives there."

"Except you," Zeke said, having long since heard the true story of my origins.

I tipped my head to the side, considering the matter. "I actually might have an idea about that." The thought was formulating in my mind, even as I spoke.

"Because of Dara, we know I'm not the only one left in the kingdoms with a power affinity. And she said she wasn't alone among the raiders—quite the opposite. What if it's having a power affinity that keeps someone safe in the fallen kingdom? My ability is like oil and water with the tainted power. Maybe my father's ability—and even my unactivated seed—was enough to keep the tainted power away from our home?"

Zeke raised both eyebrows. "It's possible, I suppose. Although your presence wasn't enough to protect us now."

I shrugged. "This was huge—I'm guessing much more than a normal concentration of tainted power. And nothing attacked me directly, like it did with you. But is this the sort of incident that's been occurring among the border villages? Even if it isn't on this scale, how could they protect themselves?"

"They can't," Nikolas said in a low voice, appearing at my side with Gia a step behind. "Which is why we can be grateful the previous instances have been so much smaller in scope. This was far beyond anything that has occurred before."

"Do you think it was a targeted attack?" Zeke asked.

Nikolas shrugged. "If it was, they've made no attempt to follow up their effort with a conventional one." He scanned the riverbank, but I didn't look with him, knowing he would find nothing. "Maybe they were expecting it to be more effective."

"It had better have been an attack," Gia said. "Because if this is the natural escalation from the borders faltering, I don't know what we're going to do." She slipped her arms around my waist, giving me a quick hug. "Hayes just filled us in on what happened last night with that raider in Evermund's suite. I can't believe you didn't mention it! How awful."

I grimaced. "There hasn't been a chance."

"It's wonderful news about your sister being safe, though." She smiled, although the worry didn't entirely leave her eyes.

"Do you think the fallen kingdom's protections could have been what killed that raider woman?" Nikolas asked, gazing down at his healed hand. "She must have come from across the border, or near it, at least. Maybe she was hit like we were, and that's why Hayes had never encountered anything like it. I've certainly never heard of anything like what happened to me."

"It seems possible that's what happened to her. Maybe Colton will work it out while we're gone." My own eyes strayed to Nikolas's healed fingers. "Are you all right now? We wanted to help, but..."

"Neither of you are healing mages, so there's nothing you could have done," he said matter-of-factly. "As I've already told Gia several times. And thanks to Hayes, my hand is now back to normal. There's no need to consider the matter further. We would all be better off putting our mental efforts toward considering how we can prevent any future such incidents."

"There you are, son." Annora rounded the corner of the cabin, stopping to survey the four of us. She inclined her head toward the twins. "Your Highnesses, I believe your parents would like to see you, to reassure themselves of your safety."

Gia sighed faintly but nodded. Grabbing her brother, she towed him away, murmuring something too low for me to hear.

"I'm glad you weren't swept overboard," Annora said in a calm tone, although I detected true worry in her eyes.

"Zeke was steady as a rock," I said. "He kept us both anchored to the rail."

"Excellent work, Zekiel." She smiled at him. "Without your efforts to protect Cadence, we might all be in the river right now."

I frowned, looking between them. Zeke looked irritated, his gaze carefully steering clear of mine. I gulped.

"But of course the main thanks go to you, Cadence," Annora said in a quieter voice than she had yet used. "I assume you took some sort of action to bring about such a sudden end to the incident. It was well-timed as some of the mages inside were faltering from exhaustion."

"I..." I once again looked toward Zeke.

"Really, Mother?" he asked.

She raised a quelling eyebrow. "I hope I am not so rude as to fail to thank someone for potentially saving my life." She looked at me, her severity falling away. "But I can see you're not ready to talk about it right now, and I assure you I don't mean to push you."

"Th...Thank you," I managed to stutter, frustrated at myself for sounding like such a fool. But it had been a long half hour, and I wasn't thinking straight.

Annora smiled graciously, giving Zeke a quick embrace before disappearing back down the side of the barge.

"You told your mother," I said, as soon as she was out of earshot.

He winced. "I'm sorry. I was going to tell you she knew before she—" He sighed. "I should have told you earlier—I know what she's like."

"She was very forbearing about it, at least," I said, placated by his obvious frustration with his mother on my behalf.

"Of course she was." He looked after her, although she was

long gone from sight. "She can be extremely forbearing if she judges it the right strategy to get what she wants."

"And what does she want with me?" I asked, going for directness now the issue was finally out in the open.

"I—" He paused. "That you'll have to ask her."

I looked at him skeptically but didn't press the matter further. Given that they'd just spent nearly two years apart, perhaps he really was unsure about the answer.

But I didn't intend to ask Annora anything of the kind. Not yet, at least. She had said she was willing to let the matter lie, and I intended to take advantage of that offer.

"I'm glad you got a thank you from someone other than me, though," Zeke said. "You saved everyone, but no one even knows about it."

I shrugged. "That's the way I prefer it. It would only make the pressure worse if everyone was looking to me to keep them safe."

Zeke hesitated. "I don't like even asking this because I saw what it did to you, but...Do you think you could keep us all safe if it happened again?"

I paled, considering whether I could knowingly let tainted power infect my ability a second time. But after a moment I nodded reluctantly.

"I'm not saying I want to. But if it came to it, I could. And, of course, I would." I shuddered, despite myself.

Zeke placed an arm around me, pulling me tight against his side. I leaned into him, resting my head on his shoulder and allowing myself to enjoy the unusual contact. I didn't know if he was offering support or trying to warm me up, but either way, I relished the calm steadiness of his presence.

"Let's hope it doesn't happen again," he said into my hair, and I nodded without lifting my head.

It had been an inauspicious start to the tour, but right now,

sitting alone in the stern of the boat with Zeke, it didn't feel
so bad.

CHAPTER 11

AIRLIE

I paced back and forth across the small living space, not worrying about who I might disturb. With Dara gone, and Quirin returning only to sleep most days, I was alone.

At least the food I had been leaving out on the table each evening was gone the next morning. It was the only sign I had that Quirin was doing the bare minimum to keep himself alive.

With a sigh, I stopped pacing as I once again reached the far wall. Endlessly thinking in circles was getting me nowhere. How many nights had I paced the living room of my old home in a similar fashion—always after Cadence went to sleep? The feeling of being trapped was a familiar one from then, as well.

Cadence had been so desperate to leave, without a thought of what might be waiting for us out in the world. But I had been terrified, knowing I was responsible for more than myself.

My earliest memory was of our father telling me to look after my sister. Protect Cadence, watch over Cadence, was the constant refrain of my childhood. According to our father, she was the future of our family—the one who would make every sacrifice worth it.

Except then he got sick and died. Without a healing mage to assist us, I would never know what it was that consumed him from the inside out. He had tried to hide the pain from me, but I had spent too many hours nursing him not to see it in his eyes.

But even on his deathbed, his focus remained the same. I needed to keep my sister safe, to prepare her for a glorious future. But now I would be alone in the effort.

When he died, I froze. He had made me promise to find someone powerful to activate me—had even told me how to trick a mage into doing so, if necessary—but I was paralyzed by uncertainty. In our home we had always been safe, so there we remained.

But the closer Cadence got to seventeen, the more I realized we had to leave. I had always known the plan—our father would activate me, but we needed the most powerful mage possible to activate Cadence. I couldn't cower forever in our safe haven, letting everything our family had fought for turn to nothing. And so we started to lay plans to leave.

Back then, I had been trapped by my own fears and our father's expectations. Now I was trapped by wooden walls, and I couldn't just make up my mind to leave. But neither could I continue to do nothing. The raiders were in the middle of another attack on Cadence, and if it failed, they would try again and again until they managed to capture her—or kill her in the process from what I'd heard about how Lawson's plans went wrong.

I had to find out what they were planning. If I knew the details, I might be able to find some way to sabotage it from here.

Just like last time, the anxiety dissipated once the decision was made, replaced with icy focus. But I could do nothing in the daylight.

I prepared the evening's food as usual, not wanting to give any indication I had unusual plans. I laid out Quirin's share on the table and retreated to my room. But I didn't go to bed.

Instead, I sat by the door, listening for his arrival. Eventually I heard the front door open. His footsteps shuffled across the floor, stopping by the table. Within moments he was moving again, his bedroom door opening and shutting seconds later.

I waited a little longer, making sure he wouldn't re-emerge before inching open my own door. The creak which had plagued it earlier in the day was gone, thanks to the cooking oil I'd lathered on the hinges.

Slipping across the living room, I opened the front door, sticking my head outside. A tall man who took the night watch outside our home several nights a week turned to look at me with an alert expression that changed to confusion when he saw my face.

"Quick!" I opened my eyes as wide as they would go. "It's Quirin! I don't know what's happened, but he's been so grief-stricken about Dara that it's like he's been sleepwalking, and now he—" I looked back inside as if something within the house had caught my attention. When I turned back to my night guard, I had assumed an even more frantic expression. "Quick!"

Galvanized into action, he hurried toward me, and I swung the door wide. The second he stepped across the threshold I hit him between his chest and stomach with the heavy metal saucepan I'd been concealing behind my back.

He dropped to his knees, winded. His eyes bulged as he struggled to suck in a breath, unable to shout or fight back. Moving at lightning speed, I whipped out a gag and stuffed it into his mouth before trussing him up with the longest length of rope Quirin possessed. As soon as he was secured, I took a long rag and double tied the gag around his mouth.

By the time I dragged him across the cabin—a difficult task given his size—and into my room, he was starting to recover from the winding. But despite his attempts to fight, there was little he could do given how tightly I had secured his bindings.

And there was even less he could do once I rolled him under my bed, a narrow space that was such a tight squeeze, I nearly didn't get him in.

I'd prepared by pushing the bed into a corner of the room, blocking access from one side. And once he was stuffed underneath, I dragged the one remaining piece of furniture—a heavy dresser—across to block the other side. With limited capacity to move, I hoped it would be a long time before he managed to wiggle his way out of such a hole.

As soon as I'd finished positioning the dresser, I ran back through the living room and out the front door, carefully closing it behind me. In normal times, I wouldn't have achieved so much without rousing Quirin, but he was too abstracted to care about his surroundings at the moment.

It was a chance I would get only once, though. If they even let me stay with Quirin after this, the guards wouldn't fall for such a trick again.

Slipping through the shadows, I clung close to the edge of buildings as I made my way to the center of the settlement, where the largest of the houses faced the central square and the gate beyond. It doubled as residence and headquarters for the General and usually sat empty when he left. Since he had led out a number of mages—including all those with a power affinity who were loyal to him—earlier in the day, I wasn't likely to get a better chance to look through his things undisturbed.

I avoided the front of the house, where the empty space between the building and the gate would leave me in full view of anyone passing by. Instead I circled around the back, searching until I found a promising window.

Hefting the cloth-wrapped rock that I'd prepared earlier, I paused. It was worth at least trying it first.

To my surprise, the window swung open at my push. Apparently the General didn't keep it locked. The unexpected good fortune made me pause, nervous. But after a moment, I shrugged. I'd come too far to just give up now.

Scrambling through the window, I landed on the wooden floorboards on the other side with a slight thump. Holding my breath, I eased the window closed behind me.

As soon as it was secured, I glanced around the room. I had entered a bedroom, but from the dust on the coverlet of the bed, it didn't see regular use. A guest room, perhaps? Although it was hard to imagine who the General would host in this isolated camp of criminals.

I hurried through the door and into a narrow hallway. I had seen glimpses through the front windows of what looked like a study, so I hurried in that direction. Surely he must keep records of some kind in there, possibly even maps.

Taking a guess at the correct door, I pulled it open and stepped inside.

As soon as I did so, I froze, but it was already too late. A single lantern perched on the desk, illuminating the far end of the room where the General himself sat, writing steadily on a sheet of paper.

CHAPTER 12

AIRLIE

He looked up at my hasty entrance, his eyebrows slowly rising as he took in my identity.

"Well," he said slowly. "This is an unexpected visit." He looked behind me, as if expecting his guard to appear. When no one followed, he surprised me by smiling. "I always had high hopes for you, Airlie."

I scowled at him, but he ignored it, gesturing for me to take one of the seats across the desk, just as if I was an invited guest.

"I imagine you're wondering about this new attack I conducted today," he said conversationally. "I'm not in the least surprised you've gotten word of it. It's so hard to keep secrets in a place like this."

Deciding to brazen it out, I matched his smile, taking the indicated seat.

"I just wish I'd received word the attack team was already back."

He chuckled. "Ah, so that's the reason for your visit. Yes, we returned just after dark."

"And were you successful?" I asked coolly.

He leaned back in his chair. "That depends on your definition of success. We didn't capture your sister, if that's what you mean."

I carefully maintained my neutral demeanor, hiding my relief at his words.

"Neither is she deceased," he added as an afterthought, loosing the final band around my chest. "May I inquire as to whether the man on guard duty at your house this evening is so fortunate?"

"He'll be fine," I said shortly. "And I have no doubt you're even now hatching some fresh scheme to get your hands on my sister."

"You've certainly got me figured out," the General said in a mild voice that only increased his sinister presence.

His close cropped, dark hair matched the military title he had bestowed on himself, giving him a forbidding look that seemed utterly at odds with his current manner. Could I risk taking advantage of his unexpectedly mild response to my incursion?

"What I want to know is why," I said, after a brief pause.

He raised an eyebrow. "That's a very broad question. Why what?"

"Why the interest in Cadence and me? You say you want to reclaim Calista, but what do we have to do with that?" I licked my lips before voicing the question I'd never dared to ask aloud before. "There have always been rumors the youngest prince escaped the massacre. Was that our grandfather? Is that why my ability is so strong?"

"Do you mean to ask if you're heir to the Calistan throne?" The General threw back his head and laughed.

I waited for his amusement to die away, gripping the seat beneath me with tight hands.

"No, my dear," he said, when his mirth subsided. "I'm afraid you are not."

His endearment set my teeth on edge, but I said nothing.

He cocked his head to the side. "Are you disappointed?"

"Hardly," I scoffed. "Only a fool would desire such a burden. The fallen kingdom is no prize."

"A very neatly delivered insult," the General said approvingly, "since I have made no secret of desiring the role." He smiled. "I believe you and I could deal very well, Airlie, if you would only see reason."

"Perhaps it is you who needs to see reason," I said calmly, despite my racing heart.

He leaned forward, his eyes narrowing. "You are but a child still, despite your strength, and there is much at play here you don't yet understand. Which is why I've been so forbearing. I still believe you will end up joining my cause by choice. It's your cause as well, after all. You might not be royal, but you're still Calistan. And you do have incredible power. By my side, you could help shape the new Calista."

He sat back, as if to let his words sink in. I couldn't deny that he had so far been much gentler than I had expected from my brief previous encounter with him. Even around camp he usually appeared commanding and brusque—expecting and receiving instant obedience to his orders.

Cold efficiency was how I would previously have characterized his manner, and I had marveled at the number of followers he had under his spell. But now I was seeing an entirely different side of him. Warm and almost charming, it was easy to see how he managed to win people over.

Here in his study, I had his full attention as he invited me into his inner circle. And I couldn't deny the temptation to feel flattered by the compliment.

I steeled myself, focusing my mind on the true nature of the man across from me. As if sensing the change in my manner, he leaned forward again.

"I have no patience for talk of lost heirs. The last thing we need is a return to the past. It's no secret that I rejoice at the destruction of the old royal family. They brought about their own downfall with pride and arrogance."

"Are you saying they're to blame for their own massacre?"

I matched him look for look.

"They are," he said, his certainty more convincing than I was willing to admit. "The young children may have been relatively blameless, but I have no doubt they would have been raised in the same mold as their parents. And their slaughter only proves why the royal family of Tartora are no more fit to rule than the Calistans were. It is time for new blood and a new era. The nomads have the right idea."

"Then you don't intend to start a royal lineage of your own?" I asked, disbelievingly.

He shook his head. "I have no wife or children. Nor do I intend ever to have them. I will build Calista up from the ashes, and when I am gone, it will be up to Calista to decide who will replace me."

I frowned. It was an unexpected sentiment, coming from a tyrant ruler.

"You see, Airlie," he pressed. "I care for the future of Calista. I might be the only one who does. In Tartora, you probably heard tell of my villainy in snatching away innocent villagers."

He paused inquiringly, and I reluctantly nodded.

"But have you seen any such captives here?" he asked.

Again I shook my head. I had been permitted to talk to anyone within the walls, and I had found no sign of other prisoners. Many of the original inhabitants spoke of the General warily, defiance in their eyes, but the newcomers all seemed to love him.

"You are the only person I have abducted—an unfortunate but necessary evil. The others I freed. In some parts of Tartora, the Calistan refugees have been allowed to blend seamlessly into the local population. But in other parts, the descendants of those who sought shelter from the destruction wrought in

Calista are treated as garbage. Is it wrong of me to liberate them from their oppressors? Did they do anything to merit such ill treatment?"

"And what of the animals and belongings you *liberated* along with them?" I asked with scorn.

He spread his hands wide. "Wealth that was rightfully theirs after generations of hard labor and sacrifice."

I frowned. His words made more sense than I liked.

"They may have been wronged," I said slowly, "but responding in such a violent way helps only those few who escape with you. Other Calistans across the kingdom will face the consequences of your actions. And is the hard life here, eking a living from a barren land, really much better than what they left behind?"

"Freedom is worth any cost. But you are right that our people deserve much more. That is why we need our own kingdom back. It's the only solution. And thus, you can see why we need mages such as you and your sister. Once our forces are strong enough, we will retake Calista, and anyone who wishes to return may do so."

I stared at him. "Is that really possible? It sounds like a child's dream to me."

"Does it? But wasn't it your father's dream as well?"

I frowned. "You know nothing of my father."

He shrugged. "Perhaps not. But I know he wouldn't listen to any of Quirin's arguments in favor of joining us. He knew there was a power affinity community here—one that could have provided support and companionship for you and your sister. But instead of joining this settlement, he raised you alone. Why?"

He paused, but I said nothing, so he continued.

"Your father knew that when Calista fell, the destruction was focused on the palace and Guild. While the massacre targeted all those with a power affinity, many among the general population escaped. At the Calistan Mages' Guild, however, your grandfather was the only one to get away—a babe in arms whose powerful parents had just been murdered."

"What's your point?" I asked, out of patience with the history lesson.

"Merely this: your father must have had a reason for refusing to put himself under the authority of this community. Can you tell me it wasn't because he had plans for you that didn't involve following anyone else's lead? Yours is the only bloodline left with a strong power affinity. You have no legal claim on the Calistan throne—the Calistan rulers were never power mages. But your father believed there was no one else left with the strength to claim it."

I struggled to keep my face calm as the full import of his words swept over me. I remembered Dara and Quirin visiting more than once when I was young and Mother was still alive. But it had somehow never occurred to me that they might have invited our family to join them here.

I could have grown up beside Renley and a whole host of other children, perhaps called Dara and Quirin aunt and uncle. When father grew sick and died, I wouldn't have been alone to shoulder the burdens he laid down.

From some of the things Dara let drop during our times cooking together, it had been a different community back then. The General had still been a young man and not yet in charge, and the camp had lived by scavenging and hunting just across the border, much as our own family had.

The original settlers had found each other after fleeing the massacre, setting up a camp by the lake when they realized Calista was barred to all except them. They had thought it only a temporary home, but the problem of the rogue protections never died down. And unlike ordinary Calistan citizens who possessed one of the other three affinities, they hadn't been able to seek refuge in Tartora or among the nomads. With a death sentence hanging over their heads, they had instead been forced to build a life here, among the ruins of their old home, their combined abilities enough to keep the rampaging protections away.

In short, it was precisely where my own family had belonged.

A sick feeling grew in my stomach as I considered my father's endless allusions to a future of glory and power for our family. He had kept us apart while telling us we were special—or at least Cadence was.

The queasy sensation grew stronger and stronger, until it began to eat away at a dam inside me. I tried to pull back, to shore up the damage, but it was too late. The cracks grew until the entire thing shattered, releasing wave upon wave of blazing anger.

It was my father's fault, all of it. He had lied to me about so many things, withholding any truth that didn't keep us under his control. He had tasked me with protecting Cadence while leaving me exposed through my own ignorance. And then he had left us, leaving me alone to shoulder all his burden.

I balled my hands into fists, my nails biting into my palms. All these years I had blindly followed his directions, holding myself to the promises he had wrenched from me. And now I discovered it was all for what? To seize the throne of a destroyed kingdom—a throne that had never belonged to our family in the first place?

He had deprived us of friends and family so that he could instead thrust us into a dangerous fight for a future neither of us had ever desired. His efforts had never been about us—it had always been about him and the legacy of our family.

I looked across the desk at the General, seeing him through new eyes. He might have faults, but at least he cared nothing for any legacy that wasn't built from his own efforts.

"You see the problem," the General said in a deceptively

mild voice, given the light in his eyes. "Calistans across the kingdoms are suffering. And they need us to come together to rebuild our home, not to each stand alone. That is all I'm asking. As a fellow Calistan, join us and leave those who murdered our families to look after themselves. All we ask for is our own kingdom returned to us. But thanks to the arrogance of those who once ruled us, we must clean up their mess first. If we are to forge our own path forward, we need those with enough strength to undo the damage they wrought."

I bit my lip. His words were enticing. Too enticing when combined with the anger still pulsing through me.

"If the throne of Calista never belonged to my father, it doesn't belong to you, either," I said, clinging to my defiance.

He steepled his hands, appearing to consider the matter. "A monarch governs only by the will of his people. Without their support, he will fall. And so, by extension, they can choose to set up a new ruler. That is what the old king failed to recognize. He believed strength was the way to secure his throne, but he was wrong. That so-called strength provoked his neighbors into destroying him—and if they hadn't, his own people would have done it eventually."

"Did the people really dislike him so?" I asked skeptically. "I thought the Calistan royal family spent generations wooing all the power mage families over to their kingdom, until they were the only ones with any power mages at all. Surely they must have liked him if they were willing to move their entire life for him."

"The most powerful mages approved of the royal family, certainly. At least at first. But the last king became erratic and dangerous, obsessed with his pursuit of power. Such a person couldn't help viewing the powerless among his own people with increasing scorn. But no one is truly powerless—especially not when they have the numbers on their side. And more and more of the mage families were seeing the danger he posed as well."

"Storing power, you mean? That seems more fanciful than dangerous. I've heard the rumors since I've been here, but it seems a fairy story."

"It's not." He sounded certain. "It's a process that requires a very specific...tool. One that has been lost to us. But it was possible once. Just as it is possible to increase a mage's strength."

"Increase someone's strength?" I shook my head. "If that were possible, I wouldn't have been so feted in Tarona."

A slow smile spread across the General's face. "It isn't possible for the Tartorans or the nomads. But how do you think I come to be so strong? Or Lawson, or my other mages? How do I have mages at all when the Guild hoards anyone with a strong seed?"

I hesitated. Renley had hinted at the same thing, and I couldn't deny some of the mages among the raiders seemed unnaturally strong. Given their small community, it certainly seemed more than flukes of heredity could account for.

The General fixed me with his piercing gaze. "Join me, and I'll tell you how it's done. Soon, you could be even stronger than you are now."

"If what you're saying is true, how come you need Cadence so much? Why don't you simply increase the strength of one of your followers with a power affinity?"

He frowned. "Unfortunately, the method only works for the other three affinities."

I snorted. Renley was destined for bitter disappointment, then.

"But you aren't a power mage," the General said. "It can work for you. All you have to do is accept my offer and help me build a new world."

I swallowed. I wasn't a power mage. Was that the crux of

my anger and resentment? Our father had been a power mage like his father before him, and he had wanted a strong power mage child to carry on the family's dream of seizing the Calistan throne. His response to Cadence made that obvious.

He had wanted a child unique in all the kingdoms. According to Quirin, my father had been disappointed when his own seed was weaker than his father's, and he had sought a powerful mage as a wife in consequence. I should have realized when Quirin said it that my father had hoped to combine his affinity with my mother's strength. But his firstborn had been born with her elements seed. What a disappointment I must have been to him—a child fit only to protect her sister.

I opened my mouth to tell the General that I would join him. But I couldn't quite get out the words.

One lingering thought held me back. Renley.

Dara and Quirin's only child worshiped the General and his cause. And yet the General hadn't bothered to tell him that his ability could never be strengthened like those of his other warriors. Renley would never be more than he currently was.

I could think of no reason for the General to withhold the truth other than to manipulate Renley, providing an incentive for his avid service. So how could I ever trust such a man?

"If I agree to join you right now," I said, "will you remove my neutralizer?"

I kept my voice bland and my lips slightly curved, as if the answer to the question was no great matter.

The General chuckled. "Have I mentioned that I like you, Airlie? But I'm afraid you're going to have to prove your loyalty first."

I narrowed my eyes. "And how do I do that?"

He shrugged. "I'm sure an opportunity will present itself."

I stood. "Fine. And in the meantime, I'm sure you'll let my guard know that I had a good reason for treating him so poorly?"

The General chuckled again before his face fell into more familiar stern lines. "None of my warriors will give you trouble. Once you're one of us, you'll see that we look out for each other."

I nodded my thanks and took my leave. But as I left—by the door this time—I reflected that his noble sentiment didn't extend to Renley.

CHAPTER 13

CADENCE

Someone must have gotten a message to the wagons to stop because they were waiting for us less than an hour downstream despite our original plan to stay on the river all day. A hive of activity surrounded the stationary vehicles as servants pitched tents for all the dignitaries.

"They're sending written messages on powered gusts of wind," Zeke said when he saw me watching the scene with a crease between my eyes. "It's an effective way to pass around messages when you've got this many elements mages on the water."

"I imagine everyone will be glad to feel solid ground beneath their feet," I said, approving the decision to stop early after the attack. "Do you think anyone will refuse to get back on the barges tomorrow?"

Zeke considered the matter. "If the king and queen are willing, everyone else from Tartora will be forced to follow their lead. And my mother would never choose to appear weaker than another leader. She'll be the first on board. And once she goes on, the other tribes will feel obligated to do the same—especially with a change of monarchy coming up." He gave me a sympathetic look. "So if you were hoping to get out of the rest of the river trip, I'm afraid you're out of luck."

"Honestly, I don't even mind," I said, after a moment's thought. "If we survived what just happened, we can survive anything, right?"

He grinned at me. "That's the spirit."

Bryce stumbled over to take up a position near the gap in the railing where we would soon be disembarking. "I'm never getting on another boat again," he said in a pained voice.

I gave him a sympathetic grimace. "Were you sick?"

"On Master Augusta," he whispered.

"Ouch. Rough." Gia joined us, looking back to her normal self. "We must have missed that part."

"Regretting being chosen over the other apprentices yet?" Zeke asked Bryce with a wicked twinkle in his eye.

Bryce glared at him, and I gave Zeke a light shove.

"Leave him alone. Being sick is not fun at the best of times." I turned to Bryce. "Unfortunately, we'll be back aboard tomorrow."

Bryce blanched. "Surely not after that attack!"

"We don't know it was an attack," Nikolas said. "While the timing was suspicious, we can't be sure it wasn't just another example of the border breaking down." He gave Zeke and me a significant look. "At least that's the official line."

We bumped gently against the bank, servants leaping forward to secure the barge. They tied it with ropes to the temporary wooden poles that had been hammered into the shore in preparation for our arrival.

"The rogue protections are part of the reason the delegations are here," Zeke said, his voice serious this time. "It's happening in the nomad kingdom, too. We're going to have to do something soon."

Bryce, his full focus on the docking process, jumped ashore

with an expression of fervent gratitude. But the rest of us hesitated.

"I wondered if that was the case." Gia sounded unhappy. "I suppose your mother has already talked to our parents about it?"

Zeke nodded. "And you can be certain they'll be doing a lot more talking after this. If the raiders have weaponized the rogue protections, then the problem just got a lot bigger."

He didn't look at me, but I felt the weight of his words. His mother knew the truth about my ability. Would she tell the king and queen? She, at least, didn't seem to feel any animosity toward me. Would she keep my secret in the hope of luring me to her own kingdom so my ability could be used exclusively to protect the nomads?

If the problem of tainted power leaching across the border was growing, and if I was truly the only one who could stop it, then that must offer me some protection. Surely no one would want to have me killed just for possessing a power affinity if it was the very ability they needed. But by the same reasoning, King Marius was going to be extremely reluctant to release me to the nomads if I decided I wanted to go with Zeke.

I bit my lip, the questions churning in my mind as I followed the others onto solid ground. Worst of all was knowing that I couldn't actually do what they might demand of me. I'd managed to help with the recent attack, but I had no idea how to deal with the situation on a broader scale.

Somewhere along the river, we had left behind a damaged, twisted section of forest because I hadn't been able to dispose of the tainted power, just move it. And even that had nearly killed me. Before I could help the Tartorans or the nomads, I had to work out a more effective way to deal with the tainted power. But the only person I had met who had known anything about my ability had been a raider.

It wasn't exactly a hopeful outlook.

"Come on, Cadence." Gia poked me, a grin on her face. "It isn't all bad. Whatever that was, we survived intact. Apparently none of the barges lost a single person. Father is pleased about that, at least." She lowered her voice to a whisper. "It makes our elements mages look good to the visitors."

I smiled weakly back at her as she led the way into the small village of tents.

"And you seemed to get less sick the longer we were on the water," she added. "Even with all that pitching around. So hopefully you just needed an initial adjustment. You should be fine tomorrow."

I shook my head at her usual optimistic outlook. Although in this case, she was right. Even without my shield, I could feel only the faintest traces of tainted power—leftovers, perhaps, from the attack. So I certainly hoped I would feel fine the next day.

"At least I wasn't sick all over one of the Triumvirate," I said, unable to help grinning a little at Bryce's expense now that he wasn't here.

Gia laughed. "Can you even imagine? What do you think her face looked like?"

We both dissolved into giggles, clinging to each other as we staggered between the tents. Out of the corner of my eye, I saw two young people I didn't recognize watching us with a disdainful expression.

The sight of them sobered me instantly. If I didn't recognize someone around my age, they must be nomads. And it made sense that the delegations would have brought apprentices of their own, just as we had.

Gia stubbornly refused to care about her position, but I couldn't help feeling sensitive on her behalf. I straightened up, but since Gia was pointing out our tent, she didn't seem to notice. She disappeared straight inside with a happy cry, while I lingered, throwing a backward glance at our audience. Neither of their expressions had changed, so I glared at them and slipped through the canvas opening myself.

Inside, it took my eyes a minute to adjust. As soon as they did, I caught sight of Karielle sitting on one of the beds. She beamed up at me.

"Isn't it gorgeous?" She ran her hand over the soft material draped over the sleeping pallet. "Much nicer than I was expecting for a tent."

Gia was rummaging through one of the bags, so I took a seat on the pallet across from Karielle.

"I certainly wasn't expecting anything so fancy for myself. Are you sure I'm meant to be here, Gia?"

"Of course you are," she called back without lifting her head out of the bag. "I insisted on having both of you. Father said my tent had to be here, in the center of camp, but I said I got to choose my tent mates." She emerged at last, triumphantly holding a pair of soft shoes which she exchanged for her boots with a soft sigh of satisfaction.

"Thank you very much," Karielle said. "I appreciate being included. This is much nicer than the tent the other female apprentices are sharing."

"I was picturing this trip being a lot of work," I admitted, rubbing my feet over the thick carpet that had been laid over the ground. "But it looks like the servants will be doing it, not the apprentices."

"I think we all had a rough enough morning to deserve a little break," Karielle said.

I turned to her. "How did you all go in the last barge? We were worried."

She gulped, shaking her head. "It hit so fast. Out of nowhere. We nearly lost Blake over the side in the first few seconds, but Master Drake caught her. I've never seen him move so fast. After that we all got hustled into the cabin. Only Carissa was allowed to stay on deck to help the elements mages." She swallowed. "I was sure we were going to sink."

"I'm glad Drake was there." I looked toward Gia. "Your parents aren't going to move him to the front barge, are they?"

She shook her head. "They wouldn't do that. Any future attacks are likely to come from that direction, and they won't leave everyone else exposed."

I nodded, breathing a little easier.

"I thought we didn't know it was an attack?" Karielle narrowed her eyes at Gia.

The princess shrugged. "Something attacked us, regardless of whether it was directed to do so by another person."

I rolled my eyes but didn't protest the semantics. That was the life of royalty. How you talked about things mattered.

"So what now?" I asked.

"We've stopped early, so we get the afternoon off." Gia looked delighted at the prospect.

The tent flap moved, Blake sticking her head inside.

"There you are, Kari! Master Augusta wants us all. Apparently we're going to have normal afternoon lessons since we're not still on the river."

She wrinkled her nose while Gia grinned unsympathetically. But her smile dropped away when Blake's gaze moved in her direction.

"You too, Gia. Master Drake is gathering the elements apprentices."

"That's outrageous!" she protested. "We just fought alongside the mages, didn't we? We deserve some time off!"

"Maybe he wants to check you're all right?" I suggested. "And discuss strategies in case it happens again."

Gia gave me a dark look but subsided without further

complaints, filing out of the tent behind the other two. From the glance she cast over her shoulder as she slipped through the opening, she considered me the lucky one.

But left alone in the tent, it didn't feel that way. What was I going to do all afternoon?

A brief visit from Evermund lasted only minutes. He wanted to reassure himself that the reports from Annora were true and I was unharmed. As soon as he'd completed that duty, he was off again. No doubt he was wanted in urgent meetings with the king and delegate heads.

His visit, short though it was, reminded me of my true purpose in coming along on the tour. Ashamed for forgetting my sister, regardless of the extenuating circumstances, I resolved to search for her immediately.

Lying on the bed, I let myself take only a moment to enjoy the softness before closing my eyes and stretching out my awareness. Sweeping around the camp, I skimmed over each of the mages, servants, dignitaries, and guards.

I took an extra moment to linger around the nomads, trying to familiarize myself with their abilities so I would be able to detect any intruders. I didn't stop too long, however, itching to begin the more important task of looking for any hint of Airlie. But after a full circle around the area, pushing to the far limits of my reach, I had to give up.

Sitting back up, I reminded myself that I hadn't really expected to find anything. We were traveling south along the Viridian River, away from Calista. I was far more likely to find my sister after we had traversed the southern coast and started north again, up the Celadon. But that didn't mean I wasn't going to check each day, just in case.

Wanting a distraction, I left the tent, wandering through the camp aimlessly. Several large open-air tents without walls had been set up to house the cooks, who were already hard at work. The delicious smells drew me in their direction, but Zeke appeared from between two tents before I reached them.

"Cadence! I was wondering where you had gotten to."

"Were you looking for me?" I frowned at him. "I thought Augusta was holding lessons for all her apprentices this afternoon."

He grinned at me. "She is. But naturally I was needed for important nomad business."

I raised an eyebrow, but his grin didn't slip.

"You are important business, Cadence. For all of us."

"I'd like to feel flattered, but somehow I don't," I said flatly.

He chuckled and grabbed my hand, pulling me between the tents. I let him lead me, wishing I wasn't so aware of the warmth and strength of his hand in mine.

"It's past time you tell me everything that's been going on," he said, as we ducked into a tiny group of trees on one edge of the campsite. "I am your influencing mage, after all." He gave me a mock stern look.

I groaned. "I don't even know where to start."

"How about with a raider woman appearing in Evermund's suite and then dropping dead?"

"How was that less than a day ago?" I rubbed my head. "It feels like a week, at least."

Zeke gave me a look, so with a gesture of surrender, I told him everything that had happened since then. It was a relief to unburden myself of all my recent discoveries about my ability, and Zeke was an appreciative audience for the theories I had formulated.

"It never even occurred to me to have you reach inward to your ability," he said. "It's a fascinating concept. Have you tried doing anything else with it?"

I shook my head. "I haven't really had the chance."

"Some experimentation is definitely in order. You could try —" He broke off suddenly, peering at my face. "But not now," he added in a stern voice. "You look exhausted. You've already done more than a full day's work."

"Thanks, Teacher," I said with a grin.

"But seriously, Cadence, what you did was incredible." His eyes turned warm and admiring. "A lot of the elements mages are flat on their beds after their efforts this morning. From what I've managed to gather from the histories, very few power mages could have handled so much power at once, even without it being tainted."

I shrugged, uncomfortable. "I did what I had to do in the moment."

He continued to eye me thoughtfully before shrugging. "Even as your teacher, I can't argue with that." He ran a hand through his hair. "And I don't think I can really claim the title. It sounds like Dara taught you more in five minutes than I've managed to in months."

"It's not that bad," I protested. "You taught me how to add power to other mages' efforts, and that's saved my life once already."

"Fine, fine," he said, laughing. "I will accept your kind words, if I must."

I groaned and pushed him in the chest. "If that was just you fishing for compliments, I'll..."

He grabbed my hand and pulled me in close against him, still chuckling. "You'll what?"

"I..." My mind seized, no words forming as his proximity overwhelmed my senses. He smelled like green things and sunlight, warmth radiating from his chest.

"Well?" he asked, looking down into my eyes as his expression slowly turned more serious, a light leaping into his gaze.

I swallowed, trying not to stare at his lips. How would they feel pressed against mine?

I frantically dredged up all the reasons why it was a bad idea to let myself fall for Zeke—the charming almost-prince who alone knew just how valuable I could be to his people. But none of the reasons seemed to hold any weight in this moment, when the one person who had always seen me and always included me held me in his arms, a smile on his lips.

"I..." Still the words wouldn't come.

He leaned toward me, his own eyes dropping to my lips. But a piercing call made him pull back with a growl.

"Zekiel!"

"Is that your mother?" I asked, almost leaping out of his arms.

He growled again. "Probably. Don't go anywhere." He stalked away, leaving me alone in the thin layer of trees.

What had I nearly done? I put a hand over my eyes. It didn't matter that Zeke felt like a safe haven from the anxiety and responsibility that plagued me. I had to be stronger than that.

"Who are *you*?" a female voice asked, her tone antagonistic.

I opened my eyes as the two nomads who had been watching Gia and me earlier stepped between the trees.

"I'm Cadence," I said haltingly.

"But who are you?" she repeated, and I realized it was my status she cared about, not my name.

"Are you an apprentice?" the boy asked. "You look about the right age."

"Oh." I tried to look unconcerned, but fresh worry made my hands damp. The last thing I needed was newcomers asking questions about my age. "No, I'm not officially an apprentice. I'm a dependent."

"A dependent?" The girl relaxed slightly, as if relieved by my lowly status. She glanced at the young man beside her. "You do look seventeen, though. How old are you?"

"Seventeen," I said reluctantly.

She assumed an expression of obviously false sympathy. "It must be hard living at the Guild when you don't have a strong enough seed for anyone to be willing to activate you. But I'm sure you'll find someone to do it eventually. There are plenty of useful roles beyond that of mage, you know."

"Very true," Zeke said coolly, stepping back between the trees.

The boy looked uncomfortable for a moment, as if caught out, but the girl squealed in delight, throwing her arms around Zeke's neck.

"Zekiel! I haven't had a proper chance to talk to you yet. I can't believe it's been two years!"

"Liara." He detached himself from her embrace, nodding to the boy. "Jaylen."

The nomad clapped him on the shoulder. "It's good to see you again, Zeke."

Although Zeke smiled at him, it didn't reach his eyes, and he took several steps to stand at my side, clearly aligning himself with me. Liara's eyes widened slightly.

"I see you've already met my friend, Cadence," he said.

My heart swelled. I had been unmoved by Liara's obvious attempts to remind me of my unimportance—these days I could only dream of being as insignificant as she thought me—but Zeke's defense still touched me. Maybe because he had first treated me as a friend before I had any ability at all.

Liara smiled at us both, but her expression didn't reach her eyes either. "We're excited to meet all your new friends, Zeke. Especially Princess Morgiana and Prince Nikolas."

"What a delightful coincidence." Nikolas poked his head through the trees, his eyebrows rising as he took in the four of us arrayed across from each other, battle lines drawn. "Because here I am."

"Your Highness!" Liara dropped into a curtsy with a giggle while Jaylen gave a shallow bow.

"Master Augusta sent me to see if your duties with the nomads were completed," Nikolas said to Zeke. "But I can see it's quite the opposite, and my own presence is also required."

For the first time in the awkward interaction, I felt my cheeks flush. Did Nikolas guess that Zeke and I had been sequestered alone in the trees before Liara and Jaylen's arrival?

If he did, he didn't seem to see an issue with it. Offering an arm to Liara with a gallant bow, he smiled with surprising charm at Jaylen. I rarely had the chance to see this side of him, but I remembered how real the charm could feel when it was directed at you.

"You already know Zeke, and you don't want to waste your time with Cadence," he told them. "But I have some Tartorans who would be delighted to meet two of the delegation members. If you will?"

With a few adroit moves, he had both the nomads at his side and was leading them back among the tents. Before they moved completely out of sight, however, he cast a final smirk back in my direction.

"Sometimes I could punch him," Zeke said through his teeth.

"I can't imagine what you mean," I said dryly.

When he remained tense, I put my hand on his arm. "Relax. This is Nikolas we're talking about. I'm fairly sure that smirk at the end meant he thought he was rescuing us."

Zeke's muscles finally loosened, his usual smile returning. "Well, he's right about that. But does that mean we owe him?"

I shuddered. "Please don't suggest something like that to him. Who knows what he would want us to do?"

Zeke chuckled before looking down at me with a shadow of concern. "When did you turn seventeen? Why didn't you tell me it was your birthday?"

I shrugged. "My birthday is in the spring. But no one asked, so I've been keeping it quiet."

"Even from me?" He sounded hurt. "I could have at least..."

"What?" I asked. "Made me a cake? For the moment, everyone seems to have forgotten all about me turning seventeen, and that's for the best. You know what will happen if Gia catches wind I've already had my birthday. She'll start badgering me to get activated, or at the very least tested. And that would be an absolute disaster."

Zeke sighed. "You're right, of course. I just hate thinking of you all alone with no celebration or even acknowledgment on your seventeenth birthday." He took my hands. "You deserve better, Cadie."

"Thanks," I said lightly, pulling my hands gently free. After the last half hour, I knew better than to let myself get caught up in the moment a second time. "But you'd better get back to Master Augusta. She seems to be getting wise to your strategies."

He seemed reluctant to go until I assured him I intended to spend the rest of the afternoon resting. It was true, too. Now that I had been ashore for a while, the exhaustion was catching up with me, and I ended up napping just as I'd promised.

The evening meal was eaten outside on long makeshift tables made of wooden planks. A breeze off the river kept the temperature from being too unpleasant, and the overall mood was lighter than might have been expected after the events on the river.

While the king and queen sat at a separate table with Masters Augusta and Drake, Evermund, Hayes, and the heads of each of the three delegations, the other nomads mingled freely with the Tartorans. I heard a number of conversations about the differences and similarities between the current trip and the usual nomad lifestyle, and for the first time, the real value of the tour hit home. It had been an inspired idea of the king's, providing a far less formal environment than the court.

"Well?" Zeke asked as we all walked back toward our tents after the meal. "Is the traveling life as bad as you thought?"

"Quite the opposite." I grinned. "As long as an entire team of servants come with me, that is."

His expression turned rueful. "You have me there. Sleep well, Cadence."

I hesitated, slow to meet his eyes. "Sleep well, Zeke."

Gia raised an eyebrow at me as we hurried into our tent, but I ignored her. I wasn't ready to talk about the warmth in his eyes, even if it kept me company in my dreams all night.

CHAPTER 14
AIRLIE

On my way back to Quirin's house, I had to duck between buildings at the sound of heavy footsteps. When the guard who I had left tied beneath my bed strode into view, I stepped deeper into the shadows.

He was heading toward the General's house, fury on his face, and I had no desire for a run in with him before he reached his destination. I could only hope the General had meant it when he assured me I would be safe from retaliation.

I waited until he was out of sight before hurrying on my way. Letting myself back into the house, I didn't bother to attempt to stay quiet as I cleaned up the chaos in my bedchamber. But Quirin still didn't emerge. I clearly needn't have bothered creeping around earlier in the night.

Eating alone at the table the next morning, I found myself staring at his closed door. Quirin was one of my captors, certainly, but after my conversation with the General, nothing was black or white anymore.

I had lain in bed for a long time, pondering his words and reliving parts of my childhood, and I had managed to retrieve memories of at least three visits from Quirin and Dara. As a child, bringing Renley to play with Cadence and me had seemed like enough of a reason for their visits. But with the greater understanding of increased age, I could see it had been more than that. Especially since my parents had always fought after they left—hushed voices behind the closed door of their bedroom.

Unlike our father, our mother must have been swayed by Quirin and Dara's arguments. A fresh wave of grief for her loss swept over me. If she had lived, would she have eventually convinced him?

Our father had kept Cadence and me isolated, but the other adults in our lives had all fought for us. Quirin had barely known either of us, and yet he had traveled a long way on more than one occasion to advocate for our inclusion in a bigger community. And though I wasn't foolish enough to think there was nothing in it for him, it still counted for something.

Crossing over to the door, I knocked firmly. When I didn't get a response, I knocked again. Quirin called something that wasn't loud enough to be heard clearly, although it might have been a command to leave him alone. I knocked again.

Finally he opened the door with a weary sigh.

I gulped at the sight of his haggard face and bloodshot eyes. He couldn't continue like this.

"Will you join me for breakfast?" I asked.

When he looked like he was going to say no, I took his arm and steered him toward the table before he could reply. After a moment's resistance, he complied, dropping into the seat with a weary sigh. And when I put a bowl of porridge in front of him, he began to eat.

I sat across from him, and we ate in silence for a while as I gathered courage for the question I wanted to ask.

"I snuck into the General's study last night," I said eventually.

Quirin looked up sharply, some of the fire from the graveyard back in his eyes. "Did you stab him?"

I chuckled uneasily. "Unfortunately I didn't have a blade handy."

"A pity." Quirin turned back to his porridge.

I cleared my throat. "He made a surprisingly convincing argument that we should all be working together."

Quirin's lips twisted up, but his expression couldn't be called a smile. "Even as a young lad, he always knew when honey would best serve his goals. Your father was right about him, and I should have listened."

"My father?" I straightened. The conversation was already going in unexpected directions. "What did my father have to do with the General?"

"Nothing much." Quirin stirred his porridge, still not looking at me. "Which was precisely his aim. But he did visit us once."

I gaped at him. "Father came here? When?"

"Just before he met your mother. He came here on his way to Tarona which is where he met her. Dara and I had invited him more than once. We were young and full of hope for the future, and we thought if he could only see the community here, he would be convinced to join us."

"But he wasn't."

Quirin sighed. "We thought he was stubborn and foolish, but he had clearer vision than the rest of us."

I frowned. "What does that mean?"

"Your father said it was obvious where things were headed here. The General was just a youth back then, but your father believed he would end up in charge. And he wasn't interested in being used by anyone—or in his children being used either."

I bit down on my tongue to prevent myself blurting out something sour. Our father might have protected us from being used by others, but who had protected us from being used by him in his single-minded quest to raise our family above everyone else?

"Do you mean the General wasn't always in charge? I thought since his ability is so strong, his family must have been the leaders here from the beginning."

"The beginning?" Quirin was surprised enough to look up. "No, indeed. His family only sought refuge here when he was a small child. He isn't even Calistan."

"What?" I pulled back, my spoon dropping from my hand. "The General isn't Calistan?"

Quirin gave me a strange look, finally roused enough from his torpor to fully engage in the conversation.

"No, he's Tartoran. His father was a powerful elements mage who couldn't accept that he was overlooked in favor of one of his rivals when the Master of the Elements position became available. He attacked the other mage and was arrested. Rather than attempt to keep such a powerful prisoner, they exiled him across the border."

"Exiled him across the border?" I stared at him, appalled. "What did they expect to happen to him over here?"

Quirin shrugged. "I imagine they thought he would die without their having to deal with anything as confronting as an execution. That's royalty for you."

"Is it?" I asked faintly. It was hard to picture the royals I had met behaving in such a fashion.

"But they didn't count on his wife following him with their young son in tow. By the time she found him, he was weakened from hunger and had injured himself as well. They kept moving, eventually stumbling on one of our hunting parties as they were making their way back here. We took them in, but by that point it was too late for the weakened mage. We didn't have anyone with a healing ability among our number back then, so…" He shrugged again.

"But his son was a powerful elements mage," I said slowly. "One who grew up here. I can see why he dislikes Tartora."

Quirin nodded. "We should have seen the direction his

anger was taking him. But those of us most likely to have intervened felt sorry for the lad and made excuses for the resentment that shaped his character growing up. By the time we realized how far his entitlement reached, it was too late. He had won enough of our people to his cause to start bringing in outsiders. And then he started training them as warriors. Soon those of us uninterested in conflict were in the minority and could do nothing but watch as he turned our peaceful settlement into a war party."

I shook my head. "I don't believe it's true that nothing can be done. It's always worth at least trying."

Quirin ran a hand over his face. "Dara and I talked about it many times. But we had a young son of our own by then. We wanted to keep him safe." He laughed bitterly. "And look how that turned out. If I'd known he would turn to the General over his own parents, I would have stood up to him sooner."

I looked down into my porridge, sympathy stirring despite my frustration with his passive response to the invasion of his home. And for the first time I felt sympathy for Renley as well. What youth, constrained to a home such as this, wouldn't choose the impassioned leadership of the General over the resigned passivity of his parents?

Even I had nearly been sucked in—and might have been completely if not for the warning provided by Renley's own experience. If the General had won me over with his words, would I ever have had this conversation with Quirin? Probably not. I would have gone on believing that the General was Calistan, just as he claimed, instead of recognizing how he twisted facts to suit his purpose—taking partial truths and turning them into lies.

"Will you take me to talk to some of the others?" I asked. "Some of the ones who don't buy the General's lines?"

Quirin looked surprised, taking several moments to consider my request. Eventually he nodded slowly.

"I suppose so."

I smiled, hoping the exercise might do something for him as well. Perhaps forcing him to talk to his old friends would help coax him back from the brink. He certainly couldn't continue as he had been indefinitely, just going through the motions.

As soon as I'd cleaned up from the meal, he led me out into the settlement. At first we walked in the direction of the graveyard, and I feared he didn't even remember our purpose. But before we reached it, he stopped at the door of a house that looked identical to his own.

The curtain at the window, made from a faded green material, twitched and then the door was thrown open.

"Quirin!" The matronly woman seized him in a sturdy embrace, her tears falling on his shoulder. "I can't believe she's really gone."

I expected Quirin to start crying again himself at the expression of sympathy and grief, but instead he straightened, patting her on the back.

"It's difficult to believe it's true. I keep turning around, expecting to see her there."

The woman pulled back, mopping at her eyes. "Of course you do! I was just the same after we lost our Sarah." She glanced at me. "She was such a wee thing. Far too young to go."

"I'm sorry," I murmured, uncomfortable to be intruding on their grief.

"That's kind of you to say." She gave me a watery smile. "It was many years ago now. But losing Dara brings it all back like it was yesterday. I'm Marissa, by the way." She swept us both inside, Quirin speaking quiet words of comfort as we took our seats at her table.

A man walked in from a back room, and Quirin immediately stood again, the two of them exchanging a shorter embrace followed by a hearty handshake. The woman, bustling around pouring hot water from the kettle into cups of tea, seized the chance to whisper to me.

"I don't care what they say about you. Bless you for bringing him here. We've all been that worried."

I blinked. "Do I dare ask what they say about me?" I added a tentative smile.

She chuckled. "Those of us who've been here forever don't look too kindly on newcomers. Not now," she added darkly.

I raised an eyebrow. "Even newcomers here against their will?"

She looked a little uncomfortable as she pressed a tin mug into my hands.

"Aye, Dara thought we were too harsh on you. But we've heard the tales of your power. And we already took in one powerful young elements mage."

I considered her answer. "That's fair."

She smiled, seeming relieved that I didn't intend to make a fuss. "Of course it's different now. We always knew Dara was a soft soul, but we didn't realize how bad it was. Not until it was too late."

I frowned. "What do you mean?"

She glanced at the two men who were now engaged in a quiet conversation of their own.

"Dara confessed it to me near the end. Quirin didn't know, or he'd have intervened. He always had a stronger will. He led the rest of us in refusing the General's demands. But Dara didn't find it so easy, especially not once Renley got involved." She sighed.

"I'm sorry," I said, "but I still don't understand. Are you saying the General was somehow responsible for Dara's death? I understood she had a fatal illness of some kind."

"Aye, it's fatal, right enough. But there's nothing natural about it. It took down too many of our grandparents and great-grandparents, and we all swore—" She broke off, gesturing me to a seat at the table as she placed the remaining mugs in front of the other chairs. When the two men didn't break off their conversation, she sat down herself with a sigh.

"It took both of my grandparents when I was just a girl. I watched them go, and it wasn't pretty. I haven't given it much thought for years, but now I can't stop picturing poor Dara—"

She mopped at her eyes with an enormous handkerchief while I took a large gulp of the hot tea. I still felt like a stranger, intruding on someone else's grief.

"It's the wild power," she said once she had herself back under control.

"Wild power?"

"Those who've come across from Tartora call it the protection." She snorted. "I can't imagine what they think it's protecting."

"Oh, the curse that was unleashed by the massacre, you mean?"

She nodded. "Curse is a better word for it. It's been a curse, right enough. I suppose someone has explained the power affinity to you since you arrived? Well, those of us who have it use our ability differently from the rest of you. We don't connect with objects or people around us but with the leftover fragments of power that linger in our environment from everyone else. Everyone here has a weak ability and can seize only small handfuls of it at a time, but even that is enough to be deadly after a while."

"Using a power affinity is deadly?" I asked, alarmed.

"Not if all you use is normal power," she said. "It's the wild stuff that's so dangerous. If you could feel it, you'd know. There's something wrong with it. Something twisted. You can't use it unless you let it infect your ability. And every time you do that, it kills a little more of your insides. That's how it feels, anyway. But there isn't much of any other kind of power out here, so our grandparents used it to build this place."

She stroked the table while fresh tears fell. I didn't dare ask if her grandparents had used their ability in its construction.

"After they grew weak and died, those of our parents old enough to have been activated stopped using their ability. And though they activated us all in case of an emergency, we all swore not to use our ability in lesser circumstances."

Her eyes narrowed. "But the General didn't like that, no indeed. He was always wheedling—asking us to do this or that feat that his own elements ability couldn't accomplish. He thought if we pushed ourselves, we could get stronger and overcome what he called our grandparents' *weakness*." She growled. "But he can't feel it like we can. Something that wrong will twist us before we can twist it. And only a fool would try."

Her brain caught up with her words, and her face crumpled again. "Or those with too loving hearts. Like Dara. When Quirin convinced her to start saying no to the General, that fiend started sending his requests through her son."

I nearly choked on my mouthful of tea. "Renley asked her to use her ability? Didn't he know?"

She sighed. "He believed the General's lies, I'll be bound. He hasn't been activated, so he hasn't felt it for himself. Of course, Dara never meant to let it go so far. She thought helping him just a little wouldn't hurt too much. But she didn't know when to stop. By the time she realized how bad it had gotten, it was too late."

I swallowed. Had I stumbled on the reason it suited the General to keep Renley in the dark? The longer he could string him along before he activated his ability, the longer Renley kept helping the General to use his mother. Any remaining sympathy for the General and his cause evaporated.

Marissa must have read my anger in my face because she leaned forward, looking alarmed. "I've been letting my tongue run free, which I'd no right to do. It's just that much of a relief to let it all out. I daren't tell my husband because he'd tell Quirin. Promise me you won't tell him yourself!"

"Surely he has the right to know what's been going on with his own family."

She shook her head firmly. "I'm sure he suspects, and one day, maybe, I'll be able to tell him the full story. But what do you think he would do right now if he found out the extent of it?"

I thought of the flashes of fire I'd seen in Quirin's eyes and realized her point.

"He'd go after the General," I whispered.

Marissa nodded. "Aye, that he would. We've just lost Dara, we can't lose Quirin as well. They were the closest thing we had to leaders before the General, you know. And some of us still have hope Quirin will find a way to get us out of this."

I looked across at the two men. They were standing close together, their faces lined and their quiet words serious. Whatever they were discussing had gone beyond condolences, and for the first time I could see Quirin as a leader. He had shown a hint of it earlier as well, when he had put aside his own grief in response to Marissa's. Maybe I'd been too hard on him.

"And perhaps you could help us as well." Marissa gave me a measuring look. "Quirin assures us you're as Calistan as we are."

"Me?" I asked warily.

"If you really are such a strong mage, you could activate our youngsters. Mayhap some of them might turn out to be stronger than their parents. A few of them were born with different seeds, too. My own eldest has a healing seed, thrown up from who knows how distant an ancestor. The General only activates his favorites, and we've been reluctant to activate them ourselves, not wanting to limit them to our level."

I held up a hand to stop her before she gained any more

enthusiasm for the idea. When she stopped talking, I pointed down at my waist.

"I have a neutralizer, remember. I can't activate anyone."

Her eyes narrowed, her gaze going to the two men. "Mayhap there's something we can do about that. If we put our heads together."

I stood. I had been unhappy when a king asked me to activate his children, and I was no more comfortable with the idea in a settlement of outcasts. I had barely had the chance to get used to my own ability before it was locked away. I wasn't ready to get mixed up in anyone else's.

But neither could I pass up the potential opportunity to be released from the neutralizer.

"If you think of something, please let me know," I said. "Maybe it would be a good idea if Quirin stays here for a few days. It's done him good to see you both."

Marissa looked over at the men again before looking doubtfully back at me. "Are you sure the General will accept that? Isn't Quirin your jailer—of sorts?"

I smiled grimly. "Let me handle the General."

Marissa grinned back. "There's an attitude we could do with more of. Very well, then. We'll keep him here. And if we come up with a plan, you'll be the first to know."

"Thank you. And thank you for the tea."

She saw me off at the door, and I walked back to Quirin's house slowly. My thinking had undergone so many changes in the last twenty-four hours, I felt dizzy.

I had thought I might need to visit a number of Quirin's friends to get a feel for the true situation, but I had forgotten that not everyone grieves by withdrawing, as Quirin did. Marissa had been almost bursting to get her anger over her friend's death off her chest.

It was possible I'd just found the allies I needed, but I couldn't shake off the reluctance that had driven me from the house. All my life, everyone had wanted something from me—first my father, then the Tartorans, then the General, and now the Calistans. And though it was true that I shared a heritage with Quirin and Marissa, I couldn't help but feel jaded after the General had attempted to use the same line on me only hours before.

Only one person—Evermund—had ever given to me while asking nothing in return. I had tricked him into the responsibility of my apprenticeship, but he had never once tried to get out of it. And when the king and the Triumvirate heaped responsibilities on my head, he had done his best to help me—fought for me, even.

I missed him with an ache that nearly brought tears to my eyes. If only he was here now so I could ask him what I should do. Because the one question that echoed around my head scared me more than any question had ever done.

What did I want?

It was the first time in my life I had fully put aside what everyone else needed from me and instead considered only what I wanted to do. And I didn't know the answer.

CHAPTER 15
CADENCE

The next morning we boarded the barges earlier than the day before, everyone putting on a show of bravery, despite the palpable tension in the air. Gia herded both Karielle and me onto the front barge with her, although I noticed Bryce had lost his enthusiasm to be included with the royals, disappearing off toward the apprentice's barge instead.

"Don't worry," Karielle said when she saw me watching his retreating back. "I don't get seasick."

"That's one blessing at least," Augusta muttered as she skirted around us and onto the barge.

According to Gia, Augusta had been largely responsible for keeping our barge together through the beating it received, her power proving remarkably effective despite the age of the wood used in the vessel's construction. Some of the other barges hadn't made it through in such solid shape, and emergency repair works had been completed overnight.

Augusta looked just as spry as usual, however, and at least a decade younger than what must be her true age. With a grin, the other girls and I followed her on board. We didn't join her in the cabin, however, this time taking up positions in the prow instead of the stern.

I drank in the uninterrupted view of the river ahead, the sun sparkling off the moving water. The way it foamed and flowed over the hull was mesmerizing, and I had to fight the desire to dive in and swim in the cool blue, as I had done so many times in Lake Aterra growing up. As the sun grew warmer, the water only looked more and more inviting, the color a beautiful contrast to the deep green of the forest along the eastern shore.

Zeke and Nikolas joined us, and as the hours passed without incident, we all increasingly relaxed. From time to time, Zeke would shoot a questioning look at me, but I could detect no rise in the almost negligible levels of tainted power around us.

Each time I nodded back at Zeke reassuringly, he looked a little more relieved. And the gaps between his silent questions grew larger.

"Isn't that fresh wind just delicious?" Gia turned her face into it and closed her eyes.

"Thus speaks the elements apprentice," Zeke said. "Personally, I'd like a chance to stop and explore that forest."

I'd noticed his gaze glued to the eastern bank instead of looking ahead—an understandable focus for a plants mage, given the unexplored tangle of greenery on that side. Karielle nodded enthusiastically, in complete agreement, and even Nikolas couldn't entirely hide his interest.

After Airlie disappeared, Nikolas had refused to allow Augusta to activate his plants seed. Apparently, he had told his parents that having been promised an elements influence, he intended to have it from one elements mage or another.

Perhaps sick of fighting with their children—or else distracted by the other crises of the moment—they relented. One of the librarians had unearthed an ancient exception that allowed royal children to be activated by a member of their family but trained within the Guild. So Evermund had agreed to activate Nikolas as long as his training happened under the Master of Plants.

Usually, Nikolas talked as if the elements influence was the only part of his ability that mattered, but every now and then he couldn't help demonstrating his interest in plants. It seemed inevitable with an ability as strong as his. Now that it was activated, he must feel a constant awareness and pull toward growing things—like I did with the power around me.

But when he caught me watching him, he quickly turned his gaze back to the river ahead of us. I shook my head and turned away as well. If he wanted to deny who he truly was, that was his mistake.

This time we sailed until the late afternoon, stopping when the campsite came into view, the tents only just starting to be raised. It was a leisurely and enjoyable way to travel, carried along by the river's current, as long as you could put aside the memory of the attack.

It took us several days in that manner to reach the mouth of the river and the sea beyond. We left the boats for the last time with the vastness of the ocean in view. Even I, who had no hint of the elements affinity about me, could appreciate the mesmerizing quality of the endless, moving water in its shifting shades.

I had never seen the ocean before, and being here now felt surreal. I just wished Airlie could have experienced it with me. When we were young, our mother's stories of the ocean had been her favorites, Airlie's eyes shining as she asked questions about its size and the elegant wooden ships that plied its waters.

"The air tastes different," I said in surprise, licking my lips. "And the salt smell is so strong."

Despite the descriptions my mother had given, it had been impossible to accurately picture it.

Zeke grinned at me. "I love falling asleep to the sound of the waves. My favorite routes growing up were the ones that took us near the ocean."

The nomad kingdom's western border was one long coast, framing a long stretch of grazing lands, so he had likely spent a lot of time near the ocean as a child. Now that I had experienced it for myself, I envied him.

"I never understood Airlie's fascination with the sea," I said. "We grew up near Lake Aterra, and I always imagined the ocean was just a bigger version of the lake. But it's different."

"I would love to see Lake Aterra one day," Zeke said.

"We're not going that far north." Nikolas strolled over to join the conversation. "The southernmost part of the lake is in Tartora, and both rivers flow from it, but it isn't the safest place to be right now. Not with most of the lake's bulk across the border in the fallen kingdom."

I frowned at his words, thinking of our little house, tucked in its valley. It sat empty now—unless the raiders had found it. Had it been hit by tainted power like the barges? It might be in splinters if so.

I shook away the thought. My world had expanded so far beyond that house that my childhood there felt almost like a dream.

"How is it going with your new friends?" I asked Nikolas.

He looked down his nose at me. "You mean the nomads? They've been nothing but kind. You should consider spending more time with them."

"I've spent enough, thanks," I said shortly.

He shook his head. "Don't let Gia hear you say that. She's already reluctant as it is. Pure foolishness, of course. Tartora needs the nomads—we rely on them for trade—and this is a rare chance to forge bonds we can use in the future. I, at least, don't intend to waste the opportunity."

He turned and strolled away, and I watched him go, struck by his words. He was right that I hadn't seen Gia interacting much with the nomads. Was he also right that she was missing a crucial opportunity—one her twin was making the most of?

But when I raised it with Gia in our tent that night, she waved away my words. I couldn't dismiss them so easily, however.

After she had left to refill her water skin, I turned to Karielle. "What do you think? You have more experience of court than I do. Is Gia making a mistake with this?"

She hesitated, concern lining her face. I could read her reluctance to interfere, but after a moment her lips twisted.

"I grew up with siblings always jostling for rank and position. And let's just say, I wouldn't sit back and let my brother forge such connections without me."

Her words stuck with me as I lay on my soft pallet once the lantern had been extinguished. The memory of Nikolas's smirk as he carried off Liara and Jaylen swam before my eyes. Maybe I had interpreted it wrong. Had he seen the situation as a personal victory?

Eventually I rolled over and forced myself to empty my mind for sleep. But not before I resolved to keep a closer eye over Gia's interests in the future. If she wouldn't do it herself, then her loyal friends would have to do it for her.

Traveling on the barges, it had been easy enough to avoid Liara and Jaylen, and even Annora to some extent. I hadn't even managed another private conversation with Zeke about my training. But traveling west along the southern coast, we rode on horseback—an enormous cavalcade that stretched along the road and out of sight, with wagons at the front and back.

When we stopped for meals, and even on the road to some extent, more mingling was possible. After my resolution on Gia's behalf, I welcomed the change. I wanted to keep a closer eye on Nikolas as well as the nomads.

On the first day, we stopped for lunch on the edge of a field, looking out over a beach of perfect white sand. I ate quickly, my eyes on the water, but I'd barely swallowed the final bite when Liara appeared. She dropped a shallow curtsy to Gia beside me before including us both in a blinding smile.

"My cousin Jaylen and I are about to sneak off to dip our feet in the ocean before it's time to ride again. Would you like to join us?"

I didn't stop to analyze the strangeness of her sudden friendliness, instead leaping in before Gia could say no.

"That's just what I've been thinking about all meal. We'd love to, wouldn't we?" I gave Gia a pointed look.

I needn't have worried, however. The suggested activity held enough hint of illicit behavior to appeal to her adventurous spirit.

"Of course we would." She jumped up, abandoning her half-eaten meal. "Zeke and Nik will want to come too."

She waved at them both, while I suppressed a sigh. I could hardly refute the suggestion, although it hadn't been what I'd had in mind.

The two boys wandered over, looking curious. Zeke was grinning before Gia was halfway through outlining the plan, but Nikolas's brow creased.

"Cadence can go, and Zeke, of course. But I hardly think it's fitting behavior for us. We're not children anymore, Gia."

She rolled her eyes. "When did you get so boring, Nik? Stay behind and make chitchat with diplomats if you want. I'm going to feel the sand between my toes and the ocean on my legs."

"Gia." He gave her a warning look, but she just blew him a cheeky kiss and breezed away.

I followed behind at a more sedate pace, worried I'd made a mistake. Maybe I hadn't thought the situation through. I had wanted to improve Gia's position with the nomads, not undermine it. I'd forgotten which nomads really mattered—and it wasn't the apprentices.

But Zeke followed along with only a swift, calculating look at Nikolas's stern face, so it couldn't be as serious an issue as Nikolas made it sound. Zeke wouldn't do anything to harm his mother's position with a change of monarch coming up.

Neither Liara nor Jaylen commented on Nikolas's choice, merely leading the three of us on a roundabout route that avoided anyone with the authority to stop us—an effort which Gia heartily approved.

And as soon as I kicked off my boots and let my feet sink into the sand, I sighed in bliss, all thought of politics forgotten. The silky-smooth feeling was like nothing I had ever experienced.

"Come on!" Zeke grabbed my hand and towed me along. "It's even better under the water."

"Oh!" I squealed and picked up the pace as we hit the part of the beach in direct sunlight. "It's hot!"

Dancing awkwardly across the sand, we raced for the line of wet sand left by the retreating tide. As soon as we reached it, we slowed, sighing in relief. The sand was packed more firmly here, making it easier to walk, but less soft, so I headed straight for the water.

Liara had already hurried ahead of us, pulling up her skirts so she could stand at the edge of the incoming waves. She gestured me over.

"Come on in, Cadence. It's cold at first, but you soon get used to it."

Zeke had turned to talk to Jaylen, so I approached her with caution, gasping when the first wave rushed up and over my toes.

"So...cold..." I gasped, and she laughed.

"You really do get used to it. I promise."

I stopped beside her, sucking in several breaths as I forced myself not to run back up onto the higher sand. But as the waves came in and out, she was right. The intensity of the cold faded, leaving only a cool, refreshing feeling.

I watched the white foam swirling around my toes as they slowly sank into the wet sand. Zeke was right. It was even silkier beneath the water, and I pushed my feet back and forth, enjoying the sensation.

"This is a beautiful beach," Liara said. "But we have some even lovelier ones along our coastline. If you come to visit Zeke, we could go see some of them."

"That's…very kind."

I glanced behind to where Gia had joined Zeke's conversation. There could be no confusing that Liara's words were directed solely at me. What had happened to the superior nomad girl I had met previously? She seemed like an entirely different person.

Liara continued to chat about some of her other favorite locations within the nomad kingdom while I contributed occasional vague answers, most of my attention on the ocean and the sand. At one point, I looked up to find Zeke watching me with an expression of amusement. I rolled my eyes at him, and his grin broadened. I reminded myself to ask him what was going on with Liara the next time we were alone.

The delight of the beach made me lose track of time, only a loud commotion from the direction of the road recalling me to our situation. I gasped and rushed out of the water.

"The meal must be over, the first riders are already leaving," I said. "We need to go back."

Liara laughed, apparently unbothered. "We'll just join at the end of the line. No one will miss us."

Gia returned her laugh, looking delighted at our new friend's attitude, but I couldn't share it. The nomads clearly had a more relaxed approach with their children, and it was true no one would be looking for me. But it was different for Gia.

Sure enough, we neared the road just as Nikolas rode by in

conversation with Drake and the head delegate from Tribe Callen. He looked at us disapprovingly on the way past, drawing the attention of the two older men. The nomad looked indulgent enough, but Drake frowned, turning slightly in his seat to watch Gia with narrowed eyes.

I couldn't hear their words, but it looked like Nikolas was apologizing for his sister. Gia's smile was undimmed, but I boiled with fury for her. The least her brother could have done was not draw their attention to us. It was almost as if he had wanted them to see her, so that they could admire the contrast with himself.

When I tentatively suggested as much to Gia as we hurriedly mounted our assigned horses, she brushed my words aside.

"He's just being Nikolas," she said.

But as we rode down the road, somewhere near the rear of the cavalcade, I found I didn't agree. Normally Nikolas stuck to his sister like glue, criticizing her decisions in person rather than from afar. His behavior on the tour seemed like something new. New and sinister.

CHAPTER 16
AIRLIE

Days passed, and the General didn't question my living arrangements. Since the nighttime guard at the door never reappeared, I wasn't even sure he knew. And even in the daytime, eyes no longer seemed to be trained on me at every moment.

The first few nights I didn't test the limits. But after a while, I couldn't resist wandering around in the dark.

No one challenged me, and I could find no trace of a tail. The General was apparently giving me a longer lead, perhaps watching to see what I would do with the increased freedom. At first, I did nothing, content to lull him into a false sense of complacency. Although I couldn't resist making one attempt to ask the gate guard to open the gate for me.

He just laughed and told me to come back another day. I grinned, giving every appearance of easy compliance. I hadn't expected it to work, anyway.

But even without Quirin's presence as a constant reminder, Dara's sad end and Marissa's words ate away at me. And the thing that troubled me most was Renley's role in it all.

The more my anger toward my father festered, the more my resentment of Renley disappeared. Scratch below the surface, and we were both the same. We had both been manipulated by adults we looked up to—adults who were too driven by their own agendas to consider what was best for us.

And while my father hadn't been the monster the General was, his betrayal was more personal and cut more deeply.

And beneath it all was an underlying sorrow that I had wasted my chance to get to know Dara better. If I had known everything I knew now from the beginning, I wouldn't have kept her at arm's length.

I had just resolved that I needed to talk to Renley when Quirin returned to the house. He still wore his grief around him like a cloak, but I no longer had to coax him to eat, and he looked marginally better rested.

While I was glad to see him returning to something of his former strength, his presence in the house complicated my new goal. I couldn't have an open conversation with Renley while his father was around.

I tried hanging around the training yard where he spent his time with the warriors, but he was never alone. But watching them at target practice, my fingers itched to hold a bow again, and an idea formed.

The next morning, I marched up to the General as he left his home.

"Let me go hunting," I said. "I'm skilled with a bow."

He gestured for the man at his side to go on without him before turning to give me his full attention.

"Our most recent hunting party has just returned. We don't have another trip planned for some time."

I shook my head. "No, let me go on my own. Just for a day. There are a few animals still scratching a living out here. I'll try for one of them."

He raised an eyebrow, an amused look on his face. "You want me to give you a weapon—which you admit to being skilled with—and let you walk through the gate alone?"

"Not alone, then. Send…" I let my gaze roam around the courtyard before appearing to latch on to Renley as he walked across the courtyard with others from his dormitory, as he did every day at this time. "Send Renley with me. You said I needed to earn your trust. Consider this the first step."

When he didn't immediately reply, I tapped the neutralizer at my waist. "Where am I going to go with this attached, anyway? As far as I know, this camp is the only place in all the kingdoms that has anyone who knows how to disable it."

Another moment of silence passed before the General nodded once.

"Renley!" he shouted in a bellow that easily crossed the courtyard.

Renley looked up in surprise, not quite able to hide his delight when he realized who had called for him. Trotting over to us, he ignored me, his focus on the General.

"Airlie is going hunting for the day. You're to accompany her and ensure she doesn't forget to return come nightfall."

"Hunting?" Renley finally looked at me.

"Yes." The General's curt voice indicated he didn't expect to be plagued with questions.

Renley straightened. "Yes, sir."

The General nodded at us both before marching off. I watched him go before turning to Renley with a fake smile.

"So, where can I find a bow?"

Several hours later, I had given up on the idea of actually catching anything. Clearly I had overestimated the number of animals that still survived on this side of the border. But at least we had made it far enough away from the settlement that it was no longer in sight, concealed behind a stand of twisted trees that were barely clinging to life.

I stopped, leaning into the wind and relishing the feel of the unfettered air. Trapped inside the wooden walls of the settlement, I hadn't felt so much as a free breeze in months. I missed the untamed elements, and the way they roared and whispered with equal allurement.

Without thinking, I reached for the air around me. I felt nothing.

My hand tightened around my bow. Even now, after all this time, I sometimes forgot about the neutralizer—like an amputee, trying to reach for something with an arm that was no longer there.

I pushed the thought away, not wanting to waste any of my precious moments beyond the walls on useless resentment.

"This is a waste of my time," Renley muttered. "I don't know what the General was thinking."

I turned to him, taking his mild criticism of the General as my opening. "He doesn't care about the hunting. It's a test. For both of us."

"A test?" He glared at me. "The General knows my loyalty."

"I don't know." I batted my eyelashes at him. "I *am* a young female. Boys of your age have proven susceptible to such tests of loyalty before."

He guffawed, a heartier laugh than I had yet heard from him. I grinned back, trying not to feel offended at his mirth.

"Sorry, Airlie," he said when his chuckles subsided. "But my parents talked about you and your sister a lot—the perfect daughters they never had." His smile twisted a little, although it stayed on his face. "I've always thought of you like a cousin, or something."

"There you go, then," I said. "Family. That's another kind of loyalty."

"If you're trying to subvert my loyalty to the General," he said in a mulish voice, but I cut across his protests, holding my hand up for silence.

When he tried to keep talking, I hissed at him.

"What?" he asked, irritated.

"Do you hear that?" I asked.

He looked around. "Hear what?"

At least he was whispering now, but I ignored him, my focus on the trees. "It's like snuffling. But it just stopped."

"I'm sure it's nothing," he said in a normal tone. "Like I said earlier, this is a waste of our time." He strode toward the trees, clearly ready to be done with the day's efforts.

"Wait! Stop!" I cried, but he didn't slow.

An explosion of movement and sound emerged from the trees as an enormous shape burst into view. It charged across the short distance of open ground toward Renley, hooves flying and sharp tusks gleaming.

I whipped the bow up, responding on instinct. Nocking an arrow, I let it fly in the same smooth movement.

It hit the hairy creature in the chest, evoking a guttural scream but no reduction in pace. The beast had nearly reached Renley.

I pulled out another arrow, having a better feel for the effect of the breeze now. This time, it hit the animal in the eye. A third arrow sprouted from its chest as it slowed, collapsing downward with an unnatural wheezing gasp.

Renley stood frozen. When the seconds ticked by and it still didn't move, he slowly spun around to stare at me.

"Thank you," he whispered.

I nodded, my mouth a thin line as I walked over to join him. Now that the danger had passed, I felt shaky and light-headed. It had been too long since I'd had a chance to practice, and I wouldn't have made those shots if I hadn't been firing at such short range.

Together we surveyed the animal.

"What...is it?" I asked.

"A boar, I think." He had regained some of his calm,

glancing at the trees behind the creature. "It's not just the vegetation that gets twisted out here."

I winced. The creature dead at our feet was far larger than any boar I'd ever seen, and his back was misshapen. Had the unnatural rage which had made him attack Renley come from pain? From the look of his body, it seemed likely. Perhaps my actions had been a mercy.

"I'm not eating any meat from that creature," I said flatly.

Renley nodded fervent agreement. "There's a reason we usually hunt across the border."

"Let's move on." I had no desire to linger beside the body.

Renley nodded, and by unspoken agreement, we skirted the trees the boar had emerged from. Once we'd made it far enough around that we could no longer see the carcass, I stopped, however. The settlement would soon come into sight again, and we still hadn't had the conversation I had brought us out here for.

Still shaken from our recent run in, I didn't beat around the bush.

"Do you know what your mother died from?"

Renley also stopped, backtracking to my side, his expression furious. I didn't back down, though, meeting him glare for glare.

After a moment, he shrugged. "She was sick. It happens." But there was pain behind the blasé words.

"Yes, it does. But Dara didn't have a natural illness. She was poisoned."

"What?" He took a step toward me. "That's nonsense. Who would do such a thing?"

"You, from what I hear," I said softly.

He growled deep in his throat, looking ready to leap forward and seize me. My hand tightened instinctively around the grip of the bow, but I kept myself still. I knew the severity of my accusation. There was a reason I was doing it away from the settlement and with a weapon in my hands.

"How dare you!" he said, his voice shaking.

"Am I wrong?" I asked. "Did you not ask her to use her power affinity to help the General?"

"Not just the General," he said. "All of us. We might already be out of this awful place if everyone just realized that we need to work together."

"But the requests came from the General," I pressed, "and you passed them on."

"What of it?" He sounded defiant now, like a child playing at adulthood.

"Didn't your father ever tell you why he wouldn't help the General?"

"He was exaggerating," Renley said. "Mother wouldn't have agreed if it was true. The General assured me any hurt was only minor and temporary. We need to accept a little discomfort if we're ever going to succeed. Ask any of the warriors. Father just doesn't want anything to change, and he's managed to convince a bunch of the other old-timers to see it his way."

His stance was still aggressive, but I could see a terrified hint of doubt in his eyes. Everything in me wanted to pull back from the wound I was about to inflict, but I steeled myself. I was done hiding the truth from others under the guise of protecting them.

"Do you really think it's true that your mother would have told you no if it was hurting her?" I asked softly. "She wouldn't be the first mother to put her child's interests ahead of her own. I understand she wasn't the...firmest of women."

Renley shook his head, but his hands were trembling, his shoulders slumping forward.

"No. No, she was ill."

"If it was an ordinary illness, what was it? Surely she would have told you—her own son."

He stared at me blankly, clearly at a loss. How had it not occurred to him to ask such a crucial question? What generality had she fobbed him off with?

"She was ill," I pressed on. "But not with any natural sickness. She was ill because of you. You say the General claimed it wouldn't hurt her, but now she's dead. Do you really think that's coincidence? She confessed to one of her friends that she'd been helping you, but she made a mistake and let it go too far. Her friend had seen it before, with her own grandparents."

"No." The doubt was stronger in his voice this time.

"It was Marissa who told me. You must know her better than me. Would she lie about the words of a dead woman? Surely your mother knew what was happening to her own body."

Horror flooded his face. "Marissa told you that? That my mother said it herself?"

I nodded. "You can ask Marissa yourself if you like. She'll confirm what I've said."

I could read in his face that he had no desire for that conversation, and I could understand why. From the anger I'd seen in Marissa, she wouldn't go easy on him. But neither could he discount her word like he could mine.

I had forced him to confront his reality—the pull between the two parts of his life—and the moment had come when he must either accept he had been wrong about the General, or fully reject the people who had raised him, branding them liars rather than just misguided fools.

"No." This time he whispered the word, his whole body trembling. "Mother...Mother would have told me."

"Would she?" I pressed, wishing I could turn and run away instead.

I didn't want to be here for this. But having lured Renley into my trap, I couldn't abandon him now.

"No," he whispered again, but this time he followed it with, "she wouldn't. She wouldn't want to hurt me."

"The General knew all along," I said. "That's why he agreed to let her go after Cadence. After handing her a death sentence, he was willing to use her final days as well, taking away her last moments with you and your father."

As I drove the final blow home, he collapsed. He didn't wail or cry, instead curling into a ball and shaking as if he had lost all control of his limbs. I stepped toward him before halting. I had no place in this moment of raw grief.

And it was more than just the fresh grief about his mother, or even the guilt. He had just lost his idol as well, his whole life's purpose crumbling around him.

I had never relished speaking the truth less. And I—one of his victims—could offer him no comfort.

CHAPTER 17
AIRLIE

The minutes drew out, each less comfortable than the last, until Renley finally gave a deep, anguished groan. Stretching out slowly, he rose to his feet, his dry eyes red with fury.

"I'm going to kill him," he said with gritted teeth, turning toward the distant settlement.

I sprang forward, racing in front of him and placing both hands out to make him stop. He ignored me, walking straight into my raised palms. I dug in my heels and pushed back until he finally halted, looking down at me in surprise, almost as if he'd forgotten my presence.

"I can understand the sentiment," I said quickly. "But think about the logistics."

The fight went out of him, the fever pitch in his eyes dulling.

"I wouldn't even get near him," he muttered.

"Exactly. What we need is a plan. And allies."

He turned to me, some of his earlier animation returning. "You! You can activate me. That's a start at least."

I put my hands on my hips. "Activate you for what? So you can use wild power like your mother? There's not a lot else out here. I'm not having your death on my hands. Besides, I can't.

One of your father's friends already asked me about that. I'm bound by a neutralizer, remember. I'm basically the same as you and every other unactivated person—I can't access any part of my power."

I hesitated, unsure if he could withstand another blow. But it was better to get it all out in the open.

"There's something else you should know. The General told me himself that people with a power affinity can't have their ability strengthened. He wouldn't tell me how it's done, but he seemed certain about that. It's why they want Cadence so badly."

He paled at my words, but after the earlier revelation, this one had lost some of its power.

"Do you know how he does it?" I asked. "How can he strengthen someone's ability when no one else can?"

Renley grimaced. "I'm not in the inner circle yet. I don't get access to his secrets." His fists tightened. "When I think of the years I wasted...What I did to my own mother trying to get the General to accept me..." He ground his teeth together.

I put a hand on his arm. "You didn't know what it was doing to her."

"But I should have." Now that his eyes were opened, he wasn't shying away from the truth, and I admired him for that. "I let myself be blinded because of my desire to be part of the inner circle—to be important and powerful. I was a fool, and my mother paid the price for it."

He paused, drawing in a ragged breath while I waited in silence.

"I should have realized after the first time that he was never going to let me in, that he was using me all along."

"The first time?" I asked.

He started, giving me a wary glance.

"Out with it," I said sternly, alarmed at his expression. "What else did you do?"

He swallowed and began walking slowly toward the settlement. I matched his stride, letting him have the small ease of not having to face me directly while he made whatever confession was coming.

"I was the one who told the General about you," he mumbled.

"What?!" I shrieked.

He winced. "I heard my parents talking about you a couple of years ago. Father was saying that if your father had agreed to come, between him and the two of you, they might have been able to keep the General from taking over. They mentioned the strength of both of your seeds, and that Cadence had a power affinity. Later, when I was trying to think how to demonstrate my loyalty to the General, it occurred to me how valuable he would find you. So I told him."

I drew a deep breath to keep myself from shouting at him.

"I'm sorry," he whispered. "At least I didn't remember where you lived, given I was six last time we went there. I assumed it must be on the Tartoran side of the border, so the General was scouring the area looking for you. Unsuccessfully, of course."

"Didn't he ask your parents where we were?"

Renley grimaced. "They told him that you moved after our last visit because your father didn't want us to know where you were. Since he'd cut off all contact, it was close enough to the truth to be convincing, although he thought you would have stayed near the border. It's the best region if you want to hide because of the number of refugees."

"So all those villages he attacked?" I asked, feeling sick again. "He wasn't rescuing persecuted Calistans, like he claimed? He was looking for us?"

Renley's brow creased as he considered the matter. "It's not as straightforward as that. He was looking for you, but also recruiting for his cause at the same time. There were plenty of disgruntled Calistans in those villages, he wasn't lying about that. I went on one of the trips myself."

I nodded, feeling marginally better. The General had already demonstrated his propensity to combine goals, and it had been an effective move on his part, even if he hadn't yet managed to capture Cadence.

"At first he was delighted with the information," Renley said. "But when he couldn't find you straight away, he said it wasn't enough. That I needed to do more to help. I should have seen through him then."

"Don't be too hard on yourself," I said softly. "I've witnessed him in action, and he's incredibly persuasive. I nearly fell for it, too. I would have if it wasn't for you."

"Me?" Renley stared at me.

I nodded. "I didn't know about your mother then, but he told me about not being able to strengthen a power ability. I realized he'd lied to you, and it all started to lose its luster." I sighed. "I'm sorry you didn't have something like that to open your eyes."

He shook his head angrily. "But I did. My own parents. I just didn't believe them."

I winced. "You wouldn't be the first youth in that situation."

Renley suddenly halted, his hand flying out to stop me as well.

"Airlie! Wait!" His eyes had gone wide. "The most recent attack—Cadence!"

"That was a while ago." I frowned at him. "The General said she survived it, and she obviously wasn't captured."

He shook his head. "That's almost worse. That must mean she fought it off. They used wild power in that attack—sending it down the river."

An icy cold sensation trickled down from the top of my skull. "What does that mean?"

"When I was younger, the wild power always stayed on this

side of the border. My parents told me there's some sort of ancient barrier there, set up by past kings on both sides. It was enough to keep the power contained in Calista. But it clings to people, apparently. And with so many of us traveling back and forth across the border on these raiding parties, it's started breaking through more and more often."

"You mean it's not chance that the wild power is destabilizing? The General is causing it?"

He nodded. "At first it was accidental, but when he realized what was happening, he encouraged it. Some of those in the settlement with power affinities are working for him—especially the younger ones. He must not be asking them to use the wild power, like he did with my mother." His voice broke, but he pushed on. "But they can still use their ability to sense the power around them. He had us ride through pockets of it so we could drag it with us. He just told us not to touch anything until we were free of it."

"Not to touch anything?"

He shrugged. "It's like healing power, I suppose. It needs physical contact to break the skin barrier. It would affect the elements and the ground around us, but it wouldn't hurt us as long as we didn't touch anything it had settled on."

"I bet those on the other side of the border didn't get the same warning. Or the animals. I suppose that's what happened to the poor boar. He brushed up against something he shouldn't have."

We both gave almost identical winces, and I tried to focus my mind on the more pressing matter of Cadence.

"Are you saying the General found a way to drag more of it?"

Renley nodded. "And before that they worked out a way to use it to get Lawson back up the river. That's how he escaped after attacking your sister."

"Surely one of those with a power affinity must have actually manipulated it in that case?"

172

"Perhaps." He frowned. "Maybe if they spread the effort out, they managed to touch enough not to damage themselves too greatly? All I know is that it worked so well, someone came up with the idea of sending some of the wild power in the opposite direction. I'm not sure exactly how it was done, but apparently the court and Guild are off on some sort of tour, and they were all in barges on the river."

"And you think Cadence fought off all that wild power?" I asked.

He shrugged. "She's the only power mage they have. Who else could have done it?"

Blind rage filled my vision, and I had to remind myself of the arguments I'd used to stop Renley racing off to physically attack the General.

"They're planning to go out again," Renley said, snapping me back to attention. "I think they might be planning a more conventional attack, but I'm not sure. The General has been keeping the details of this one close. He wants to make the most of the opportunity of the tour. They're all much more exposed than usual."

Panic clawed at me. "When are they leaving?"

"I'm not sure. In the next day or two?"

I increased my pace. "We have to get back. We have to think of a way to stop them. Maybe we can convince the General to send us along. We could—"

"Actually, Airlie," Renley said with sudden regret, "I don't think that's going to be possible."

"Why not? We just need to—" I stopped talking as I followed his pointing finger with my eyes. "What's that?" I faltered, trying to bring the distant haze into focus. "It looks like a dust cloud."

"That's exactly what it is. That's what happens when a large group of mounted riders travels over ground where no grass grows. I think the attack party has already left."

The settlement was well and truly in sight now, so I picked up my pace, nearly bursting through the gate. A crowd must have assembled to see the group off because they were still dispersing. And on the other side of the square, in front of his home, the General stood.

Our eyes met across the distance, cold washing over me. I had thought I was manipulating him, creating an escape for Renley and me, but he had been the one sending us away. And since I had suggested the trip myself, neither of us could accuse him of excluding us from the attack team's departure.

He must have known we would both want to be included, and in one effective move he had protected himself from our recriminations. Moves within moves. This was how he maintained loyalties while manipulating everyone around him.

I swallowed, forcing my face to remain impassive. If I had any hope of outmaneuvering him, I couldn't tip my hand. Not yet.

The General would pay. But not today.

CHAPTER 18
CADENCE

It took us a week to travel between the mouth of the Viridian and the Celadon. During that time, three villages and two large towns came within the range of my ability. But I continued to find no sign of Airlie.

I cornered Evermund as we neared the western river, but he had been equally unsuccessful in uncovering any clues.

"We'll be turning north soon," he told me. "We'll have more luck in that direction."

Outwardly, I agreed, but privately I was feeling far less hopeful. Nikolas had been right when he said the border region was too dangerous for the tour. After the run in with the rogue tainted power, I was certain the royals would end the tour early rather than continuing up the Celadon past Tarona and into the northern part of the kingdom. Which would mean the whole trip was for nothing as far as the search for Airlie was concerned.

"But not for nothing overall," Zeke reminded me. "We needed you back there on the river. I, for one, am glad you came."

I smiled, but my heart wasn't in it. It had been days since I felt so much as a twinge of tainted power, and although I couldn't guess at the intent of the unfamiliar people who came in range of our group, none of them ever behaved in a suspicious manner or approached close enough to cause concern. As far as I could tell, the tour was safe.

Which meant I had nothing to do and no purpose. Even my attempts to train myself using my recent breakthroughs had fallen flat. While I could manipulate my ability into any shape within my own body, I couldn't push it past my skin. And neither could I draw the power that lingered all around me into myself or another object. I could grab the loose power and push it away—as I had done on the river—or I could grab it and merge it into the power someone else had already shaped—like I had during Lawson's attack. But I couldn't work out how to do anything else with it.

It began to feel as if I was on the tour only to keep Gia company. Although that in itself felt like a full-time role sometimes. Now that our escape to the beach had given Gia a taste of rebellion, I had to head off such suggestions every day.

But having been involved in leading her astray once, I didn't want to do it again—even if Liara encouraged us to join her on more than one occasion. The nomad girl often appeared, ready with a friendly overture, or sat near us at mealtimes. And she hadn't once broken character from her new persona as a hopeful future friend, bestowing smiles on me and seeking me out at regular intervals. I sometimes wondered if I'd dreamed our first encounter.

As we stopped for lunch on our final day near the coast, however, I caught sight of her from afar. She stood with Annora and an older woman who looked enough like Liara to be her mother. The younger girl had a petulant look when she turned in my direction, and I had to quickly spin the other way to avoid being caught staring.

When I dared glance back again, she was approaching me, an enormous smile pasted on her face. I greeted her as I usually did—politely but without her own enthusiasm. But out of the corner of my eye, I watched Annora and Liara's mother. Both of them were focused on me, and from the pleased smiles on their faces, Liara was doing her duty as instructed.

I immediately scowled, making Liara falter. I couldn't believe I'd been so naive as to miss the reason for her apparent change of heart.

Clearly it had not been her own choice, but the result of an instruction from her tribe. Between when she confronted me on the first day and when we next met, she must have been informed I was a person of interest to be courted.

I had thought Annora was being remarkably forbearing in giving me space, but in fact she had merely been sending a delegate she imagined to be more appealing than herself.

"Excuse me," I said roughly. "I've just remembered..." I let my words trail into a mumble, not bothering to come up with a good excuse for my hasty departure. If Liara was only interested in talking to me because she'd been instructed to do so by her mother, I felt no compunction to continue the conversation.

My foul mood lasted the rest of the day as we finally reached the Celadon River. A sizable town sat on the eastern bank of the river mouth, a trading hub with the nomads whose lands began on the other side of the Celadon. Our party skirted around the town, setting up camp on the riverbank just north of its main gate.

Our journey would continue on horseback, although we would follow the river road now, instead of the coastal one. I knew from Evermund that a great deal of thought had gone into whether the Guild could come up with a way to propel the barges back upstream. If the mages accomplished it—instead of the usual team of donkeys—it would be a mighty show of strength in front of the nomads.

Several ideas were put forward, but in the end, the idea was abandoned. With the protection curse on Calista going rogue and jumping across the border, as well as increasingly daring attacks from the raiders, it didn't seem like a good idea to exhaust a significant number of mages in an unnecessary exercise.

And neither did it seem ideal to sail the barges all the way up to Lake Aterra where they could cross over from the Viridian to the Celadon. In the past, plenty of barge captains had done so, despite the need to cross briefly into Calistan territory. But now, with the protections growing weak, I doubted anyone would attempt it. Our barges remained on the Viridian, and we would remain on our horses.

Evermund had informed me the previous day that we would follow the river road as far north as Karielle's father's estate before heading back to Tarona. His estate sat only slightly further north than the capital, but at least it was in the right direction. And he had informed me that if we made it that far without another attack, he intended to ask King Marius to allow us to break away from the tour and continue north to search for Airlie.

The news gave me fresh hope, driving off some of my dark cloud, as I headed to the evening meal with Gia and Karielle. Before we reached the long tables, however, Zeke caught my attention from off to the side. Given the subtlety of his gesture, I excused myself to the other girls and slipped over unobtrusively.

"What is it?" I whispered, looking around in all directions.

"Probably nothing."

I gave him an unconvinced look. "This is a lot of subterfuge for nothing."

"It might be foolish, but I have a bad feeling. Like an itch at the base of my neck that won't go away." He stretched his head, rotating it around as if the itch he described was a physical sensation he could expunge. "I don't know how else to describe it except that something around me isn't right."

I had taken to leaving my ability shaped into a protective shell, so I tried to remember how long it had been since I last cracked the shell to check for tainted power. When I realized it hadn't been since the day before, I silently scolded myself, immediately sampling the air around me. But there was nothing.

"If there's something wrong out there, I can't feel it," I said.

"Which probably means there isn't anything wrong." He frowned. "Maybe I'm just getting edgy after so long without any signs of trouble."

"I remember when that was a good thing."

"It is," he said. "As long as it's real." He hesitated. "What about the town? There could be raiders lurking there. It's big enough that not all the residents would know each other. They might not have noticed suspicious newcomers."

I glanced back toward the distant lanterns at the town gates.

"There are a lot of people in there. From this distance they're all a big blur." When the concern didn't drop from his face, I suppressed a sigh. "Would you like to take a walk? If we got closer, I could tell you if there's anyone there of unusual strength."

His expression lifted, immediately rewarding me for the sacrifice of missing the meal. Hopefully Gia would save me something, or I could beg from the kitchen staff who had accompanied the tour. Some of them might remember me as the princess's friend.

We turned together and strolled out of the campsite, side by side. No one stopped us, and from the amused looks of the servants we passed, they thought it was romance that motivated our escape.

I couldn't deny that walking through the pleasant evening air beside Zeke was an enjoyable activity. Nor could I deny the strong desire to slip my hand into his. But one overpowering doubt held me back.

Tribe Nicabar.

It wasn't the false promise of Liara's friendship that had fueled my bad mood all day. It was the uncomfortable thought that maybe Zeke had received the same instruction from his mother. I had thought his interest seemed to be increasing lately, but what if that was only because his mother had arrived? Had she told him to make sure I accepted her upcoming invitation to visit their tribe?

I watched him out of the corner of my eye, feeling slightly sick at the disloyal thought. Was I wronging him?

If I took his hand right now, how would he respond? And would his response be entirely fueled by his own emotions?

As if sensing my gaze, he turned his head to look at me, a rueful smile on his face.

"I'm wasting our time, aren't I? The feeling is already fading. And our meal is growing cold."

I smiled back at him, unable to resist the apology in his expression. "I don't mind. We should be close enough soon."

His gaze dropped down to my hand, and for a breath I thought he meant to take it. But his eyes moved on, leaving me to wonder yet again what was going through his head.

"Here," I said, stopping abruptly. "This will do. Just give me a minute."

It was still light, thanks to the long summer days, although twilight was approaching, and the sky had slowly begun to darken. But sight wasn't the sense I needed right now, and my ability worked just as well in the dark as in the light.

I reached toward the town, skimming over the power I sensed inside it. Several mages lived here, but they were spread out in what seemed like a natural pattern. Three healing mages clustered together with a group of ordinary people who had the healing affinity—presumably in some sort of healing center.

And I found several plants mages, one of whom was out in the fields to the east of the town.

I pulled back. "I don't think there's anything out of the ordinary. The General certainly isn't there. I didn't sense any elements mages at all."

Zeke let out a long breath, turning back toward the camp. "Good." He gave me a grin and a shallow bow. "Please accept my humble apologies and excuse my overanxious nature."

I shook my head, although a small smile crept up my face. "I haven't noticed that trait in you before, I must confess."

"It must be the old age, then. I'm told it's a common symptom of the condition."

I snorted. "Just because you're graduating, doesn't mean you're getting old. Must I remind you that you're not even nineteen yet?"

He rubbed the back of his head, looking at me sideways as we walked. "About my graduation…"

I tensed. If he was going to invite me to come with him when he returned to his tribe, I wasn't ready to hear it. Not after the day's earlier revelation.

"I've heard there's going to be a ball," I said hurriedly. "Put on by Karielle's father, since she's due to graduate as well."

A slight expression of disappointment slid across his face, but he suppressed it quickly.

"That is certainly the rumor. I don't think I can claim it's for me, however."

"I'm sure they'll let you dance at it all the same." I smiled at him broadly in gratitude for being willing to let the other matter go.

He started to reply, only to cut himself off.

"That's odd." He pointed to someone who appeared to be having a nap in the walkway between two tents.

"Yes, it is," I agreed.

It wasn't just that they were sleeping on the ground, in the open, either. Something about them felt strange.

I hurried forward, toward the person. "There's power coating their head. It's not a lot, almost like a thin film, but I've never felt anything like it before."

I stepped between tents into an intersection of pathways, only to stop abruptly.

"Zeke!" I cried, louder this time.

He reached me in two strides, his mouth falling open. From this vantage point, we could see the end of one of the long tables. A number of people had slumped forward, sleeping with their heads on the table, while those that remained upright swayed slightly, not seeming to notice the strange behavior of their companions. As we watched, one of them sank slowly down, placing his cheek into his plate of food and starting to snore.

We both took off running at the same moment. As I got closer to the table, I saw Karielle, stretched out on the long bench seat. Scanning the area around her, I found Gia, flat on the ground a few steps away, as if she'd sensed something was wrong and tried to leave.

I dropped to my knees beside her and shook her shoulders roughly. She only snorted slightly and tried to roll over.

Frantically, I looked up at Zeke.

"She won't wake! What do we do?"

Zeke had stopped beside Karielle, conducting a much more clinical analysis of her condition. Perhaps it was from his mother being cross-influenced with healing, but he knew enough to look competent at least. He met my eyes, although he still held her wrist between his fingers.

"Her pulse is steady. It seems to be sleep, but obviously not a natural one. You said that other woman had power around her head? What about the rest of them?"

I drew in a couple breaths, forcing myself to set aside the

panic and respond helpfully, like Zeke was doing. As soon as I went looking, I found the same phenomenon on all of them. I took a second to do a more thorough evaluation of Gia, my forehead wrinkling.

"Yes, they all have it as well. But it's more than just their heads. I can feel it inside them too. Here." I touched Gia's middle, just below her ribs.

"The stomach." Zeke let go of Karielle, violently pushing her plate away, as if it might infect him by proximity. "There must have been something in the meal."

I gulped, trying to think.

"What if it was some sort of plant or herb? Like that one you used on the librarian back at the Guild. Didn't you say that if you'd put it in his tea, this is what would have happened?"

Zeke nodded. "It's possible. It would explain why you can sense the power in both their stomachs and their heads, since the head is the part it's affecting." He slammed a fist onto the table. "If only I hadn't dragged you away. You would have been here to feel the power in the meal and warn everyone not to eat it."

I stood up and joined him. "Or I might have missed it—it's only the faintest trace of power. I don't think I would have noticed it on any of them if I hadn't been looking especially. And then we'd both be asleep right now, too."

"If everyone is asleep..." Horror slowly filled Zeke's face. "This must be the raiders. They're just waiting for everyone to fall asleep before they attack. It'll be a massacre!"

CHAPTER 19

CADENCE

"No," I said firmly. "It won't be because we're going to wake everyone up."

"How will we do that? Can you pull the power out of them?"

I reached for Gia, drawing out the power that clung to her head and stomach. She moaned and stirred, but she didn't wake up.

"It didn't work," I cried. "Why didn't it work?"

"When my mother makes her sleeping potion, she only uses power to augment the natural properties of the herb," Zeke said. "It makes it more potent than any natural plant, but it's the herb which is causing the effect. And maybe once it's started working, the plant is enough to keep it going for a while on its own?"

I wrung my hands. "Then what do we do? I can remove the power, but I don't know how to wake everyone up. We need a healing mage."

"Or better yet—my mother. Come on, this way. She always eats with the king."

We dashed down the long table, turning a corner into a small square with several more tables. People lay everywhere, but we didn't stop beside any of them until we reached the smaller, royal table.

I shivered at the sight of the king, queen, Evermund, Drake, and Augusta all slumped over their meals. Movement made us both jump, whirling toward a man with a sword.

But he wore the blue and gold livery of the royal guards, and at sight of us, he looked ready to weep.

"Oh, thank goodness! Someone else is awake!"

"How did this happen?" Zeke asked. "Didn't you realize something was wrong?"

"It happened so slowly that by the time the first people started dropping, everyone had already started eating."

"Were you the only one on guard duty?" Zeke asked, sounding surprised.

The man shook his head. "There were four of us here guarding Their Majesties. I sent one of the others to warn the sentries, one to run for the town to raise the town guards, and the other to gather everyone here in camp who's still awake. There must be some servants who weren't eating with everyone else." He sounded grim. "We'll need everyone still on their feet to form a guard around Their Majesties until the forces from the town have time to arrive."

"I doubt the raiders will wait that long," Zeke said in a voice of command. "We need to act now."

The change in the guard was visible. Clearly he was relieved to have someone else assume the responsibility of command.

"What else can we do?" he asked. "You're the first mage I've seen who isn't asleep."

"I need to wake my mother." Zeke pushed past the guard and dropped down beside her. "Just a moment."

He rummaged through her robe, pulling out packet after packet of seeds and herbs. Finally, he settled on one, holding it to his nose.

"Phew!" he held it away again, his eyes watering. "This is

the one. She always told me to use this if she inhaled too much smoke while brewing her concoction. Hopefully it will work against whatever this is, too."

I nodded, having already pulled the lingering power out of her while he searched. Watching with bated breath, I awaited any signs of alertness returning.

Holding the small pouch at arm's length, Zeke tipped it out into his palm. Crushing the small herbs in his fist, he opened his fingers again and held them under his mother's nose.

She stirred, sitting up slowly, although her eyes remained unfocused. Zeke made an irritated noise and stuffed the herbs into her mouth.

She gave a loud exclamation at that, coming fully awake and spitting them out. As soon as her mouth was completely clear, she spoke.

"Zekiel! Don't you ever do that again! Those herbs are not meant to be consumed." She shuddered. "The taste!"

"Look around," he said. "There wasn't time for anything else."

She turned to survey the fallen people all around her, her eyebrows rising higher and higher toward her hairline. Her gaze finally moved from the lone guard to her son and then to me. Understanding filled her face, meaning we didn't need to waste time on explanations.

"What's the fastest way to wake them all?" Zeke asked. "Do you have more of this?" He shook the now empty pouch.

"Not prepared like that was. But I have the seeds." She thrust her hand into one of the internal pockets of her robe, pulling out another pouch.

With brisk, efficient movements, she shook the seeds into his hand. "Place them in the ground and make them grow. You need to stretch those seeds as far as they can possibly go. We need to make as much of the herb as your power can produce. And make it strong—I need it as aromatic as possible. Enhance its natural properties. I'm sure Augusta will have taught you that."

He dropped to the dirt at our feet, thrusting both hands flat against the soil. It was hard packed and dry, but his mother took the nearest water pitcher and upended it over his hands. I grabbed the one from in front of the king and did the same, earning an approving look from Annora.

"What about you?" I asked. "Are you going to help him?"

She shook her head. "I need my power for something else."

The first shoot of green thrust up from the wet earth, growing at an unnatural rate. As soon as the first row of leaves unfurled, Annora reached over and snatched them from the ground.

The guard had hurried over to stand expectantly behind the king, but Annora moved toward Augusta instead.

"The mages first and then the guards," she said. "Everyone else can wait."

Pressing the herb over Augusta's nose, Annora let her power fill the greenery and then travel through into Augusta. She glanced over at me, taking in my wide eyes.

"It's my healing influence," she said. "If I'm touching some-one, I can push my power into them, like a healer."

"You can heal people as a plants mage?" I asked, astonished.

"Not properly. Not like a healer. But I've worked out that if I'm using a plant with medicinal qualities, I can push those qualities into them. It's not as good as a healing, but it's faster and more potent than if they just ate the herb."

She pulled her hand back, letting the withered herbs drop to the table. Augusta jerked away from her, nearly falling back-ward over the seat.

Annora grabbed at her, steadying her. "It's an attack," she said. "Help Zeke."

To Augusta's credit, she grasped the situation nearly as

quickly as Annora. Without asking any questions, she sprinted over to join Zeke in the dirt.

I dashed after her, ripping up two handfuls of the herbs that had already sprouted. Running back to Annora, I thrust them at her.

"Will there be enough seeds?"

She stepped over to Drake. "I don't know. But my power will probably be the bigger problem. It's likely to run out before the herbs do."

I hesitated, glancing back toward Augusta. But she was fully occupied with Zeke.

"I can help," I said quietly. "If you use only a dollop of your power, I can augment it."

She looked at me for a single measuring second before nodding briskly.

I felt the difference this time when she pressed several leaves of the herb under Drake's nose. She was only using the tiniest sprouting of power. Seizing some of the leftover power that always swirled around the tour, I poured it into the pattern Annora had created.

Drake bellowed, rearing back and crashing to the ground. But he was on his feet a second later.

"An attack is expected imminently," Annora said crisply. "For now, you have him." She pointed at the lone guard. "More will be coming."

Drake's eyes swept the eerie campsite littered with sleeping people, dwelling for a moment on Augusta and Zeke with a creased brow. But when his gaze landed on the sleeping royals, he straightened.

Neither Annora nor I stopped to listen as he began barking orders at the single guard. Instead, we moved on to Hayes. As soon as he was awake and apprised of the situation, Annora asked if his healing power could wake people more effectively than she could.

He immediately offered to attempt it. Putting his hand on Evermund, who was sitting next to him, he pushed power into the sleeping mage. Evermund's eyes fluttered open, his expression sleepy and bemused.

Hayes looked up at us. "Your method is more effective, and from the amount of power that just took, more efficient, too. The herb is doing half the work." He grimaced. "And it smells so appalling, the patient wakes fully alert."

Annora nodded. "In that case, save your energy for casualties. I won't be able to help there. Get Evermund to Drake and then bring me more herbs."

She moved to the next table where a number of nomads had been sitting. I trailed behind her, while Hayes took over my job. He ran back and forth with fresh handfuls of the herb, not asking why I clung so close to Annora.

As soon as she had woken most of her people, sending them all to Drake, she turned back to me and Hayes.

"You direct me from here. I want elements mages first, then plants mages, then guards. We won't wake any more healing mages until the fighting actually starts."

"You think it's inevitable, then?" I asked, trying to keep my voice steady.

"Not if we can move quickly enough. They won't attack unless they have the advantage."

"Him." I pointed at an elements master at the next table. "And then her." I pointed at the woman sitting next to him.

Moving further and further away from the royal table, we woke mage after mage. At some point we ran out of mages and moved on to guards instead. When we ran out of those, Annora finally relaxed. Hayes had just delivered another load of herbs with the message that it was the last to be eked from the seeds.

Annora nodded. "We'll use these to wake a handful of your healers, Hayes. You can wake everyone else in a more conventional style. But take your time. I haven't heard an attack yet—

surely a good sign—but your services may still be needed tonight for other healings."

Hayes nodded, leading us to a cluster of healing masters. Once we'd woken them, Annora gestured for me to follow her back to the royal table. When we reached it, she revealed a final cluster of leaves in each hand.

It only took moments to wake King Marius and Queen Celestine, although it took a lot longer for first Annora, then Augusta, and then Drake to report on the situation. I hung back, unnoticed in the background, relieved to hear Drake's assessment that an attack was no longer incoming.

"They were there, sure enough, Your Majesty," he said. "Waiting to the north of our campsite."

Zeke and I exchanged a look. We'd walked in the wrong direction.

"I sent out a couple of scouts, and they reported back to say that a large group of mounted warriors was moving upriver as fast as they could ride."

"Are you in pursuit?" the king asked, fury in his eyes.

Drake shook his head. "By the time the report came back, Captain Huxley was awake and able to assess the situation. He advised that we didn't have the troops to both ensure the safety of the tour and pursue the criminals. Especially not when we haven't had the chance to do a full sweep and confirm there isn't a second party hidden somewhere nearby."

King Marius didn't look happy, but neither did he dispute the captain's decision.

"Many people have yet to be woken," Annora said crisply. "And I'm sure we would all like a complete check by a healing mage to ensure sleep was the only effect of whatever concoction they used. Plus, we still need to investigate how a drug was slipped into our food in the first place. I am in complete agreement that we are in no condition to go chasing down a violent party of unknown strength."

The king inclined his head. "You raise excellent points. Has anyone seized hold of the Master Cook?"

A guard shouldered his way forward, dragging an older woman who was shaking with sobs. At a barked order, she pulled herself together and curtsied to the king.

I expected him to start issuing threats. But to my surprise, it was the queen who stepped forward, a look of sympathy on her face.

"You have been with us for decades, Priscilla. I cannot believe you would turn against us now. But can you explain what happened here in any other way?"

"Of course I would not betray you, Your Majesty," the cook declared, straightening to her full height. "Never would I do such a thing! It was those girls."

"Explain," the king said, in a shorter tone, but his face remained open.

She curtsied again.

"A number of my people came down sick, leaving me short-handed for the evening meal. So, since we're camped so near a town, I hired some girls to help out until we leave tomorrow. Lovely young things they seemed to be, too, but I see now they were snakes in the grass."

"Where are these girls?" Captain Huxley asked, appearing from out of the night.

"Gone!" she wailed, throwing up her hands. "I went looking for them as soon as Hayes woke me, and not a sign can I find of them anywhere."

The king drew a long breath. "Very well, then. We have our answer. Captain, you'll wish to interview the rest of the kitchen staff, but I have no doubt you'll hear the same story from all."

The cook began to cry again, whether with lingering guilt or relief, it wasn't clear. The guard led her away, much more gently this time, and the king turned to Annora.

"It was a neat trick, and a devious one. But I would like to understand more fully how it was foiled. Was someone able to resist the effects, or were we saved by someone's lack of hunger?"

Annora hesitated, glancing at me.

"It was Zeke," I blurted out, knowing an explanation was needed and that Zeke would be reluctant to put himself forward to receive all the credit.

Everyone turned to look at me, and I gulped at the weight of so many important eyes.

"We were late to the evening meal because he was telling me about his concern that something was wrong. He couldn't tell what exactly, but he could sense that something around us wasn't right. When we came to eat, we discovered everyone already falling asleep. At that point he identified it as a sleeping herb and was able to use a counter herb to wake his mother. The rest you know."

"A sense of wrongness?" Augusta stepped forward to frown at me. "What does that mean, precisely?"

I could see Zeke over her shoulder, watching me with confusion. There hadn't been a chance to tell him my theory, so he was hearing it for the first time along with everyone else.

"While I was assisting Annora, I was thinking it through. I don't believe it's a coincidence he had the sense just as the meal was being prepared. Since it was a plant that was put into the food—its properties boosted by both a healing mage and a plants mage, most likely—I believe Zeke was able to sense its presence. When we moved a short distance from camp, he said the feeling eased—probably because we moved too far away."

For a moment there was silence as everyone considered my explanation. I stood my ground, convinced I was right and needing them to accept Zeke's involvement without pushing further. It was true that he'd done most of the work.

"Is that possible?" King Marius looked from Annora to Augusta, the two most powerful plants mages present.

Annora regarded her son through narrowed eyes. "It is within the realms of possibility, although I must congratulate Augusta on her strength. I didn't know she was capable of such feats—and therefore of bestowing such capability on my son. I can see I made the right choice in sending him to her to be activated."

Augusta slowly shook her head, a thoughtful look on her face. "Reluctant as I am to reject a compliment, I don't believe it's earned. I sensed no such thing."

My heart sank.

"You disbelieve the theory, then?" the king asked.

"I wouldn't say that," she said, causing my spirits to lift slightly. "I hope I'm woman enough to admit when someone outperformed me. I just worked beside young Zekiel in a moment of intense stress and pressure, and he utilized greater strength than I can draw on."

Drake spoke into the deafening silence that followed. "We're getting old, Augusta. Painful as it is to acknowledge it."

"Speak for yourself," she snapped with her usual spirit. "My physical body might be starting to weaken, but my ability is not yet failing. I'm telling you, Zekiel showed himself stronger than me tonight."

A hubbub arose at her declaration, although when my eyes found Zeke's he was silent, his face frozen in an expression of shock. The head of the delegation from Tribe Patrin stepped forward.

"That is now two young people under Tartoran tutelage who have shown greater strength than their influencers. What secrets are you hoarding, Marius?"

An angry murmur sounded from the scattered huddles of nomads, but King Marius turned a scalding look on each of them in turn.

"I am as eager for an explanation as you. If anyone has one, we are all of us listening."

Another heavy silence descended on the group as everyone's eyes darted around the rough circle, seeking anyone willing to speak. No one did.

"Consider for half a moment," King Marius said when the silence had grown too long. "If we had such a secret weapon, would we use it on Annora's son?"

Annora laughed, breaking the tension. "That much I will believe, and readily."

The man from Tribe Patrin hesitated only a moment longer before bowing his head toward King Marius in a gesture of acceptance and apology.

"If I didn't know better," he said in quieter tones, "I would suspect you of having—"

"Hold your tongue," the king snapped, some sort of silent communication passing between them as he added, "It is impossible, as you well know."

The nomad leader subsided, giving no response to the piercing look that Annora threw at both him and the king. Whatever he had referred to, Tribe Nicabar didn't know about it. And from the looks on the faces of Augusta and Drake, the Triumvirate didn't either.

Interesting.

"Whatever the cause," the lead representative from Tribe Callen said, "it's in all our interests to identify it. If we are to fight this insidious force that is escaping from the fallen kingdom, then we need all the strength we can gather."

"We had barely started examining the elements girl when she disappeared," Augusta started.

"When she was abducted, I think you mean," Evermund said firmly.

She glanced at him before continuing. "Before she was abducted, then. But Zekiel has been under my care and training for two years now. There has been no shortage of opportunity to watch him utilize his ability. And while he has always been a fast learner and a promising student, I saw no hint that his strength was such as to defy the laws of power. Unless Annora can shed some light on the situation..."

"Absolutely none," Annora said immediately. "If Tribe Nicabar had such a skill, we would share it freely. This is not a time to be hoarding strength."

The other nomad delegates nodded approvingly, while I watched in fascination. There was no doubting Annora's political skill.

Slinking back through the crowd, I positioned myself at Zeke's side.

"I'm sorry," I whispered. "I had no idea I was throwing you into...this." I waved around at the crowd of important people who were continuing to discuss the matter.

"How could you?" He sounded dazed. "I didn't suspect it myself."

"Really?" I gave him a closer look, watching for any sign of hesitation. "You never suspected you were stronger than Augusta?"

He had certainly always possessed confidence commensurate with such a belief, but there was no sign of anything underhand in his manner now.

"Not once. In fact, I would have sworn I wasn't."

"Do you mean you think your strength has grown?" I frowned. "Then that's not the same as Airlie. She was more powerful than Evermund right from her activation."

"I have no better explanation than anyone else." He turned to fix me with burning eyes. "I swear to you, Cadence. I'm not interested in hiding anything from you. Not anymore."

I slipped my hand into his, warmth filling me.

"I believe you. Which means we'll just have to work this out for ourselves."

CHAPTER 20
AIRLIE

As usual, I started my morning at the tallest spot in the settlement. The paths between the clustered buildings and tents were quieter than usual, the attack party not yet returned. Sometimes I told myself their continued absence must mean they had been defeated, but I knew it was too soon for it to mean anything in actuality.

Steps sounded from my right, but I didn't turn my head to greet the new arrival.

"Why do you still come here every day?" Renley asked, standing beside me and looking out as I did, as if he wanted to see the view from my perspective. "Nothing ever changes."

"Nothing has changed *yet*," I corrected him.

He shook his head. "I've lived here for nineteen years. It always looks the same."

"Hope is important. No matter what, we need to hold on to hope."

He remained silent, clearly unconvinced.

"Very well, then." I finally turned to face him. "How about this? One day the General will slip up. He's going to make a mistake, and I refuse to miss it because that was the one day I chose to stay in bed."

"Now that is a good reason to come."

I faced forward again. "It's the only reason."

Ten minutes later, we walked back to Quirin's house side-by-side.

The next morning, when I arrived at my usual position, he was already there, surveying the view. For a moment we stood in silence while I completed my scan. Then he spoke.

"Nan would like to meet you. She's asked me to bring you over for a cup of tea."

"Nan?"

"She's Marissa's mother, but we all call her that."

"Where does she live?"

"Come with me. I'll take you there."

We walked downhill in silence while I contemplated the meaning of the invitation. It was the first I had received since my arrival, and I felt an unexpected trepidation. Between the Guild and our isolated childhood, I had never had much to do with the elderly. Even here they were few in number. It was a hard life in the settlement with limited resources and no access to anyone with even a weak healing affinity until very recently.

The house he led me to looked just like all the others except for the bright and cheerful yellow curtains. He knocked once and entered without waiting for a reply, leading me into a neat room that looked much like the main living space of Quirin's cabin.

"Renley!" A tiny, cheerful woman greeted him with a broad smile, her eyes glinting with pleasure. Her sparse white hair had been carefully brushed away from her face, and a beautifully carved walking stick leaned against the chair next to her.

He walked around the table to place a kiss on her cheek.

"This is Airlie, Nan."

"Ah, Brantley's girl. It's a pleasure to meet you at last, young lady. I'm glad they changed their minds and decided it was safe to send you, after all. I can see at a glance you've a good heart."

"Actually," I said awkwardly. "Brantley was my grandfather."

"Oh yes, of course he was," she said, undaunted. "Your father looked just like him. Handsome young men, both of them. But please, do sit down. I have the tea all ready, as you can see."

I slipped into the seat across from her while she turned to Renley.

"Run along now, dear. You can let the others know she's here. But tell them there's no hurry. We haven't had a chance to get to know each other yet."

Renley grinned and left, leaving me to stare at Nan in confusion. "Others?"

She cackled. "A bit of subterfuge is good at my age. It gets the blood flowing."

I raised my eyebrows. "Subterfuge?"

"They'll be angry if I steal their thunder, so I'll leave the tale to them, but it wasn't really me who summoned you here today. I'm just providing a convenient meeting point." She clucked her tongue. "I think Marissa wants me to feel relevant still, poor dear."

I suppressed the desire to pepper her with more questions on the matter, instead accepting the mug of tea she poured me.

"I didn't know anyone here knew my grandfather."

"Oh, aye. I didn't know him as well as your grandmother, of course, but I met him several times."

"My grandmother?"

She put three large spoonfuls of sugar in her tea before offering the bowl to me. When I shook my head, she tutted.

"You'll learn by my age to accept whatever sweetness you can get."

I smiled politely, trying to restrain my curiosity. "How did you know my grandmother?"

"Why, Louise was my dearest friend growing up. So many

years ago now, but the memories haven't faded. You have her look around the eyes, you know."

"No, I didn't know," I said softly. "She died before I was born."

"Of a broken heart, I'll be bound," Nan said with a sigh. "Brantley was so tall and so determined. And such strength. It was a marvel to us—a whole community without a single strong ability. It seemed like he could do anything." She shook her head. "None of us were surprised when Louise left everything to marry him. Any of us girls would have done the same—although no one was surprised when he chose her. Louise was the most beautiful of us, inside and out."

Her eyes grew moist. "Such a tragedy, how things turned out."

"His death, do you mean?" I asked. "I know he died when my father was young, but Father never talked about him."

"Some things are hard to relive." Her hands stilled. "My own parents went the same way, and it was hard to watch."

"Your parents?" I frowned. Marissa had mentioned her grandparents' deaths. "Did my grandfather die from using too much wild power? I thought your generation knew better."

"Aye." Some of the spark returned to her eye. "We tried to tell him. But men! They can be stubborn."

"Not just men," I muttered, thinking of Cadence.

She snorted. "True enough, my dear. True enough. He would have done better to listen, though. He thought he was different. He thought because he was so strong, he could tame the wild power and bend it to his will. He talked about retaking Calista and turning Louise into a queen." She shook her head. "Not that the promises were why she married him. She was besotted."

"My grandfather tried to clear the wild power from Calista but died from contact with it?" I said the words slowly, trying to absorb the revelation.

"That's what we heard. Louise never visited again after that, but Quirin's parents went to see her. I would have gone along as well, but I was expecting at the time. She refused to come back here with your father who was just a boy still—said it wasn't what Brantley wanted for his son."

"She should have come," I said hotly. "She should have chosen community over empty dreams of power."

Nan looked at me steadily. "You're different from your father."

"You met him, too, I think you said? Was that when he visited here?"

She nodded. "Aye. When he first turned up, it was like history repeating itself. He looked that much like his pa. We thought at first he'd come with the same intent as his father— to find a bride with an ability like his own. But he didn't stay long. After he left, Quirin told me Louise had instructed her son to go to Tarona to find a bride."

I listened silently as she confirmed my guesses about my family's history.

"Brantley was disappointed when his son turned out weaker than himself—a result of Louise's weak ability, no doubt. His choice had ensured him a child with a power ability, but he wasn't the heir Brantley desired."

A surprising fellow feeling swept over me as I imagined my father's childhood. He had always been so competent and assured that it was hard to picture him as a boy. But my sympathy quickly soured. How could he do the same thing to me that his father had done to him?

"So my grandfather decided his son should gamble in the other direction," I said, not quite able to keep my voice neutral. "He would marry a mage bride from a different affinity and hope at least one of his strong children received his own power affinity."

"Aye, that about sums it up," she agreed. "At least he was

wise enough to swear off using his ability—at least on this side of the border. That's natural after seeing his father die."

My mind whirled. It explained why I had never seen my father use his ability. But I couldn't wrap my mind around the fact that he had intended for Cadence to attempt the very thing that had killed his own father.

Before I could express any of my simmering resentment, the door behind me opened, and a stream of people entered the small room. I stood, exchanging greetings with Quirin and Marissa and sending Renley a nod.

My earlier curiosity about their purpose in sending me here resurfaced, driving down the emotions about my father. I didn't have to ask any questions, though, because Marissa burst immediately into speech.

"I hope Nan hasn't been talking your ear off. Her age certainly hasn't dented her tongue."

I assured them both it had been a pleasure, hiding a smile at the source of the accusation. Nan herself seemed to find the whole thing amusing, cackling at random intervals and saying provoking things that made Marissa scold her.

"We don't want to be seen gathering at my house," Quirin explained while Marissa pottered around, re-boiling the kettle. "The General hasn't forgotten that some people used to see me as a leader of sorts."

"What have you been meeting about?" I glanced at Renley. "You didn't mention anything about this."

"We didn't want to say anything until we knew if we could make it work," he said.

"Make what work?" I looked between them.

"Renley stole a neutralizer." Quirin clapped his son on the back, pride on his face.

Renley shrugged, clearly uncomfortable with his father's praise. Quirin had been transformed since his son's change of heart, but I knew Renley hadn't told him the reason for his about face, and it weighed heavily on his conscience.

"A neutralizer?" I raised an eyebrow. "Daring. But why? If you're hoping to use it on the General—"

"Nothing as dramatic as that," Quirin assured me. "We just wanted the chance to test one out. Marissa told us you'll activate our young people if we can get yours off, but none of us have ever had reason or opportunity to attempt such a thing."

"And?" I asked, skipping over the fact that I'd never actually made that agreement.

If they could remove my neutralizer, it would be a price worth paying. And since they were Calistans in Calista, I thankfully wouldn't find myself legally bound to the entire group.

"Physical proximity doesn't seem to be necessary for it to function," I added. "I've tried removing it at night, of course, but it doesn't make a difference. It's possible a greater distance would have an effect, but I daren't remove it outside the cabin."

"We worked it out," Renley crowed.

"But it isn't good news, I'm afraid," Quirin added quickly, dashing my hopes just as they were leaping high. "It turns out it works like a miniature power storage device. Any time you reach out with your ability, it sucks the power you produce straight into itself. So it takes someone with a power ability to unlock one."

I looked from him to Marissa. "I thought you both had power abilities? Isn't that good news?"

Marissa bustled over, a frown on her face. "We thought so at first. But we tried it on several different volunteers, and it seems the person doing the unlocking needs to have equivalent or greater strength than the person bound by the neutralizer. Which means no one here is strong enough to release you. Not even the General himself can do it."

"In fact," Quirin said, his eyes on me. "I believe only one person in all the kingdoms could unlock you."

"Cadence." My eyes widened. "No wonder the General was furious when he only managed to capture me. My strength can't do him any good bound in a neutralizer."

"Aye, but it can't do him any harm either," Marissa said. "Which is a great pity for all of us."

"So that just means I need to find a way to escape without my ability." I tried to sound matter-of-fact and capable, but inside I felt sick.

Even with my ability, escaping would be difficult. The General himself could nearly match me with strength—as impossible as that should be—and several of his warriors were powerful mages. Without my ability, the task seemed impossible. Especially since the window of opportunity created by the absence of the attack party was rapidly closing.

Given the disappointing end to their experiment, there didn't seem much point in further discussion. But we all stayed anyway—as much to satisfy Nan as anything. We sat around the table, drinking tea and rejecting every idea anyone suggested.

After a while no one had anything new to put forward, and Marissa gathered up our mugs, insisting that Nan stayed sitting while she washed them up. Nan ignored her, however, following her over to the small tub against the far wall.

"I'm no power mage," I said while we waited. "But I thought it was impossible to store power. How is it that this... thing can do it?" I gestured toward the neutralizer strapped to me.

"It's actually a seed," Quirin said. "From the paser tree."

"I've never heard of a paser tree. What's so special about it?"

"Legend says it comes from beyond the northern mountains, past the nomad lands. But I have no idea of the truth of it. Whatever its origins, the tree has—or had, I should say—the unique trait of being able to store power."

"A tree that can store power?" I stared at him. "How have I never heard of that?"

"I'm guessing the Tartoran kings didn't spread the information wide given their mistake in cutting them all down."

"It was a stupid thing to do," Renley said, unexpected fury in his voice.

His father shot him a look of mild surprise. "It wasn't wise, certainly. But greed seldom is." He looked at me. "The Calistan kings were the only ones with access to the seeds. They grew a small grove of the trees in the palace walls, and after they had wooed all those with a power affinity to Calista, they began to store power within the trees. When the Tartoran and nomad kings rode in at the head of their combined army, they chopped every paser tree down. My grandfather always said their intention was to cart the logs back to their own kingdoms, thinking it would allow them access to the power inside."

"I'm guessing it didn't work that way?" I asked with foreboding.

"No," Quirin agreed. "When the last tree came down, the power stored in all of them was released. There was healing, elements, and plants power, all mixed up together and directionless, and it exploded out across the kingdom. And it would have kept spreading further, if the old protections at the border hadn't stopped it."

"That's where the wild power came from? You mean it had nothing to do with massacring the royal family?"

"That was just a convenient explanation to put the blame on the dead king, I'm guessing," he said.

"There must have been an enormous amount of power in those trees." I considered the desolation that had been wrought over an entire kingdom for nearly a century.

"You don't invade a kingdom for a small amount of stored power," Quirin said grimly.

"But even so, we think it's more than that," Renley said.

"Mother had a theory, remember?" His voice hitched at mention of Dara, but he recovered and continued. "She always thought it was somehow multiplying. When the power broke free, it twisted and warped, and some aspect of that process has allowed it to feed off the land and grow stronger."

I gulped. "So, after all this time, it might be stronger than the force which killed my grandfather?"

Quirin nodded, his brow creasing. "I wouldn't recommend your sister attempt to wrestle with it."

"No!" I shook my head, horrified. "I should think not!"

"There, that's done." Marissa returned, wiping her hands on her apron. "I'll be back to visit tomorrow, Mother."

We all stood, taking our leave of Nan and exiting in single file. We dispersed quickly, only Quirin staying at my side as we returned to our own cabin.

"So there are no paser trees left?" I asked quietly as we walked. "Which means no opportunity to make new neutralizers?"

"As far as I know, yes. Which makes it a great pity the General already has several of them."

"A very great pity. Where did he get them?"

"From us." Quirin grimaced, holding open our front door and gesturing for me to precede him. "One of our ancestors managed to grab a stash of them as they were all fleeing."

"I don't suppose they managed to take some paser seeds as well?" I asked. "I guess not, or the General would already be growing his own grove."

"No, they didn't. Although..."

"Although?" I looked at him expectantly.

After a moment's hesitation, he continued. "I was surprised you didn't know about the paser trees. Once when we were lads, your father boasted that he had a whole stash of the seeds, and that he would one day grow a power grove of his own."

"Father had paser seeds?" I stared at him. "He never spoke

of them to me." I grimaced. "But that doesn't mean much. There were far too many things he didn't trust me with."

"A pity. That means they're lost, if they ever did exist."

"But is it a pity?" I asked. "It seems like they caused a lot of trouble the first time around. Maybe it's for the best they're gone and no one can access any more neutralizers."

"I'll be more inclined to agree with you when the ones in the General's possession are gone," he said.

"Can Renley get his hands on all of them?" I asked.

"No." Quirin spoke quickly, shaking his head emphatically. "Just getting one was dangerous enough. I would have forbidden him from trying if he hadn't done it on his own without consulting us first. He just showed up with it one day."

Beneath his irritation, he sounded pleased at his son's daring and initiative. But clearly he wouldn't permit us to ask Renley to repeat the feat. And I could understand his concern. Stealing one might go unnoticed, but it would be a different thing to take or destroy them all.

"Then we'll just have to think of something else," I said before escaping into my room. I had run out of energy to pretend that I was hanging on to any more than the tiniest sliver of hope.

CHAPTER 21

CADENCE

The chaos from the attempted raider attack kept us camped in the same spot for a second day. Investigators interviewed not only the tour kitchen staff, but also residents from the nearby town, but they found no trace of the missing workers. According to Zeke, who was kept informed by his mother, the girls had clearly been planted by the raiders.

Gia spent the day in a bad mood—although more at having missed all the excitement than at the raiders. Karielle, on the other hand, was grateful to have missed it but could barely sleep at night from the anxiety. So between the two of them, I had almost no rest and spent the next day in a sleep-deprived, exhausted daze.

I kept expecting Annora to corner me, intent on discussing my role in the events, but she seemed occupied with the other high-ranking officials. The following morning, we broke camp and rode out with an overwhelming feeling of collective relief. Everyone was glad to see the last of that particular site.

As a day passed, then two, then three, everyone slowly relaxed again, just as we had after the encounter with the tainted power on the river. Slowly but surely, talk shifted to the upcoming visit to Karielle's family estate. From the chatter around me, I learned that the entire tour had been invited to the ball being held in honor of the graduating apprentices.

Gia finally let go of her disappointment over having been drugged and transferred her attention to clothes. Apparently, unlike me, she had known about the ball before we left the capital and had packed accordingly.

"It's too bad Karielle is so much taller than you," she announced one morning, measuring us both with her eyes. "Otherwise you're a similar size. You could borrow one of her gowns."

I grimaced an apology at Karielle, but she waved it away.

"It's an excellent idea. And as it turns out, one of my older sisters is a similar height to you. I'm sure something from her wardrobe would fit." She joined Gia's open assessment of me.

I groaned. "It really doesn't matter what I wear. No one will be focused on me."

"Oh, won't they?" Gia threw me a knowing look. But when I sent a warning glance Karielle's way, Gia subsided, looking guilty.

"If that little silent conversation was on my behalf, you needn't bother," Karielle said in a carefully light tone. "Zeke might be utterly delicious, but I'm holding out no hopes in that direction."

I flushed, remembering the warning she had given me at the one and only previous ball I'd attended. But when Karielle continued, it was in a thoughtful tone, not a warning one.

"Once I would have cautioned you the same, Cadence. In fact, I think I did. But I don't know what it is about you." Her brow creased, her lips quirking to one side. "The nomads seem to love you, and Zeke is always at your side. It makes no logical sense—no offense—but perhaps you have a chance after all."

I ducked my head, horrified by more than my embarrassment. Who else had noticed Tribe Nicabar's attitude toward me? And what did they make of it?

"Of course she has a chance, if she wants one," Gia said. "Zeke has always singled Cadence out."

Karielle, emboldened by the conversation, gave Gia a long look. "I always assumed it would be Zeke and you, Gia. If the rumors are right, and his mother wins the throne after Fenix dies..."

"Me?" Gia shook her head vigorously. "I love Zeke, but I'm not interested in ruling a kingdom at his side."

I stiffened despite myself, hurrying to fold my clothes into my bag to hide the involuntary movement. Zeke might use his charm liberally, but he was kind-hearted beneath it, and he had intelligence and strength as well. He would make an excellent ruler. If Gia couldn't see that, she wasn't much of a friend to him.

I relaxed suddenly, laughing at myself. Or perhaps a friend was exactly how she saw him. Which was a good thing, since I had no desire to compete with my best friend in the romance arena.

I tried to focus on the upcoming celebration like everyone else, but it was hard to do when I kept expecting Annora to confront me at any moment. How had Airlie done this? The constant pressure felt like a weight, driving me into the ground. And even with only a handful of people in the tour knowing my true role, I was plagued by doubts as to their real feelings toward me. How had Airlie trusted anyone at the Guild?

I let Gia and Karielle's chatter about gowns wash over me as I sat at the evening meal. Zeke hadn't appeared, and Nikolas had chosen to eat at one of the other tables with several nomads. Gia continued to brush off any attempt to bring up the subject of her brother's changing behavior, but I watched him anyway, my eyes narrowed.

Just as he got up from the meal, Evermund approached him. The two exchanged quick words before Evermund disappeared again. Nikolas looked in our direction, not noticing me as his eyes focused on his sister. He stepped toward us before stopping again, indecision twisting his face. Pausing for a moment, he shook his head and spun the other way, walking off with a determined pace.

I looked from him to Gia, who remained oblivious to the entire thing. Had I missed a fight between the two of them? The situation had moved up in intensity if Nikolas was now avoiding his sister completely.

I couldn't think of any non-hurtful way to relay the incident to Gia, so I let it drop, continuing with my evening like normal. I was distracted enough to make that easy—a distraction I realized with some chagrin had its roots in Zeke's absence. How would I cope with his imminent graduation if I looked for him constantly after an absence of mere hours? At the Guild we had often gone for large parts of the day without seeing each other, but I was growing used to the almost constant contact the tour allowed.

He finally appeared just before I withdrew for the night, stepping up to join me where I stood at the edge of the tents, watching the flow of the river.

"It's a similar size to the Viridian," I said softly, "but it's interesting how different the effect is with grasslands on the other side instead of forest."

"The Celadon flows through forest further north," he said. "But that's a different effect again because it's forested on both sides of the bank."

"I'd like to see that," I whispered.

"You will." He sounded confident. "One day. Once you get a taste for travel, it's hard to stop."

I tried to smile, but it didn't quite stick. I couldn't imagine a future where I got to go wherever I wanted. Accepting an invitation to Tribe Nicabar would provide me with movement, at least, but I wouldn't be free to choose our destination. But, then, maybe that didn't matter. Maybe just the act of constant movement would feel like freedom?

I wrapped both arms around myself.

Zeke frowned down at me, seeming to sense my mood.

"Is everything all right?" he asked.

I shrugged. "Airlie's been abducted, tainted power is coming out of Calista, and the raiders keep attacking every time we drop our guard. I don't know that I'd say all right is an accurate description."

"But what about now?" he pressed. "Tonight. You seem abstracted, and Gia never showed up. Is everything all right?"

I turned away from the river, my brow creasing. "Gia never showed up for what?"

"I just got out of a grueling marathon of standing still for hours while powerful mages tried to work out what's wrong with me." He said the words lightly, but there was tension underneath.

"Nothing is wrong with you!" I said hotly before curiosity got the better of me. "Did they find anything? I assume they were trying to work out why you're stronger than Augusta?"

He nodded. "I'm afraid it was a fruitless exercise. But Gia was supposed to be there, only she never showed up. Nik said he tried to bring her, but she wouldn't come. King Marius didn't even try to hide his anger with her."

I sucked in a breath. "*Nikolas* was supposed to bring her? Is that what Evermund was talking to him about?"

Zeke frowned. "Probably. He was sent to let them know about it. I thought she would be excited that they actually wanted her input for once. The theory was that the twins have spent as much time with me as Augusta—far more than anyone else—so they might have some unique insight."

"Excuse me," I said abruptly. "I need to speak to Gia."

"Cadence!" Zeke called after me as I hurried away, but I ignored him.

Racing to our tent, I stormed inside, confronting Gia. "We need to talk."

Karielle took one look at my face and stood. "I'll leave."

"Thanks." I didn't turn from Gia.

She slipped outside, leaving the two of us alone. Gia stared at me, confusion on her face.

"What's the matter? Is something wrong?"

I threw my hands up. "Yes, something is wrong! Your own twin is trying to steal your throne, and you refuse to see it!"

Wariness entered her eyes. "I don't know what you're talking about. Nik—"

"Do not give me a spiel about how loyal he is," I cried. "Maybe he was once, but he's changed lately. You were supposed to be at an important meeting tonight—one where they actually wanted your input. I saw Evermund give Nikolas the message—and then I saw him decide not to pass it on to you. Apparently your father is furious that you flouted him like that. And in front of the nomads, too. The most important people in the kingdom were there, and you looked childish and irresponsible next to your brother's responsible diligence. He planned that, Gia."

She deflated, her shoulders slumping as she sank down to sit on her sleeping pallet. But when she looked up at me, it wasn't betrayal on her face.

Her eyes, half embarrassed, half hopeful, fixed on me.

"Do you really think it came across that way?"

"Of course I do. How else could it come across?"

She sighed. "You're a good friend, Cadence. I should have told you sooner. But my parents made me swear years ago not to talk to anyone outside the family about it, and the habit stuck."

"Not talk about what?"

She took a deep breath. "I don't want to be queen."

I frowned. "I imagine it's a daunting prospect. But hopefully you won't have to be queen for decades yet. You have time to grow into the role. And I know you'll be a great—"

"No." She cut me off. "I don't want to be queen ever. And I don't want to be crown princess now."

I shifted uncomfortably. "It isn't the kind of thing you get to choose, unfortunately."

"Actually," she said, straightening, "it is. I was fourteen the first time I read about abdication, and I've known ever since then that it's what I want. I love my family, but I don't want my birthright."

I sank down onto my bed. "You want to abdicate?"

She nodded, looking lighter already, as if it was a relief to get it off her chest. "I've been fighting about it with my parents ever since. They said I was too young to make a decision like that and made me promise to wait until I came of age at nineteen at least. I countered by saying that I would abdicate immediately unless they let me have my two apprentice years as a regular apprentice."

"Apprentice Gia," I breathed.

She nodded. "They thought if I experienced life as a non-royal, I would quickly realize the advantages of my position. But I love it, Cadence. I love the freedom and the lack of constraint. I love being able to say and do what I actually feel instead of needing to weigh every tiny word and action."

"Surely it's not that bad." I snorted. "Nikolas doesn't seem to weigh his words that closely."

She rolled her eyes. "Nik is...Nik."

"So, all this time you've been plotting an escape?" It was hard to absorb. "But why do your parents want you to be queen if you're so wildly opposed to the idea? That doesn't seem like it would lend itself to a good rule. And your brother doesn't seem to share your aversion, so they wouldn't be left without an heir."

She grimaced. "Back before I knew abdication was an

option, I poured all my energy into learning to be Princess Morgiana, heir to the throne. I was good at the role—too good. Nikolas, on the other hand, is…"

"Selfish, unpleasant, and power hungry?" I supplied.

She laughed. "Poor Nik. He's not that bad, I promise. But according to my parents, he doesn't have the natural temperament to rule." She sobered. "He's convinced himself it's just because of his seed that they're so opposed to the idea of him becoming the heir."

"Oh…" A lot of things became clearer in light of this information. "So the way you've both been acting on the tour…"

"It's a play being enacted on a public stage," she said. "We're not going to get a better chance to convince my parents that Nik is their only hope at a responsible child who will fulfill his duties diligently."

I shook my head. "It's a risky move. What if all you do is turn public opinion against your family entirely?"

Her mouth twisted, her hands clasping together in her lap. "I hope not. That's why I haven't been too outrageous." She turned large eyes on me. "Have I?"

I considered the matter before shaking my head. "No, I don't think so. I've noticed, and it's been driving me crazy, but I'm sure some on the tour haven't noticed anything at all."

She let out a sigh of relief. "I hope you're right. Poor Nik has been working so hard."

"Poor Nik…" I shook my head again.

Gia snorted. "Don't look so shocked, Cadence."

"It's a big adjustment," I said indignantly. "I'd worked myself up into a righteous fury against your brother, and now I find out I should feel sympathy for him." I looked across at her. "I still think it's a risky move, though, bringing the nomads into it."

"You're right, of course." She sighed. "We were hoping Nik would look better to the Triumvirate by comparison."

"The Triumvirate? Not your parents?"

"Well, them too, of course. But I don't think they'd be so opposed to the whole idea if it wasn't for the succession laws."

"What succession laws?"

"Didn't you study them at school?" Gia asked before correcting herself. "No, of course not. You didn't go to school. I forgot. Succession goes first to the eldest child of the ruling monarch. But if he or she dies before ascending the throne—or is unable or unwilling to accept the crown—succession doesn't automatically go to the next in line."

"What? Why?"

She shrugged. "I think whoever was part of the Triumvirate at the time the law was written would have preferred a system like the nomad one. This was their compromise. The monarch has one chance to provide a suitable heir, and if they fail at that, then the Triumvirate gets the chance to accept or reject the next in line. Only the firstborn in each generation has an automatic right to the throne."

"And you think the Triumvirate would reject your brother?" I asked, shocked.

She shrugged. "We don't know for sure because my parents refuse to so much as mention the idea of my abdicating to anyone. They're not confident enough of the Triumvirate's opinion of Nik to risk letting me have my way. Not that they've said that," she added, "but I can tell."

"King Nikolas," I murmured softly, trying it out. Gia watched me, so I smiled for her benefit. "I suppose I could get used to the idea."

She didn't smile back. "Now if we could just convince my parents and the Triumvirate of that."

"At least he won't be murdered in his sleep by me now," I offered. "That's something at least."

That attempt did elicit a weak chuckle as she jumped up and rushed over to give me a hug.

"You're a good friend, Cadence. I'm glad you came to the Guild."

I paused for a moment, considering my answer. "Some days it's harder to remember than others, but I really am too."

And I meant it. As much as I missed Airlie, and worried for her safety, as much as I stressed about the weight of trying to do my part to keep everyone safe, I couldn't imagine still living in my old home, talking to no one but Airlie and knowing nothing of the power that floated all around me.

"I would have never seen the sea," I added. "And what sort of life would that have been?"

CHAPTER 22

CADENCE

It took us a week to get from the ocean to Karielle's parents' estate. When the Celadon split, we stayed with the eastern branch, leaving behind the border with the nomads which followed the western branch of the river all the way up to the mountains. Instead we continued on the course that would eventually lead to Lake Aterra and the Calistan border.

Before we reached that far, however, we arrived at the final destination of the tour. If I had come here before ever seeing Tarona, I would have considered Karielle's childhood home a palace. The enormous manor house had rooms enough to fit all the senior members of the tour and more than enough grounds to comfortably fit the collection of tents that housed everyone else.

I would hardly have qualified for a room if Karielle hadn't generously offered to share her bedchamber.

"It seems like the least I can do when you and Gia hosted me the rest of the tour," she said, laughing off my attempts to point out that I had been a fellow recipient rather than host in that situation.

Blake, Augusta's other current female apprentice, also

joined us. She was a short, lively girl who bemoaned Karielle's upcoming graduation almost as much as she gushed about the ball.

"It won't be the same without you," she assured Karielle as she pinned her friend's curls to her head.

Karielle just laughed. "Don't be silly. You'll love ruling the roost and ordering the boys around. And I'm sure Augusta's next pick will be just as nice as me."

Blake looked unconvinced but promised to do her best to give the girl a chance. She glanced at me in the mirror as she spoke and must have seen the bemusement on my face.

"Augusta likes to always have a minimum of two female apprentices. She claims she can't abide being surrounded by boys." Blake giggled, as if she didn't entirely agree with the sentiment. "So now that Karielle is graduating, Augusta has another female apprentice lined up."

"Does she only ever have two at a time?" I asked.

"Oh no," Karielle said. "A couple of years before me, they were all girls. Two is the minimum."

"It won't be all girls again any time soon," Blake said with another giggle. "The prince has only just started his apprenticeship."

"What's it like living with Nikolas?" I asked. "He's sour enough after his breakfast, I can't imagine what he's like first thing in the morning."

Both girls laughed, but Blake ended it on a sigh. "But he's so handsome. And he's a prince."

I grimaced. "That's not enough for me."

"You just say that because your prince is handsome *and* charming," Karielle said with a wink that sent Blake into a fresh round of giggles.

"He's not my anything," I sputtered. "And he's not even a prince yet. His mother might lose the vote."

Both girls instantly sobered.

"Oh no, surely not," Blake cried. "That would be much too sad."

"All the nomads on the tour clearly look to her," Karielle said thoughtfully. "She might not officially be their leader yet, but they treat her like she is."

"That's what I said to Zeke." I took Karielle's seat, ready for Blake to arrange my hair as well. "But he tells me it only seems like that because the other tribes here are Patrin and Callen. Patrin got to choose who came—they still have the throne for now—and they've put their support behind Nicabar as the next rulers. So they chose another supportive tribe as the third representatives. Apparently Tribe Alia were seething."

"The previous ruler before King Fenix was from Alia, wasn't he?" Karielle asked. "I suppose they're hoping to retake the throne."

I shrugged. "This is all secondhand information, but that's what Zeke says."

She sighed. "I suppose I should have realized it was a little too civil and convenient. When is politics ever like that?"

"Forget politics—we're going to a ball!" Blake twisted my hair this way and that while she considered how to arrange it.

As she got to work, I had to fight back tears. Blake was nice, but I couldn't help the memories of preparing for my last ball. I missed Airlie and the camaraderie of our long history. No one knew me like she did and, despite our fighting, no one was so comfortable to be around. Because, at the end of the day, it didn't matter what I said or what I did, she still loved me anyway.

As soon as Blake finished, I thanked her and hurried over to the window to surreptitiously wipe my eyes. In the weeks since Dara's revelations, I had been too focused on all the weight that remained on my shoulders to recognize the weight that had been lifted. Airlie hadn't been so offended by my words she'd abandoned me. She hadn't even mentioned them to Dara in all the weeks of her captivity.

Airlie hadn't left me, she'd been taken from me.

Determination rose inside my belly. After tonight, with or without Evermund, I was going after my sister.

When I turned back around, I had a smile on my face, but it changed into a gasp of surprise when I saw the dress Karielle was holding toward me. I hurried over to run gentle fingers over the fabric.

"Are you sure your sister won't mind me wearing this?" I asked. "It's so beautiful."

The cornflower blue gown had a full skirt of the softest layers I could have imagined, swishing satisfyingly as Karielle waved it back and forth enticingly.

"Of course she doesn't mind. She's not even here. She was married two years ago and has her own home and a baby now. She left some of her dresses here, and they're still in her old wardrobe. In fact, you should keep it."

"I couldn't do that," I said fervently before grinning up at her. "But I might be able to be convinced to wear it tonight."

"Excellent." Karielle pressed it into my hands. "Let's see it on you."

It fit even better than I'd hoped, and I couldn't help swishing the skirt as I walked back out of her dressing room. Gia had arrived some time during my absence, so an audience of three waited for me.

They all exclaimed in delight, telling me no one would guess the dress hadn't been made for me. And when I looked in the mirror, I couldn't help agreeing. With my hair up in soft curls, I hardly recognized myself.

"Here, I'll tie this for you." Gia skipped over to twist the long blue sash into a bow at the back, letting the two ends drape elegantly down, almost reaching the floor.

"You look incredible," I told her when I spun around and got a proper look at her red gown.

It had simple, elegant lines that only made it more striking —a perfect match for the vividness of her personality.

"My parents will hate it," she said with satisfaction.

"You're hopeless, Gia," Karielle laughed before disappearing off to get into her own gown.

It was only a short walk from the family wing of the house to the large ballroom, but a sizeable crowd had already gathered before we arrived. Despite its generous size, the room couldn't accommodate half the court plus the nomad delegations, so the long row of double doors on the opposite side of the room had been thrown open, giving free access to the equally large stone terrace on the other side.

With the warm summer air making the outside even more pleasant than the inside, the crowd flowed freely back and forth, dancing on the stone as happily as on the polished wooden floorboards. Green vines and bright, colorful flowers had been wound around the stone balustrades and draped along the walls of the ballroom, giving the two spaces a unified look.

"It's beautiful," I breathed to Karielle, who blushed prettily.

"I spent most of the day on the flowers. Do you like them?"

"I love them! And congratulations again on your graduation."

Gia sidled up next to me, a grin on her face. "Someone's looking for you."

I looked around, suppressing the nervous desire to rub my palms down my skirt. "Who? Where?"

She just snorted as my eyes landed on Zeke. He stood in one of the double doors to the terrace in conversation with Liara and Jaylen. But he was no longer looking at them, his face turned toward me.

Our eyes met, and my heart skipped at the warmth that

leaped across the ballroom from his gaze to mine. Seeing the expression on his face, the last of my doubts fell away. And with them went the deceptions I had been using on myself.

This was what I had been dreaming of since before my first ball back in Tarona. Zeke was the reason I was standing here at all. I had no desire to dance with anyone but him.

Zeke didn't break eye contact, abandoning the other nomads to come straight to my side. I caught a hazy glimpse of disgust on Liara's face, but nothing could puncture the happy feeling growing inside me.

When Zeke reached us, he bowed low.

"Cadence. You look beautiful tonight. As always."

"Thank you, Zeke," Gia said gravely from beside me. "We all appreciate your heartfelt compliments."

"You look equally incredible," he said, still not looking away from my face.

Gia snorted. "You're hopeless."

That made him finally break the breathless moment between us, looking over at her with a grin.

"You do all look lovely, ladies. But I'm going to steal Cadence away now."

"Just as long as you bring her back," Gia called after us, as he led me away. "I want my best friend back!"

I laughed as her voice faded into the distance. "Are we running away from Gia?"

"If necessary for me to have you all to myself," he said, his warm hand squeezing mine.

Liara and Jaylen remained where Zeke had left them, but he pulled me toward one of the other doors and out onto the terrace. The crowd was only slightly less thick here, but he swept me into his arms and joined those dancing in the center of the space.

The first time I had been wrapped in his arms for a dance, it had been thrilling—heady and exciting and like nothing I'd ever experienced before. This time his solid strength felt comfortable and familiar. The sense of belonging was one I had only ever felt with Airlie, but with Zeke it had transformed into something entirely new. Exhilaration lent my feet wings, my pulse pounding out a beat along with my feet, and warmth filling me from the inside out.

He pulled me closer, and I almost forgot to breathe.

"Why are you so captivating, Cadie?" he breathed in my ear. "From the first moment I saw your bewildered blue eyes staring up at the Guild building, I haven't been able to look away from them."

"That's not very complimentary," I said, although my laugh came out a little shaky. "Do I have to come up with a list of my own virtues? Starting with confused, apparently."

He chuckled, pulling me even closer. "The confusion just makes your bravery all the more admirable. You clearly had no idea where you were, but you didn't falter for a moment. Even when everyone fawned over your sister, abandoning you entirely."

"That's because I had you," I said, remembering the moment as if it had just happened. "I would have been lost without you to show me around. Literally."

He shook his head. "You would have found your way. I don't doubt it for a second. Just like you've always been there whenever you were most needed, ready to quietly shoulder the burden for everyone. How many times have you saved me now?"

I couldn't recognize myself in the picture he was painting. "Are you sure you're not thinking of Airlie? I'm the rebellious one, always trying to get away and be free. She's the responsible one."

"Maybe," he said. "And maybe there's a family pattern. Are you sure you wanted to be free? Or did you just want to step out from under her shadow? You certainly accepted her mantle fast enough. Nothing you've done since her departure has been the actions of someone thinking only of herself and her freedom." He dropped his voice even lower. "Like Gia does. If that was what you wanted, you could have walked out of the Guild the same night Airlie disappeared and never looked back. Gia would have done it in your place."

"But I couldn't leave. Everyone would have been in danger without someone to monitor for…" My voice trailed off, a flush rising on my cheeks. "Oh. I see what you mean."

He laughed softly before turning serious again. "I'm not saying Airlie's had it easy—at the Guild or in your old life. But at least she's always been recognized for her efforts. It's easier to bear the burden of responsibility when you're the acknowledged leader. But you've borne the same weight without a single bit of recognition or assistance. To me that's even more admirable."

I detached one hand from his back to briefly cup his cheek, marveling at the feel of his rough skin beneath my fingers.

"You're forgetting," I whispered. "I've never been unrecognized. And I've always had you to assist me."

He turned his head and brushed his lips against my palm in the softest of caresses. A shiver ran over my skin, and he pulled me tighter.

With great strength of will, I forced myself to return my hand to his back, pulling away the slightest bit. We were still in the middle of a crowd, and I needed to find a way to step back from the intensity of the moment.

My searching mind remembered his comments about my friend.

"I used to think Gia and Nikolas were opposites," I said. "But I can see it's not so simple. You're right that there's a selfishness in her, as there is in him. But isn't that true of all of us?"

"You don't act on yours, though," he said.

"Of course I do. We all do, sometimes, in some things. And,

anyway, I don't think it's pure selfishness to recognize you're not suited to ruling. There's a nobility in that honesty. She has no desire for power, and I admire that."

"Even if that leaves the kingdom in Nikolas's hands?" He gave me an unconvinced look.

Zeke might not know Gia had developed an actual plan to abdicate, but he hadn't been friends with them for two years without seeing that she didn't want her rank. And given he was more astute about both people and politics than I was, he had likely guessed the truth already. But while I wouldn't confirm it without Gia's permission, I couldn't help arguing for her.

"Decades of resentment, anger, and pain won't forge Gia into a better queen," I said. "But they might turn her into someone who would do Tartora more harm than good. She wants the chance to use her strengths to do good in the world, and why shouldn't she be allowed to? There are others with the strengths to rule—and maybe Nikolas can become one of them." My mouth twisted to the side. "I know what it's like to be always overlooked, a superfluous younger sibling. If he has the chance to step to the front, maybe it will change everything for him, too."

"Maybe." Zeke looked down into my eyes. "But why are we talking about Nikolas right now?"

I laughed. "Would you like to talk about the ball and the dresses and the flowers instead?"

"If you wish it," he said promptly. "I'm willing to talk about anything you'd like. Especially if you promise you'll come back to Tribe Nicabar with me."

I froze, stumbling over the next step. Zeke halted as well, a beat behind, and ushered me out from among the dancers. Pressed against the stone balustrade, I fanned my hot cheeks, embarrassed.

"I'm going home after the tour, and I don't want to leave you behind, Cadie," he said. "I'm not asking you to commit to a life among the nomads—just a visit. I thought you wanted to travel and see life beyond Tartora."

I looked out over the dim garden, almost hidden now in the evening gloom. The pull to say yes was overpowering. I could stay with Zeke, travel further, and even study freely. Among the nomads I wouldn't have to hide who I was.

I opened my mouth to agree, but still something held me back. Out of the corner of my eye, I caught Liara watching us from the other side of the terrace. Zeke wasn't the only member of his tribe, and I didn't know if trusting him was enough to trust them all.

"Think about it? Please?" he pleaded. "I'll go get us some drinks and give you a minute to yourself."

He disappeared before I could speak. I wished that a minute or two of solitude was all I needed to resolve my confusion. But I had already spent far longer than that wrestling with the question.

If it wasn't for Airlie, I would have said yes by now. Once Zeke left, I would have no one to help me with my training. And eventually someone would realize I must be seventeen, and then the real trouble would begin. But I couldn't commit to going to Tribe Nicabar when I had every intention of leaving to find Airlie. And it was Evermund and Tartora who were going to help me with that goal.

So didn't that mean I owed them some loyalty? I felt loyalty toward Evermund, at least.

I stood up, hurrying along the balustrade, suddenly eager to be out from under Liara's gaze, however distant. But the crowd pressed in on me, so I kept going, stepping down the shallow stone steps and into the garden.

Among the dim greenery, it was cooler, and I managed to draw an unfettered breath. I wandered slowly along, keeping close to the terrace and its lights, but enjoying the illusion of being on my own.

When I heard Zeke's voice, I turned, though. Hurrying directly toward it, I ended up some distance from the steps, separated from where he stood by the balustrade. I intended to call out, suggesting he jump over and join me, but the sound of my name stopped me.

He wasn't calling for me but referring to me in conversation with someone else. From my vantage point, I caught sight of him talking to his mother, the two of them visible in the light from the ball's lanterns, although I was hidden in the dark of the garden.

"Have you seen Cadence? I left her here."

"She's looking particularly attractive tonight," his mother said in an approving voice. "You should know better than to leave her unattended, son. I'm sure some other young man has stolen her off to dance."

I grimaced. Now it would be awkward to reveal myself.

"Really, Mother." Zeke sounded exasperated.

She patted him on the cheek, an unusually indulgent smile on her face. "Don't worry. I've seen the besotted expression on her face when she's looking at you. She'll be back soon enough."

I flushed, my hands fisting around my skirts. Is that what everyone thought of me? She made me sound like a foolish puppy, following Zeke around.

"I knew your looks and charm would serve Tribe Nicabar well," she continued, distracting me from my own humiliation.

I frowned. What was she implying?

"I'm glad I meet with your approval," Zeke said, although his voice sounded strained.

"Adolescents can be boringly predictable," she said, "but you really do make an irresistible package for a young girl, considering not only your personal charms but the strength of your ability and your future rank."

"My future rank is not a sure thing." Zeke shifted slightly, moving out of my view.

"You leave that to me," Annora said. "I haven't worked my whole life to see us fail now. You just need to finish what you were sent to Tartora for—win the heart of the only remaining power mage and ensure she's loyal to only you." She smiled again. "As I said, I don't doubt your success for a second."

I stumbled back, my hand flying to my throat. Whatever Zeke answered was lost in the pounding of my pulse through my ears. That couldn't be right. I must have misheard.

Zeke had chosen Tartora for his apprenticeship in order to seek information on power mages, not for me. He had arrived long before I did—long before I even knew I was going to the Guild. I shook my head, still stumbling backward. It couldn't be true.

But Dara and the raiders knew about my family. The insidious thought crept into my brain. Was it so impossible Annora had heard rumors as well? Had she heard a single power mage remained and that he had two daughters the same age as her own son?

She was right when she said Zeke was irresistible. She had sent him to sniff me out, and as soon as I turned up, I fell straight into his trap.

A branch brushed against me, and I nearly screamed, only just cutting the sound off in time. I trembled violently, waving my hands frantically to ward off anything else that tried to touch me. I needed to get away.

CHAPTER 23
CADENCE

Fleeing through the garden, I stumbled and slipped several times before kicking off my dancing shoes. Giving the lighted building a wide berth, I fled through the rows of tents, heading blindly for the river.

Everything fit. Zeke—who always knew what was going on—was waiting in the courtyard the day of our arrival to greet the new apprentice with unrivaled power. How many times had I clung to the thought that he noticed me before he knew anything about my power? But it was all a lie. He had known from the beginning, had been searching for me even.

And those first weeks, while Airlie was still there. He had been more circumspect then, paying court to us both, perhaps trying to work out which of us was going to prove more valuable. But she had seen through him and had tried to protect me. And I had rejected her.

The tears fell faster. The edge of the river forced me to stop, but my thoughts barreled on.

Once Airlie left, his attention had grown more concentrated. Of course it had. Especially after he received a demonstration of my ability the night he activated me.

I ran an angry hand over my face, swiping away the tears.

Like a lovesick fool, I had been so close to agreeing to go with him.

No one else was in sight, but I still felt exposed. Ducking beneath the trailing branches of a weeping willow, I found a wooden bench, tucked within its protective cover.

I sat, my eyes now adjusted to the moonlight which glinted off a small spur of the river which inched almost to the edge of the seat. The shallow stretch of water lacked the current of the main river, and I could easily imagine Karielle and her siblings playing under and around the tree as children, splashing in and out of the water.

I looked down at my bare feet, now covered in dirt and muck. If I stretched them out fully, I could just dip my toes into the edge of the inlet.

But as soon as my skin touched the river, my stomach rebelled. Instinctively, I recoiled, and the feeling faded. Moving more cautiously this time, I reached for the water again. And this time I also reached with my ability.

Sure enough, there in the water, was a trace of tainted power. I wanted to leap to my feet and run to warn everyone, but I made myself wait and analyze it first.

Not wanting to miss any warning signs, I had fallen out of the habit of shaping my ability into a shield. I was unprotected now, and yet my reaction had nothing of the severity of our first day on the Viridian. Even searching with my ability, I couldn't sense the tainted power at all until I made contact with the water. Whatever was here in the Celadon, I didn't think it was warning of an imminent attack.

I ran the matter back and forth in my mind. Three attacks had now happened on or near a river—if you counted the one in the Guild where Lawson had escaped up the river. But the Viridian and the Celadon were half a kingdom apart, and I had found no trace of tainted power between them. Which meant it must be the rivers themselves bringing the power so deep into

Tartora. And this branch of the Celadon flowed from the same source as the Viridian—Lake Aterra.

I stood, bunching up my skirts and running for the front doors of the manor house. Every time the raiders intruded on Tartora, they dragged tainted power with them. That must mean they were coming from an area where it congregated. The lake, perhaps?

Two footmen gave me a surprised look, but no one tried to stop me as I barreled through the front door and up the stairs toward my temporary room. All I had ever needed was somewhere to start looking, and this lead was good enough for me. Maybe I could even track the tainted power back to them.

I stripped off the gown, changing into dark clothes that would hopefully help me stay inconspicuous. I left the dress draped carefully over the bed while I shoved my most practical clothes into my bag. Thankfully I had packed some basic survival tools as well—the same ones I had always taken on my hunting trips with Airlie.

Food would be a problem, however. Without her bow, I would only be able to scavenge edible plants—and those only until the border. Pushing aside a brief moment of guilt, I decided to stop by the kitchens on my way out. They would be chaotic with the ball underway, so hopefully I could stock up my bag without drawing too much attention.

I paused halfway through securing my bag to wonder if I should be talking to Evermund before I left. It would be difficult to extract him from the ballroom, but I might be able to send a message with a servant, asking him to come out.

After a moment's consideration, I resumed wrestling with the clasps of my bag. This was not going to be a sanctioned departure. Evermund had said he would approach the king if there were no other attacks between the ocean and this estate. And that hadn't been the case.

I was on my own.

No sooner had I thought the words than a knock sounded on the door. I froze, unsure if I should answer. It sounded again, louder this time, along with a familiar voice calling my name.

"Cadence? Cadence, are you in there?" Zeke sounded worried.

My anger surged afresh, and I marched over and pulled the door open.

He stepped back, the momentary relief on his face replaced almost instantly by confusion.

"What are you wearing? I've been looking for you everywhere." His eyes traveled past me into the room, widening as they reached the packed bag on my bed. "Are you leaving? What's going on?"

"I heard you," I said, quivering in anger. "I heard you and your mother talking."

Color flooded his cheeks, and he swallowed.

"I'm sorry, Cadie. I—"

"Don't call me that," I snapped.

The color drained away, leaving behind a stricken expression that pinged at my heart despite my intentions.

"I know it was wrong of her," he said. "She should never have done it. I'm furious with her myself."

"Wrong of her?" I gaped at him, breathless at his effrontery. "And what about you? You're the one who looked me in the eyes and pretended to be my friend. Who told me only days ago that you didn't want secrets between us."

"I don't!" He ran a hand through his hair, frustrated.

I tried not to notice how adorable he looked in his confusion. Even my anger was hard to hold on to when he looked so thoroughly bewildered. But then, he must be an excellent actor to have played his role so convincingly for so long.

Somehow I had fallen back several steps, allowing him to take one long stride into the room. I tried to tell him to get out, but he spoke first.

"You said you heard us talking. What exactly did you hear?"

"I heard enough," I said stubbornly. "I thought you were my friend—that you noticed me when no one else did. But you were searching for my ability from the beginning."

"No, I wasn't!" He stopped, taking a deep breath. "If you heard our conversation—our whole conversation—you would have heard my shock at what my mother said. She never told me about you, Cadence. I swear it. She told me I was going to Tartora to find out more about power mages. She never said anything about meeting one."

As his anger grew, my own faded, replaced with shame. How quick I had been to assume the worst without even staying to hear his response. Annora's words had confirmed all my own fears, and I had closed my eyes to everything except what seemed to back them up. I had been all too fast to forget Zeke's many moments of true friendship toward me.

"I can't believe her!" he cried when the storm cloud had consumed his face. "She knew that if she suggested any such thing to me, I would have rejected it outright. So she sent me to Tartora, knowing I would be fascinated by any power mage I met, and hoping events might fall in her favor. It's outrageous."

"So you didn't know I was a power mage when we first met?" I asked in a small voice.

He shook his head. "I heard there was an impossible new apprentice on the way, and curiosity sent me out to the courtyard to watch for your arrival. And then when I saw you climb out of the carriage, looking charmingly confused, I couldn't resist speaking to you."

"And this..." I gestured between us. "This has nothing to do with your mother's plans?"

He stepped forward, closing the gap between us. "Everything I've said to you and felt for you has been real, Cadie. I couldn't care less what my mother thinks on this topic."

I swallowed. "But at the beginning, you always seemed more interested in Airlie."

He ran a hand across the back of his neck, looking shame-faced. "I was always interested in you for you, Cadence. But it was more than that as well. I guessed there might be more to your ability than initially seemed obvious. Especially after that test. I was afraid that if I made my interest in you too obvious, it might draw other, less friendly attention in your direction. Everyone was focused on Airlie, so I let it seem like I was, too. I was trying to protect you, in a roundabout way." He paused. "And in the interests of total honesty, I was also serving my own curiosity. I didn't want anyone else to discover your secrets before I could."

"Oh." I let out a shaky breath. "I suppose I can forgive that if you can forgive me for assuming the worst tonight."

He stepped forward again and took both my hands. "After what my mother did? Of course I don't blame you. You have every right to be furious. I certainly am." He gave a low, reluctant chuckle. "The worst of it is that she's getting exactly what she wants."

"She is?" I whispered, shaken by what I saw in his face as he looked down at me.

"She hoped the rumored power mage would fall in love with me," he said in soft tones. "But instead I fell in love with you. And now—no matter how much I want to disoblige my mother—I will never stop trying to win you over."

"You don't have to try," I said. "I've been a little in love with you ever since that first morning when Airlie walked away, and you stayed behind."

"Just a little?" he breathed, leaning down toward me.

"On that first day," I whispered. "And a little more every day since."

With a satisfied sigh, he pressed his lips down against mine, letting go of my hands so he could sweep me into his arms and crush me against his chest. I leaned into the kiss, wrapping my arms around his neck and plunging my fingers into his hair.

Warmth and light exploded inside me, the weight that had worn me down for months gone. At any moment I would lift into the air and float away, I felt so light.

But when I deepened the kiss, he groaned, pulling back.

"So does this mean you'll come to visit my tribe with me? Or has my mother scared you away?"

His eyes jumped to the pack on the bed beside me, as if he'd forgotten it for a moment. A crease appeared between his eyes, and I did what I'd wanted to do for so long and smoothed it with my fingertip.

He laughed, capturing my finger and dropping a kiss on it. Delightful shivers chased down my hand, but his next question brought the weights that usually resided on my shoulders crashing back down.

"Where are you going?"

I sucked in a breath. How could I have forgotten Airlie? What sort of flighty sister was I?

"I'm going after my sister." I made my voice strong and certain. "I have reason to think the raiders are somewhere near Lake Aterra, and I'm going to find Airlie."

"On your own?" Fear sounded beneath Zeke's horrified words.

I turned away, fiddling with the bag, although it was already packed and closed.

"Evermund said he'd come only if there were no other attacks. But then the raiders drugged our food, so..."

"And what about me?" he asked.

I turned, putting my hands on my hips. "I was angry with you up until ten minutes ago, remember? I was hardly going to invite you to run away with me."

His arm whipped out and caught me around the waist, pulling me close, a smile on his lips.

"Is that an invitation? I would enjoy running away with you, Cadence of Calista."

"Hush!" I pulled back, batting at him and eyeing the open door. "I'm not running away—I'm running to Airlie. It isn't the same."

"No." He sighed disconsolately. "It does sound a lot less fun."

I gave him an unimpressed look, and he turned serious.

"Of course I'm coming, whether I'm invited or not. I'm not letting you go on your own."

I gave him a measuring look. "You're not going to try to stop me?"

"Of course not. She's your sister. I couldn't be more enraged with my mother right now, but I would still go after her if someone abducted her. And good luck to anyone who tried to stop me."

I bit my lip. "It might be dangerous."

"Might?" He gave me a disbelieving look. "You're off to tackle a settlement of raiders, on your own, in their home territory—which just so happens to be a cursed wasteland—and you're warning me that it *might* be dangerous?"

"Sounds like my kind of trip," Gia said from the doorway. "When do we leave?"

"Right now, if Cadie's packed bag is any indication," Zeke said without missing a beat.

"And you were going to leave without us?" Nikolas asked, completely deadpan. "How could you?"

"Nobody asked you to come," I shot back at him.

"Excellent," he said promptly. "Come on, Gia. We aren't wanted here."

She ignored him, surging into the room and looking between Zeke and me with interest. "Were you really going to go off just the two of you?"

"It was just Cadie fifteen minutes ago," Zeke said, an undertone of displeasure in his voice.

"Then I can assume we're off to rescue Airlie?" Gia asked happily. "I've been wondering when we were going to break away."

"Are you really going to come with me?" I asked in disbelief.

"Of course we are."

"Both of you?" I looked at Nikolas.

He sighed. "Both of us, apparently." Something else lurked in his eyes, but I was too shocked to try to puzzle out its meaning.

I looked to Zeke. Suddenly the reality of what we were doing seemed far more dire. Could we take the first and second in line to the throne into the fallen kingdom with us?

"I can see what you're thinking," Gia said, her expression turned serious. "But there's no way I'm letting you go off after the raiders with only Zeke along. It's too dangerous—and besides, you'll never succeed in rescuing Airlie. You told me that yourself a hundred times while you were forced to wait around at the Guild."

"But I didn't mean I wanted to take you!"

"If there's one advantage to being royal," she said, "it's that we have strong abilities in our bloodline. Nik and I might only be apprentices, but we're already more powerful than most full mages. We can help."

"But what if something happens to you?" I looked to Zeke for assistance, but he was watching Gia with narrowed eyes.

"That's my risk to take," she said. "If you want to save Airlie, you need us. You've known all along you can't do it on your own. You need help, and we're all you've got."

I wanted to protest further, but one glance at the determined look on Gia's face told me I was either taking her with me or not going at all. And for Airlie I was willing to defy a king.

"Very well, then," I said. "Pack quickly."

Zeke and Nikolas disappeared, hurrying off in the direction of their own rooms.

"Are we walking?" Gia asked as she threw a haphazard collection of items into the first bag she could find. "Because they might come after us." She sounded apologetic, although I couldn't see her face.

"Let them try." I laughed, a crazy idea occurring to me on the spot. "We're riding the Celadon up to the lake, and I defy anyone to catch us."

"Riding upriver? How are we going to manage that?"

"The same way the raider plants mage did. We'll harness the Calistan protections."

She stopped, turning large eyes on me. "We can do that?"

I shrugged. "I think so. Do you want to back out?"

"Are you kidding?" Her eyes gleamed. "I'm with you all the way."

"Great." I swung my bag onto my back. "In that case, let's go."

CHAPTER 24

CADENCE

We strolled out the front door while the music from the ballroom still drifted over the manor.

"Aren't you supposed to be a guest of honor back there?" Nikolas asked Zeke as we made our way through the formal gardens that stretched in front of the building. "Won't they notice you've disappeared?"

"Aren't you supposed to be a prince?" Zeke asked back with a cheerful lilt. "Won't they notice *you've* disappeared?"

"One can only dream," Nikolas muttered, earning him a glare from Gia.

"It doesn't matter if they notice," she announced. "Because Cadence has a plan that's going to get us well beyond their reach."

Both boys turned to me with almost identical raised eyebrows.

"The tainted power," I said. "If the raider mage could use it to pull him upriver, so can we."

Zeke whistled softly while Nikolas continued staring. "Tainted power?"

"The Calistan protections," Gia explained gleefully. "I have no idea how Cadence is going to pull it off, but I have full faith in her."

"Look, there!" I pointed to the quiet inlet that spread under the willow.

To one side of the tree, a small wooden boat had been secured. It was nothing like the barges that had taken us downriver, clearly intended for short, recreational trips in the vicinity of the manor. But it was big enough to seat eight which made it good enough for our purpose.

"We'll have to find a way to pay Karielle back for taking the boat," I said as Zeke and Nikolas untethered it and pulled it over to the edge of the main river, where the current was waiting to snatch at it.

"That's no problem," Gia said. "I'll send them a new boat when we're back in the capital."

"Being a crown princess has some advantages," I muttered, earning an approving look from Nikolas.

I carefully refrained from making eye contact with him, however. I still hadn't fully adjusted to the idea that Gia was appreciative of his efforts to undermine her during the tour, and I wasn't ready to share a moment with him, however small.

"Are you sure about this?" Zeke asked, catching my gaze.

"Not at all," I said boldly. "Are you still coming?"

I had given Gia an out, so it only seemed fair to do the same for Zeke.

"Do you even need to ask?"

I smiled at him, and he smiled back, his gaze softening as the seconds passed by. Gia cleared her throat ostentatiously, breaking the moment, and Zeke turned back to the boat.

He held it in position while we threw our packs in, and then he gestured for me to climb in first. I hesitated, however. Was I really going to do this?

Memories of my sister filled my mind, and I stepped over

the side of the boat. I wasn't doing this for myself, and I couldn't back out now.

Gia and Nik followed me, Zeke jumping in last. He immediately started searching around for an oar.

"We'll need to give ourselves a few pushes to get out of this inlet and into the current." He glanced at me. "Or can you do that, too?"

"I think so? Give me a minute."

He nodded, and I closed my eyes. My nerves thrummed with tension. I would look foolish now if I couldn't do what I'd so rashly claimed.

I put my protective shell in place, although it had done nothing to help me last time, and reached out with my ability. At first I could feel nothing, but as soon as I dipped my hand over the edge of the boat, trailing my fingers in the water, I sensed the tainted power.

It was still very faint and dispersed, but it was there, stretching away in both directions. As usual, it tried to slip away from me, each tangled knot of vines slipping free and slithering away as I reached for it. I gritted my teeth and grabbed for one, pushing myself faster than I'd moved before.

Grasping it, I braced myself for the nausea. But it still made me pitch forward onto my knees, the intensity robbing me of breath. I had thought I was prepared, but only now that I was experiencing it did I remember how it actually felt.

"Cadence!" Zeke's worried cry reached my ears.

I ignored him, all my focus on finishing my dealings with the tainted power as quickly as possible. I let it wash over me without struggle, digging its claws in and twisting my ability to match itself. My body protested, but I ignored that, too, pushing through the pain that seemed to come from everywhere at once.

Now when I reached for the remnants of tainted power, they came eagerly, leaping to my grasp as soon as the thought was formed. On the previous occasion, I had thrust them away from me, sending them hurtling through the air. I wanted them to do a similar thing now—but taking the boat and the topmost layer of water around it with them.

I would have assumed it was impossible except that I knew someone had already achieved it. Which meant there must be a way for it to work.

I called more and more of the tainted power to me, collecting it in the water directly beneath the boat. The surface began to bubble and foam, and I felt the boat lurch, rocking violently as someone leaped into it.

I tried to open my eyes to see what was happening, but my body was no longer responding to my commands, all its efforts centered on self-preservation. It was hard to think through the pain, but the only way to relieve it was to make this work.

I imagined the power like waterweeds, directing it to wind itself around the boat from beneath. As soon as it had a good latch, I pushed it away from us. But unlike with the power I had gathered during the attack on the Viridian, I sent it gently, merely directing it toward the center of the river.

It went, dragging the water around us and the boat along with it, in the same direction.

Gia let out a cheer as warm, strong arms wrapped around me, lifting me from where I had slumped in the bottom of the boat.

I had expected the tainted power to resist my attempts to shape it, as normal power did, but it offered no resistance. Only the slightest push was enough to make it merge with the power further upriver. It wasn't stable and stationary, like ordinary power, but instead all the vines and strands and roots of tainted power seemed connected with a pattern I couldn't grasp. It wanted to join together, the momentum to seek out other tainted power increasing with only the smallest encouragement from me.

As our boat began to move upriver, a shout rang out on shore. Another voice joined the first and then another. They were probably clamoring for our return, or calling a warning, but I didn't lift my head to look in their direction. The pain was growing worse, and I was running out of time.

The boat jerked and shuddered but held together, following the thin stream of water on the surface that was moving against the current, dragged along with the tainted power. Whether the power felt a call back to its place of origin and proper location, or whether it was merely the draw to greater concentrations of tainted power, I didn't know. But whatever the cause, it was achieving our aim. We already moved far faster than the downstream flow of the river.

"We've gone far enough," Zeke whispered in my ear. "They won't catch us now. You need to disconnect."

I shook my head, or tried to, anyway. I wasn't sure if I'd actually moved. I had to find a way to make the upstream pull continue without my input.

Sinking the power that surrounded us further into the wood of the boat, I anchored us to the forward movement. The momentum had increased again, the tainted power that clung to us leaping forward to join more like itself and taking us along with it.

I pulled myself free of the weeds of power, but nothing happened. I remained entangled. I tried again, with more force this time, and popped free. It took too many precious moments, but I managed to find a shred of regular power, pouncing on it like a cat on a mouse and holding it tight until it smoothed my ability back to normalcy.

I shuddered, sweet release filling me at the sudden absence of pain. Taking a moment to assess our situation, I noted with satisfaction that our pace hadn't changed. If anything we seemed to be moving a little faster.

"What in the history of power was that?" Evermund asked.

My eyes flew open as I twisted toward his voice, my mouth agape.

"Evermund? What are you doing here?"

"Contrary to your obvious assumptions, I like to keep a watchful eye on minors under my charge," he said blandly.

I continued to gape at him, trying to absorb the significance of his presence. Had he followed me from the ballroom? How much that I thought had gone under his notice had he actually observed?

"Might I inquire where you're all off to in the middle of a ball?" he asked.

"We're going to rescue Airlie." I kept my voice level and strong. I didn't think he could do anything to turn us around, but I wasn't sure.

Would he even want to? The Royal Mage and I had always dealt well together, and he understood why I had to do this more than anyone.

At least I hoped so.

"I thought that might be your aim." He eyed the boat. "You'll excuse my skepticism, but this seems like an insufficient vessel for the task." He glanced at the swiftly passing shore. "But then, it seems there's more going on here than I yet understand."

"Do you mean to stop us?" Gia asked defiantly.

He raised an eyebrow. "That depends on where, exactly, you're going. If this is the start of a second lengthy tour—this time through barren and dangerous lands—then I might be forced to attempt my insufficient best. Although I confess, I have no idea how to stop this boat, and I'd prefer not to dump you out into the river."

"We're going to Lake Aterra," I said, making the split-second decision that he could be trusted with my plan. "I have reason to believe the raiders might be based beside the lake."

"That," he said slowly, "is a very interesting piece of information. May I ask how you arrived at such a conclusion?"

"Well…" I looked at Zeke before turning back to the others. "I think the time for secrecy is well and truly past. At least with you three. There's something you should know about me."

"That much is obvious," Evermund said gently.

"I'm a power mage." I dropped the words baldly.

"Excuse me?" Whatever Evermund had expected me to say, that clearly wasn't it.

"I'm sorry I let you believe my seed was weak and not yet activated. Zeke activated it the night Airlie disappeared which is also when I found out I'm a power mage."

"Zeke activated you?" Evermund looked between the two of us, his expression unreadable.

"He knew about power mages from his tribe, and he guessed that's what I was. We wouldn't have driven back the raider attack that night without my ability."

"This story just keeps getting more and more interesting," Evermund said dryly.

"But you can't be a power mage," Gia exclaimed, her eyes almost bulging out of her head. "There aren't any power mages left."

"Actually," I said, "there's one. Me."

"And she's powerful," Zeke said, looking at Evermund. "Very." He gestured around us. "Which is how we're doing this right now."

"Did I mention my extremely great interest in this story?" Evermund leaned forward. "I don't suppose you've told it to King Marius?"

I shook my head quickly. "No one knows but Zeke."

"No one at the Guild, at least," Zeke said with a hint of guilt.

"Ah, I see. So Annora knows. That does explain a few matters that had been puzzling me." Evermund's enigmatic eyes rested on me.

Had he noticed Tribe Nicabar's interest in me? Karielle had and wondered at it. And perhaps he had also questioned my role in helping Annora on the night of the drugging.

"I can now see why you thought you might be able to take on the raiders without me," he said. "In fact, you find me completely humbled. I can see that while I envisioned myself as a noble savior, I am in fact a mere bystander."

His eyes gently mocked me, but I was still too bemused at the situation to take offense.

"Is that why you jumped into the boat?" I asked. "To save us?"

He inclined his head. "I had clearly arrived not a second too soon, and there was nothing to be done but seize the moment. It seemed a marginally better option than letting you leave without me." His gaze turned on the twins, his eyes thoughtful.

"Thank you," I whispered.

He shrugged. "I like you, Cadence. But I'm not doing this for you."

I nodded, struck by the expression in his eyes. Was he coming to protect the twins, or was it someone else who had inspired his impulsive inclusion in our rescue attempt?

I drew a deep breath. "The rogue Calistan protections that have been causing so much trouble are made up of tainted power—twisted and warped power that has somehow been let loose to run amok. I can sense it in the water of the river, and I'm going to use it to pull us all the way into Calista where I'm hoping I can then track it back to the raiders. Given the prevalence of tainted magic in the two rivers, I believe it must be congregating in Lake Aterra, and I believe the raiders must also be there, given how much use they're making of it."

"That is a much more solid plan than I thought you had when I leaped into this boat," Evermund said.

"Where's your faith?" Zeke muttered with a grin, but the

expression dropped away. "Cadie left out the part where connecting with tainted power makes her seriously ill."

"I witnessed that for myself." Evermund weighed me with his eyes. "If that happens every time, then we're not doing that again. You looked like you were about to die. We'll have to find another way to rescue Airlie."

"I agree," Zeke said fervently.

"You're really not going to stop us?" Nikolas gave Evermund a contemptuous look. "Aren't you the responsible one?"

"Oh, let it go, Nik!" Gia snapped. She turned to the rest of us. "Nik is just sour because he talked to Drake at the ball. Apparently our little play during the Tour hasn't worked. The Triumvirate still haven't softened to the idea of Nik as our future king."

"Gia!" Nikolas hissed, looking as if he wanted to throw her overboard.

She flicked her hair. "Relax. I'm sure Zeke and Evermund have already guessed exactly what's been going on." She gave them both a knowing look, and neither of them disputed the charge.

"But it's not any of our fault," she continued, looking back at her brother. "So I won't have you taking your bad mood out on us." She looked at me. "Nik might pretend he's being dragged along against his will, but he's got his own reasons for coming."

Nikolas glared at her but didn't protest again, perhaps realizing his sister was too annoyed with him to be silenced.

"I know you too well not to understand exactly what's happening." She poked him in the chest. "You're once again convinced that the issue is your affinity, and you were just looking for a chance to prove how strong you can be despite being a plants mage. And then this opportunity fell into your lap—with the added bonus that you're on a mission to recover someone of value to the Triumvirate." She shook her head. "It's not going to serve your purpose—they're all going to be furious with us, whether we succeed or not—but don't pretend you're only coming for me."

"What does it matter if we put ourselves in danger?" Nikolas asked bitterly. "You're not sticking around no matter what, and they don't want me. We might as well both get ourselves killed as not."

"Your parents hardly feel that way," I said, filled with belated alarm. "What are they going to think when they realize the two of you have just disappeared?"

Caught up in the heat of the moment, I clearly hadn't thought this through enough.

"I'm fairly sure a few people got a good look at us back there in front of the manor," Nikolas said. "So we hardly vanished into the air. And besides, I left a note."

"Oh well done, Nik!" Gia cried, patting him on the shoulder, her good humor with him apparently restored. "That was excellent thinking, given they can't do anything about it." Her mouth twisted. "They will be angry when we get back, though." She looked across at Evermund. "With you, too."

"Whatever do you mean?" he asked with a lurking smile. "I'm merely doing my duty to the crown by protecting the two of you."

"All the way into Calista?" Zeke asked dryly.

"Of course." Evermund gave him an innocent look. "We were swept up by the raiders' power. What else could I do?"

"Unbelievable," Gia muttered. "You'll probably get away with it, too. You always did get away with everything."

Evermund shrugged. "I didn't get chosen by the Triumvirate as the youngest ever Royal Mage by not being my own man. I can handle your father."

Nikolas, who had been gazing over the side of the boat with increasing concern, looked up and interrupted. "We aren't really caught up in this tainted power without any direction, are we?" He sounded alarmed.

"Tainted power isn't like normal power." I cleared my throat. "Normal power doesn't do anything at all unless directed. The leftover pieces just sort of...hang there."

"Leftover pieces?" Gia sounded fascinated.

"That's what power mages use. Everyone else's leftovers."

"Not always leftover," Evermund said. "Sometimes mages are still using it when the power mages snatch it away."

His words were true. I had done that myself, and it was clearly one of the parts of a power mage's ability that the other kingdoms considered dangerous. But it wasn't relevant to the issue at hand.

"Tainted power is different. It's active—like we saw on the Viridian—although without sense or purpose. And it's all connected, somehow. That's the only reason it's still carrying us along without any more input from me. I just had to connect us in and then start the momentum."

"That's convenient," Nikolas said.

"Is it?" I frowned. "It probably means it would all need to be removed at once to do any good, and I don't think any mage could ever be strong enough to deal with it all at once."

"Then it's a good thing we're trying to rescue Airlie, not free Calista," Evermund said, his eyes holding a warning.

I bit the inside of my cheek but nodded.

Even traveling at such a fast pace, it took time to move so far up the river. We took turns sleeping, curled awkwardly on the bench seats of the small boat, and always leaving at least two people awake in case of trouble.

But this section of the Celadon was broad and free of rocks, and we encountered no issues. The only concerning moment came when several of the planks of the boat sprang small shoots—one even going as far as to unfurl a bud. But after waiting with bated breath, no leaks appeared, and we all breathed a sigh of relief except for Zeke who looked a little sick.

"Is that what it's doing to your insides whenever you connect with it?" he whispered—a question for which I didn't have an answer.

I slept for a time and woke for a turn on watch just as dawn was breaking. But as I turned my head to gaze at the river ahead of us, I saw the glint of water stretching wide on each side.

"The lake!" My words woke the sleepers, Nikolas and Gia stirring groggily while Evermund came instantly awake.

"What's the plan now?" he asked, looking at me.

"If we're already approaching the lake, we've crossed the Calistan border," I said, considering the matter. "I don't think we want to risk getting swept out into the actual lake, though. We need to direct ourselves toward the shore just at the point where the river and the lake converge."

"How are we going to do that?" Nikolas asked.

"I'm guessing those." Gia pointed at the four oars which had lain idle on the bottom of the boat until now.

It took a little bit of maneuvering, but we set ourselves up in the right positions, Gia and I sharing the fourth oar as we waited for the river to carry us the small distance remaining. Evermund, positioned in one of the front two spots, shouted when it was time to pull, and we all dug our oars into the water.

At first we seemed to make no progress, and fear seized me. What had I led my friends into?

But then we found our rhythm, the oars digging deep, and the boat shot across the water. Our momentum freed us from the tug of the tainted power which flowed away without us toward the center of the lake.

At first, we pulled toward the closest stretch of shore, but a murmured word from Evermund directed us slightly further north.

"What is it?" Gia asked, twisting to look around him.

"I can see something." His voice sounded strained from the physical exertion of rowing.

"Very descriptive," Nikolas muttered.

"It might be an enormous building, or perhaps a wall?" Zeke sounded surprised. "Surely it must be the raiders! I didn't think we'd find them so easily."

"Finding them isn't the hard part," Nikolas said, effectively quenching the rising excitement in the boat.

We bumped gently against shore, all clambering out to stand in a loose huddle, no one quite sure what to do next. Evermund looked at each of us in turn.

"There's every chance that is a settlement of raiders over there. So just remember—we're not going there to capture any of them, or destroy the settlement, or do anything else to end their threat to Tartora. There are only five of us, and all four of you are apprentices. We're going to get in, get Airlie, and get out. Does everyone understand?"

We all nodded.

"The best thing we can do for both Tartora and the nomads," he added, "is to survive this and get back to report on the raiders' location. Then a proper force can be sent."

A brief silence followed his words, broken by Nikolas.

"Well, let's get this over with, then."

CHAPTER 25
AIRLIE

A cool breeze blew over the walls, despite the warmth of the coming day. The dawn winds were an unexpected benefit of my increasingly early visits to the small hill that gave me a vantage point over the walls.

Since the return of the unsuccessful attack party, everyone had been lying low as much as possible, avoiding the General and his rage. But a tall figure still walked slowly toward me, looking barely awake.

When Renley reached me, we nodded a greeting. The ritual had become familiar enough now that no further comment was needed. But curiosity prompted me to question him.

"Aren't you concerned your old warrior friends will notice how much time we're suddenly spending together? Or worse, the General himself might notice?"

"I already told them I'm working on winning you to the General's cause. The General himself has hinted that if I succeed in the task, I'll finally win the chance to be activated." His bitter tones conveyed what he thought of such a prospect, but a moment later he smiled. "So, you see, they all imagine me to be corrupting you rather than the other way around."

"How is that going?" I asked, smiling into the wind.

"I'm not sure. Are you feeling corrupt?"

"I'm—" I froze halfway through the light-hearted banter. "What's that?" I tried to keep my voice low and manner unexcited, but it was hard to contain myself.

"What?" He tried to follow the line of my gaze, and I immediately swung around to face the other way.

When he tried to follow my movement, I hissed at him to stop. "Look where I was looking before. I only turned because I don't want to attract anyone else's attention to it."

"I don't know what...Wait! Is that...?"

"People." I whispered the word. "It looks like people. People coming from the direction of the lake. But there are no hunting parties or attack parties out at the moment. Everyone from the settlement is within the walls."

"Do you think it's a rescue party?" He sounded doubtful. "It isn't a very large group."

"Who else would be here in the middle of the fallen kingdom?"

"I wouldn't say middle," he muttered, but I ignored him.

"They'll be down in that hollow in a minute or two, and out of sight. We need an excuse to get outside the walls." He didn't answer, and I continued on, thinking out loud. "I could ask if we can go hunting again. Although our lack of success last time doesn't speak in our favor. I hope they don't run into something like that boar! Cadence is a terrible shot."

"If it is your sister, she's not alone," Renley said. "I think their bigger problem will be the hunting party due to ride out shortly. They're heading over the border to try to refresh our food supplies, and there's every chance they'll see this group on the way."

"The hunting party! That's how we get out. We'll ask to be included."

Renley frowned. "Have you forgotten you're a prisoner?"

"But you're so convincing, Renley." I gave him a fake look of adoration that made him snort. "Now that I've been exposed to your influence, I want nothing more than to join the General's cause. I just need a chance to prove myself."

"Do you really think that will work?" Renley, at least, didn't sound convinced.

"Maybe not, but we don't have time to think of something better. My rescuers will be here soon. Come on." I started down the slope at a light jog, leaving Renley to catch up as I reached flatter ground.

"Where are you going?" he asked in alarm.

"To the General's house, of course."

"Right now?"

"You said the hunters are leaving soon. There's no time to waste."

"But I—"

"You don't have to come. You don't have to be involved at all. In fact, maybe you shouldn't be. This might not end well."

"All the more reason for me to be along to help," he said staunchly.

I nodded approvingly and increased my pace.

We arrived in the square between the General's house and the front gate just as he stepped out his door. Rushing over to him, I positioned myself in his path.

"Airlie." He gave me an unnerving look.

"I've just heard there's a hunting team going out today," I said, trying to steady my breathing. "I want to go with them."

His eyes tightened, but otherwise his face remained impassive as he looked at my companion. "And I suppose you want to go, too, Renley?"

"I could keep an eye on her, sir," he said crisply. "She wants to prove herself, and I'm willing to assist in any way I can."

I silently saluted him. He was a far better actor than I'd given him credit for.

254

"I note that all your attempts to prove yourself seem to involve a weapon," the General said to me.

"Without my ability, my skill with the bow is all I have to offer."

"Come now." A hint of amusement entered his voice. "I'm sure you're underselling yourself. But why the sudden hurry?"

"I can't sit around here for another day doing nothing." I let all my true frustration leach into my face and voice. "I need to do something active."

The General turned his head toward the gate, a calculating look in his eye. When he turned back to us, he had a small smile on his face that sent chills up and down my spine.

"Why not?" he said in a deceptively soft voice.

I watched him warily, unable to believe it could be so simple.

"Be ready to leave in ten minutes. We won't wait for either of you."

"We?" I stared at him.

"I, too, grow weary of these walls." His smile grew. "And I should like to see your loyalty in action for myself, Airlie."

"I..." I pulled myself together. "I'll be at the front gate in five minutes."

Whisking myself away, I stopped as soon as I was out of sight, putting my back against the closest house and taking deep breaths.

"Are you all right?" Renley asked.

"No!" I hissed back. "The General is going himself. That's the opposite of what I wanted."

"Hopefully King Marius sent his best people." Renley sounded grim. "Or it's not going to be much of a fight."

I focused on my breathing for a moment, tuning him out. Once I'd regained the strength in my legs, I straightened.

"This changes nothing for me. This is my chance, and I have to take it. But you can—"

"No. I'm coming."

"Are you sure?"

"All I've ever wanted is to get out of these walls. I thought the General could give me that, but his promises are empty. You're different, Airlie. I misjudged you at first, but I can see that now. Besides, do you know how to instruct Cadence on removing your neutralizer?"

I froze. "No, I don't. I should have asked about that before now."

"No matter. I know how it's done. I was there for all the experimentation."

"Thank you." I tried to meet his eyes, but he looked away.

"It doesn't come close to making up for what I did, but I know my mother would approve of this. She would want me to look out for you."

I nodded, accepting his decision. "We don't have time to pack. If this works, we won't be able to take anything with us."

"There's nothing here I need." He was silent for a moment. "At least not anything I can carry away with me."

"In that case, let's get to the gate. I'm not giving the General any excuse to leave us behind."

We hurried toward the gate side by side, reaching it just ahead of the raiders making up the hunting party. As I scanned their number, my heart sank even further. While they weren't a huge group, they were made up entirely of the General's warriors. I couldn't see a single face from either the original settlers or the non-combatant new arrivals. Usually resupply groups included at least a couple of older, experienced hunters and several women who were experts in preparing the catch for travel.

I told myself that the General must have some secondary plan for this excursion. It couldn't have anything to do with the rescue party outside the gates since they had only just appeared.

As soon as the General himself strode up, the gates began to open, pulled by an enthusiastic pair of lads who gazed admiringly at the outfitted hunters.

I had claimed I wanted to hunt, but no one offered me a bow, and I didn't have the chance to ask for one before I was filing out the gate at the back of the group. As the gates swung shut behind us, I gave a single, lingering glance back.

I regretted not having the chance to say goodbye to Quirin and the other settlers. My experience within the walls had been far more complex than I had expected when I was first dragged through them, and I struggled to know how to feel about the settlement's existence. As a war camp, I would welcome King Marius razing it to the ground. But as the last Calistan settlement, I felt more at home there than I had anywhere else.

I shook myself, facing forward again. Home was Cadence, and a place where I didn't walk around with part of myself shackled. This wasn't the time for sentiment, or for looking behind.

Two warriors brought up the rear, their presence making any immediate attempt to slip away from the group impossible. But I couldn't resist scanning the surrounding area, looking for the people I had glimpsed from inside the walls.

I could find no sign of them. The land dipped away from us in the direction of the lake, the closest hollow partially obscured by one of the stands of deformed trees. Had they taken shelter among them?

If the rescuers managed to evade our group, what would Renley and I do? We might be able to make our escape later, circling back to find the rescue team.

Before I could formulate plans for how such a thing might be accomplished, my eyes caught on the General. He had turned slightly in the direction of the stand of trees, his face raised into the slight breeze, and his head faintly cocked.

Something about the stance rang a familiar chord. Ice raced

through my veins. I had once turned into the breeze for information on those around me, but I had forgotten the General had the same ability—as impossible as that was supposed to be.

Had he picked up the presence of the newcomers from the air before we ever left the settlement? Looking at the rest of the hunting party, I could no longer pretend it was coincidence they were all warriors. This was an ambush.

Desperately, I tried to think of a way to warn the incoming Tartorans. But there was nothing I could do at such a distance without my ability.

Still testing the wind, the General changed course, no longer heading for the border. Instead we walked toward the stand of trees. I tried to hang back, hoping to break away, but one of the men behind me pressed close, forcing me to stay with the group.

When the General reached the edge of the clump of trees, he gestured to the men behind him. They disappeared among the trunks, moving silently as they took possession of the only significant shelter between the lake and the settlement.

I stopped completely, and the man behind me grabbed my elbow, roughly shoving me toward Renley who stood by the closest tree, frowning back in our direction. Our eyes met, the concern reflecting back between us.

Had the General truly believed I was now loyal to his cause to the point of attacking a group of people come to rescue me? Or was my inclusion in the group a sign of his confidence in his victory?

He must think I was no danger to him, weaponless and without my ability.

Without thinking it through further, I sucked in a deep breath and screamed, the sound piercing the quiet morning.

An angry shout from the General echoed my cry, and sound and movement erupted from the far side of the trees. I wrenched my arm free of the man beside me and plunged into the trees. The canopy was denser than it should have been, and something that looked terrifyingly like an enormous spider lowered itself toward me.

I put both arms over my head protectively and charged forward, doing my best to ignore everything around me. It sounded like Renley had tackled the raider I'd just escaped, preventing him from going after me, but I didn't look back.

The trees around me groaned and creaked, the branches above me rustling loudly. I burst out from among them, straight into the face of a gale force wind. I screamed again, but this time the sound was snatched away from me.

I swayed, trying to catch my balance just as the wind whipped in the other direction, spinning its way into a tornado. It swept past me with such force that I felt myself being tugged upward.

Before I could actually leave the ground, however, something lashed up from the dirt, twisting around my ankle and anchoring me in place. I looked down to see a green vine twined around each leg. The dirt beneath me shifted, covering over both feet and securing me to the ground.

The wind howled, gathering fury and making me glad for the restraints that held me in place. I strained to see past the dust that had been lifted into the air, trying to identify the combatants.

Zeke caught my eye first, his gaze trained on his own feet which were slowly sinking into the ground. When he finished securing himself in the same manner as me, he looked up. When he caught me watching him, he winked.

So he was responsible for keeping me from being sucked away into the vortex. I appreciated his efforts, but I hadn't expected to see him here. For all his natural power, he was still an apprentice. Surely the Tartorans had sent experienced fighters.

The whipping wind moved slightly, revealing Gia and just beyond her Nikolas. My stomach seized. There was no way King Marius would have sent his two children on an elite rescue mission. Which meant this was an unsanctioned expedition, not a selection of the Guild's most talented mages.

A garbled scream gave me warning to duck as the wind whipped a flailing raider past my head. A moment later it spit him out, a sickening thud sounding as he hit the ground.

I looked behind me, scanning for any sign of Renley, but he hadn't emerged from the trees. As I twisted back toward the lake, the wind suddenly cut off.

The deafening stillness revealed the General standing menacingly in the center of the destruction, facing off against a figure so familiar it made my heart twist inside my chest. Evermund.

I tried to pull free of the vines and dirt clinging to my feet to run to him, but they held me firm. Looking desperately toward Zeke, I caught his eye and gestured toward them. He nodded, and the vines instantly let me go, the ground pushing me gently upward.

While I waited impatiently, a much larger vine, this one covered in thorns, erupted from the earth beside Evermund and lashed toward him. Just before it made contact, however, it burst into flames and crumbled into ash.

My feet released, but I hesitated. My frustrated grip closed around the neutralizer. If I ran to Evermund, I would just distract him. I could do nothing to help in such a battle.

Instead, I scanned the rest of the rolling plain that stretched from the trees down to the lake. Lawson stood within the shadow of the trees, his eyes fixed on Evermund as two more thorny vines pushed free of the dirt.

I raced over to Zeke, grabbing his arm and pointing to Lawson.

"It's him," I said. "And he's the one who attacked you in the Guild, too."

Zeke's brows drew together, and the ground beneath Lawson shuddered and cracked. His concentration was shattered, and the vines lashing at Evermund dropped to the ground. At least one of them had made contact, though, from the red that streaked its thorns.

Lawson turned toward us with a growl, and I backed away from Zeke. Once again, I was worse than useless, a dead weight needing protection.

But Nikolas stepped into my line of sight, moving toward Lawson from the other side, his eyes darting between Zeke and the raider mage. Lawson, his focus still on Zeke, stepped sideways, his foot slipping on a sudden crater that formed in the earth behind him.

Zeke and Nikolas stepped toward him in unison, closing from both sides. I turned away, still looking for the one familiar face I both wanted and dreaded seeing.

Instead, I found Gia. She stood further toward the lake, in the direction Nikolas had come from, her attention on her brother's battle.

Two raiders stepped out of the trees behind her. I tried to shout a warning, but she was beyond my reach. Catching her by surprise, they seized her by both arms.

She responded with fury instead of fear, however. Tongues of flame sprouted from the raiders' clothing, and both of them let her go, shouting in alarm. I grinned, my gaze traveling on.

If Zeke, and Nikolas, and Gia were here, then surely...

There. I breathed a sharp breath in and out. Cadence.

My sister had come for me.

CHAPTER 26
AIRLIE

The paralysis of uncertainty that had been keeping me stationary disappeared, and I flew across the distance between us. She turned in time to see me just before I collided with her.

"Airlie!" she screamed, wrapping her arms around me just as I did the same to her.

"What are you doing here?" Tears ran down my cheeks unheeded. "You're going to get yourself killed."

"No, I'm not." Her face had a determination I didn't recognize, her eyes gleaming with a new look of confidence and experience. "You're not the only one with power now, big sister."

"NO!" I screamed, pushing her so hard she fell into the dirt, hopefully breaking her concentration before she could call on her ability.

"What are you doing?" She scrambled up again, glaring at me. "I'm not going to let us all get killed, Airlie."

"And I'm not letting you kill yourself saving us. You can't use the wild power, Cadie. Promise me you won't."

"Wild power?" She frowned. "You mean the tainted power? I can take the pain, Air."

The whoosh and crackle of flames made us both look behind me. My face paled as I saw the column of bright flame where Evermund had been standing.

A cloud appeared over his head, dumping a deluge of water that quenched the flames. I drew in a shaky breath as he appeared, his clothes partially ash, the rest marred with long, bloody rips. But he was still standing, facing the General with the same determined expression as before.

He was losing, though. In a battle of pure power, even Evermund's great strength couldn't match the General's. I ground my teeth together, wishing with every fiber for access to my ability.

"I can't let him win," Cadence said, pulling my attention back to her. "I can handle the tainted power."

"No!" I grabbed at her arm. "You don't understand. It will kill you, Cadence. It already killed Dara."

I almost cried with frustration when I remembered that would mean nothing to her. She didn't know Dara.

But something in my words made her halt.

"It was using tainted power that killed Dara?"

I nodded, relieved that she knew what I was talking about. "There's no way to use it safely. It killed our grandfather, too, and he was strong like you."

One of the closest trees exploded, sending spears of wood in all directions. I jumped for Cadence, sheltering her with my body as I sent us both crashing to the ground.

She pushed me off straight away, looking toward the remaining trees where Zeke was visible, now fighting hand-to-hand with Lawson while the trees writhed, reaching for first one and then the other with thick, dangerous boughs.

"I can't just stand here and do nothing!" she cried, her heart in her eyes.

"Then free Airlie." Renley appeared from nowhere, seizing my hand and hauling me to my feet.

His hair was tousled, and dirt streaked his face and clothes, but he seemed to be in one piece. Cadence eyed him warily.

"That's what I'm here to do."

"This is Renley, Dara's son," I said. "He's a friend."

She raised an eyebrow, her skeptical expression suggesting she knew how I had been lured away from the Guild. We didn't have time for that now, though.

"They're keeping me bound with a neutralizer." The words tumbled out so quickly they were almost garbled. "Only you can release me, and only Renley knows how. That's what he means."

"Oh!" Cadence's wide eyes latched on to the large seed secured at my waist.

"It's been sucking her power in and storing it every time she tries to use her ability," he said. "The power needs to be removed again. Once it's empty, it will no longer have an attachment to her."

"That's all?" I asked. "That's so simple."

He shrugged. "We never said it was complicated. Just that we needed a power mage—one strong enough to handle all the power you've been pouring in there."

I bit my lip. "So if I'd never used my ability in the first place, it wouldn't have ever connected with me?"

A tree fell, the thump it made as it struck the ground making everyone freeze for a minute.

"Never mind, don't answer that," I said hurriedly. "Quick, Cadie!"

A look of concentration came over her face, followed by one of surprise.

"It's not tainted power. It's normal."

Renley nodded. "Stored power was always intended to be used—it just needs to be retrieved by a power mage."

Cadence's eyes gleamed, her face turning back toward the

trees and her friends. "I can use this. I'll look after the others, Air. You help Evermund."

I ripped off the fastenings of the neutralizer, throwing it away from me as full awareness came roaring back. I shouted in exultation. I was whole again.

All around me, the elements called to me. The water of the lake, deep and cool and strong, and the wind, whooshing, and leaping and flying. I could feel the moisture in everything, and the crackle of something stronger lurking high above us in the air.

Teeth bared in a wild grin, I ran toward Evermund. Finally it was the General's turn to be afraid.

"You protect the others," I cried. "I'll deal with the General."

I stepped forward, looking my captor directly in the eye. A strange gleam leaped into his gaze, almost as if he relished pitting himself against me.

His mistake.

He held out both hands, flames appearing in his open palms. I didn't bother to form a cloud, as Evermund had done. Instead, I called to the moisture lurking in the air around us. It coalesced over his hands, dropping in two sheets which extinguished the flames. His face darkened.

A wind sprang up again, and though it wasn't a natural one, I reveled in the feel of it whistling around me. It could no more whisk me away than it could him. It could hurt my friends, though.

Reaching up my arms, I called to the distant crackle above us. It burned so brightly that, for a second, I feared I might be consumed. But when I concentrated, it came to me, twining around my outreached power.

I jerked my hand down, and the bolt of pure light came with me, sizzling through the air to strike where the General stood, the clap of thunder coming almost simultaneously.

He screamed, an ugly, guttural sound, and I hit him with a second lightning bolt.

"Airlie!" Evermund took my arm, pulling me in the direction of the lake. "We only came for you. Come on! We need to go!"

I resisted for a moment, caught up in my fury with the General, but three raiders appeared between him and the trees, hurrying toward their fallen leader. He stirred, pushing himself up onto one arm and looking at me with death in his eyes.

I called silently to the water of the lake. It formed an enormous spout that reached up into the air and bent over, growing longer and longer as it stretched for the raiders.

The General's eyes widened, and he thrust up his arms. As the water hit, a bubble appeared around him and his closest men. I kept the stream of water going, hammering at his bubble and keeping them pinned as I turned my back and ran with Evermund toward the distant shore.

"Watch out!" Evermund put out an arm, trying to sweep me protectively behind him even as we ran.

I followed his gaze in time to shout, "No!" just as a ball of flame appeared on Renley's sleeve.

Renley shouted and batted at it, but it died as quickly as it had appeared.

"Renley's with us," I panted to Evermund. "He's my friend."

Evermund's step faltered for half a second before he regained his stride, his eyes slipping from Renley to me.

"Your friend?" His voice held a note I couldn't read.

We both slowed, and I nodded, finally catching my breath.

"Thank you for coming for me, Evermund," I whispered, wishing I could tell him how much I'd missed him, but unable to speak the words now that he was actually here.

"Of course," he said, his voice low, and his eyes locked on mine. "You're my apprentice, Airlie. I'll always come for you."

I shivered, our eyes locked together, as I tried to convince myself it was only my imagination reading a deeper promise in his gaze.

Renley broke the moment, running the final steps toward us and letting out a shout. He was looking back over his shoulder, so I followed his gaze. My absorption with Evermund had broken my concentration. My funnel of water was gone.

In the distance, the General and his men were regaining their feet.

"Over here!"

We all turned toward the shout to see Cadence waving frantically for us to join them. She, Zeke, and the twins had untethered an open boat from a small wooden dock that I hadn't noticed before.

Gia and Cadence clambered in as we raced to join them, the two boys holding it steady. When we reached the edge of the water, Evermund scooped me up as if I weighed nothing, depositing me on one of the seats. I didn't protest, although I could have climbed in myself.

He gestured the three younger men in after me, holding the boat steady until they'd found their footing. Several shouts reverberated toward us as the raiders neared.

Evermund pushed the boat away from the dock, running forward across the top of the water for several strides before stepping over the edge of the boat. When he caught me watching him wide-eyed, he grinned.

"Remind me to teach you that trick one day."

I grinned back, reaching without effort for a wind to push us toward the too-distant river mouth. Another wind sprang up, working against mine, and I looked toward the shore where the General had nearly reached the lake.

But Evermund sat down beside me, and the force of wind at our back strengthened and grew, sweeping away the General's breeze. I smiled up at Evermund.

"We make a good team."

"That we do," he agreed.

The current caught us, the boat lurching and then gathering speed.

Zeke shouted a warning, using an oar to push us off a rock that jutted out into the flow of water. I turned my attention from the wind, sinking my awareness into the water beneath us and shaping it around the boat.

We rushed forward toward the center of the river, our progress now smooth.

"I'm glad we're going downriver this time," Zeke said, casting a hooded glance at Cadence.

She slipped her hand into his, and he looked down at her with a warmth that sent both my eyebrows flying toward my hairline. What was he doing looking at my baby sister like that? I'd warned him...

My thoughts petered out as she rested her head against his shoulder, and he put a gentle, protective arm around her. Her soft sigh spoke of heavy burdens shared, and I remembered the new depth I had seen in her eyes earlier.

I had been gone too long. Cadence wasn't my baby sister anymore. And apparently she wasn't only mine anymore, either. While I had been a captive, she had grown up.

I squashed down a foolish flare of resentment. I was happy for her. And if Zeke was actually serious about her, she'd made a good choice. His tribe would soon have the authority to keep her safe from the many people who would want to use her ability.

So why didn't I feel better about the prospect of relinquishing my heaviest burden to someone more qualified to bear it?

Cadence looked up and met my eyes, a delighted smile spreading instantly across her face.

"I can't believe we did it," she exclaimed. "And you're safe." Her brow lowered. "You are all right, aren't you?"

I nodded. "Now that you got rid of that awful thing binding me. Thank you for that, by the way."

Her hand tightened around the pack at her feet, drawing my eye. When I looked back at her, she had a familiar defiant light in her eyes.

Had she rescued the neutralizer I had thrown away and stashed it in her pack? I had to fight down an instinctive rush of revulsion, slowly replacing it with admiration at her quick thinking. From Quirin's experiments, I knew they were reusable, and it was a powerful tool to have in her possession—especially given no one else in Tartora could utilize it.

"I've missed you so much," I said softly, and tears sprang to her eyes.

"I've missed you, too."

"I want to hear everything that happened while I was gone," I said. "Starting with how you found out you had a power seed and got activated. I was in shock for days when I was told there's a fourth affinity."

"Then it's a good thing we have a long trip ahead of us," Zeke said cheerfully. "Because it's a long story."

"And one I'm equally curious to hear." Gia popped up beside Cadence. "I may have been there, but clearly I didn't really know what was going on."

She sounded mildly put out, and I looked between them with interest. Cadence hadn't told Gia about her ability?

Zeke looked over his shoulder at Nikolas. "What about you? Are you burning to hear about Cadence's journey of discovery?"

Nikolas just rolled his eyes.

"I hope at the very least that little tussle back there taught you a greater appreciation for our affinity," Zeke added, a slight barb in his voice. "As you saw, it's not only elements mages who can be useful in a fight."

I looked between them, trying to understand the undercurrent beneath his words. Clearly I'd missed more than just

Cadence's transformation—starting with the twins' obvious activation by someone other than me.

It felt longer than a few months since I'd been part of this world. They had grown closer together, while I had become an outsider. I never thought I could feel that way about Cadence.

And I'd never dreamed I'd feel so much a part of the world I'd been forced into. I looked back toward the lake, straining to catch a distant glimpse of wooden walls. What would happen to Quirin, and Marissa, and the others now the Tartorans knew the location of their settlement?

I would gladly lead the fight against the General myself, but would the Tartorans listen if I told them not all the Calistans were equally guilty? I met Renley's gaze where he huddled silently in the back of the boat, out of place and conscious of it.

I would simply have to try.

"This is Renley, everyone," I said. "He's an old friend of the family, and he helped me escape."

Everyone murmured greetings, his eyes growing wider as they each introduced themselves and he discovered the illustrious company my sister kept these days. I thrust down another misplaced stab of resentment and turned to her, letting my eyes rest on her familiar face.

"Now about that story. I really do want to hear everything."

CHAPTER 27

CADENCE

We slipped quietly into Tarona several days later, but our entry into the Guild wasn't nearly as surreptitious. An outcry arose as soon as we were glimpsed, and mages swarmed on us from every direction.

Drake rescued us from being mobbed, carrying us off to the palace with the rest of the Triumvirate. The king's interview of Airlie lasted a full hour, but she still didn't tell him everything she'd told me on the journey back to Tarona. I approved of her decision, given how many of her discoveries related to our personal history, but I couldn't help wondering if she'd applied the same selective filter to the facts she told me.

I shook off the cynical thought. That was part of the past. Airlie and I had a new start, and I would have to work not to hold such things against her.

At least the king appeared satisfied with her account as it stood. He dismissed us, along with Zeke and Renley, who had been given permission to stay on at the Guild, at least temporarily, given his service to Airlie.

Thankfully when it was established he had a weak seed, no further questions had been asked, so we had avoided awkward questions about his affinity. On the journey home we had decided as a group to keep the information about the continued survival of the power affinity to ourselves for now, a decision that had pleased but surprised me. I wouldn't have thought Evermund would be willing to conceal important facts from the king and Guild.

Glancing over my shoulder, I shot Gia a sympathetic look. It felt cowardly to walk out on her, but I could hardly defy the king's dismissal. Even if he was obviously sending us away so he could deal more severely with them.

Zeke offered to take Renley in hand, setting him up in a room in the apprentices' section. When I looked at him gratefully, he gave me a knowing smile in return. My heart warmed at his understanding. As much as I wanted a quiet moment just with him, time with Airlie had to come first. It had been too long since the two of us were alone.

I led the way to Evermund's suite, but as we reached the door, Airlie pushed past me, opening it and stepping inside first. My teeth clenched, but I forced them to relax, scolding myself for the instinctive reaction. Airlie likely hadn't even realized she'd done it. She was just used to leading the way. And what did such trivialities matter compared to finding her alive and well? There had been too many days when such a happy ending seemed too much to hope for, and I refused to waste any of it in pointless arguments.

I followed her inside, closing the door behind me.

"It's strange to be back here." She looked around the living space with a bemused look in her eye.

"I'll give you your room back, of course," I said hurriedly. "We just thought it was sensible for me to stay there while you were gone."

"You can share it with me, if you like," she said absently, shaking her head. "Although it's odd to think of just going back to being an apprentice, like none of it happened."

"Do you not want to?" I asked. "Unfortunately, I don't think you have a choice, given the laws and all."

"No, I'm happy to be back." Her eyes lingered on Evermund's closed door.

"I'm glad to hear it," I said. "It's been hard without you, Air. You left big shoes to fill. I'm so used to everything being about you, it took me awhile to find myself."

"All about me?" She reacted sharply, making me reconsider my words.

"I didn't mean to criticize," I said quickly. "Just to explain how strange it's been. I know it wasn't your fault our lives were always about you."

"What are you talking about?" She stared at me with utter bemusement. "From my earliest memories, it's always been about you, Cadence!"

"Me?" I gaped back at her, completely thrown off my mental track. "But you were always Father's favorite."

"Favorite? Is that what you call the endless pressure and demands? Always having to make allowances because you were younger. I had to be stronger and wiser and more restrained. I could never relax, never make a mistake in case something happened to you. My whole life has been nothing but my duty to look after you and keep you safe."

I put my hands on my hips, my irritation rising, despite my recent resolution that I would never fight with her again. "Your whole life? So every time a boy walked straight past me to fawn over you—that was somehow about me? When I begged for us to leave our home after Father died, but you overrode me time and again and insisted we stay—that was about me? What about when you kept secrets from me and lied to me and dragged me to the Guild in your wake? Was that all about me?"

Airlie flushed. "I was afraid, all right? I was terrified of being alone and responsible for you—and apparently the fate of Calista into the bargain. And I didn't even know why or how! I didn't want to keep secrets! I kept them because Father told me keeping them would keep you safe."

"Did you ever once consider how I might feel about it?" I asked. "You hated it when Father refused to answer our questions, telling us half-truths or refusing to say anything at all. Surely, once we came to the Guild, at least, you could have told me everything. Father had been gone for years by then!"

"I—" She started an angry retort, only to stop herself, her demeanor changing. Taking a deep breath, she started again. "You're right. I told myself I was protecting you from the healing mages who could read deception, but that was only part of it. I could have told you more once we'd made it through the initial testing, at least. But it was such a habit by then—thinking of you as someone who needed to be sheltered and protected, even from herself."

She looked down. "And, if I'm being completely honest, it was more than that. Do you know how it felt that for once someone was interested in me for my own sake, not for the service I could perform for you?"

"I wouldn't know anything about that," I said, but the words were quiet rather than angry, my emotions deflated by her admission. "No one has ever been interested in me, separate from you."

She raised an eyebrow. "Really? Zeke looks pretty interested to me. And I suppose there's been no interest in you at all since your power was activated?"

I stared at her. She was right, of course. I was talking nonsense—a lifetime of ingrained thinking and reflexive resentment that no longer made any sense.

"At first it was still about you," I said slowly, putting up my hand to stop her when she looked upset by my words. "I was just filling in for you, keeping your position open for your return. But then it changed." I looked across at her. "I'm sorry, Air. I understand now how it must have been hard for you, with everyone depending on you like that. I've hated all the pressure."

I gave a shaky laugh. "While you were gone, I was your staunchest supporter—the one person convinced you would never just walk away. I devoted myself to rescuing you, and when we escaped from the raider settlement, I was so happy to have you back. I promised myself I would never fight with you or take you for granted again."

Airlie chuckled. "When was that? Thirty minutes ago?"

I snorted. "More like fifteen."

She threw her arms around me, squeezing tight.

"I love you, too, Cadence. But I'm not promising never to fight with you. Seventeen years of history isn't that easy to overcome."

I squeezed her back before pulling away. "Were you really afraid? Those two years we spent alone in our house? You always seemed so sure of yourself."

She sighed. "Because I was afraid that if I cracked even the tiniest bit, I would crumble completely. Father told me to find someone powerful to activate me—he even instructed me how to trick someone into doing it. I was supposed to be powerful so I could protect you and make sure you ended up with the right influencer—even activate you myself, if need be. He instructed me on all sorts of dangers we might encounter."

"Even neutralizers?" I asked, remembering the assassins who had burst into Evermund's suite and thinking about the large, harmless looking seed currently stashed in the bottom of my pack.

She nodded. "But when he died, I just...froze. It was only when you were approaching seventeen that I was finally pushed into action. But now, with everything I've found out since..." She shook her head. "I've been so angry with him, Cadie. There were so many things he didn't tell me—lies he told. Like telling me we were safe from the protections because we were Calistan. All the time he knew about it all—the wild power, your ability, Quirin and Dara's settlement. We could have lived there, you know. With friends and family."

She glared into the distance. "He took so much from us. But do you know what the worst of it is?"

I decided it was a rhetorical question and stayed silent. Sure enough, she powered on without waiting for my input.

"While I was in the settlement, there were times when I felt lost. And when I didn't know what to do, it was Evermund I thought of. I wished I could tell him all about my predicament and ask his advice." She turned to me. "I missed you, and I worried about you, but in those moments, it never occurred to me to talk it all over with you and ask you for advice."

"Wow, thanks," I muttered.

"Exactly!" she said. "Why wasn't it you I was wishing for? We're only two years apart, and I'm closer to you than I've ever been to anyone. We've lived almost our entire lives together, and you understand me better than anyone else still alive. But there was always a wedge between us—one of Father's making. We were never equals. I had to be the adult, to lead and protect you—all so that one day you could step into the spotlight and save Calista."

I frowned. "I don't think I can do that, Airlie. I have no idea how to control so much wild power, let alone to safely get rid of it."

"You don't have to do it," she said firmly. "It's just another error to lay at Father's door. He took so much from us, and for what? Just so he could send you out to attempt a task so dangerous it killed his own father? What kind of parent does that?"

"One more obsessed with what our family lost than with the future we could make for ourselves," I murmured.

She nodded. "In that future, I want to be best friends with you, Cadence. I don't want to lead you, and—to be honest—I don't want to follow you, either. I just want to be sisters. Do you think we can do that, despite all the ways Father manipulated us?"

I bit my lip. "I'd like to try. And I'm glad you don't want to follow me because I have no idea what I'm doing."

She laughed. "I can help you out there. I rarely knew what I was doing. The trick is *looking* like you know what you're doing. It's remarkable how often everything works out if you start out that way."

I shook my head. "I can't believe it. Perfect little Airlie was just pretending all along."

She grinned. "Well, I wasn't pretending about everything. I am, for instance, a far superior shot to you."

"Of course you'd bring that up," I grumbled. "The one thing I could never do, no matter how hard I tried. And how you loved to rub it in!"

She looked guilty. "Sorry about that. I always knew I was missing the crucial thing Father wanted—the thing you had—even though I didn't know what it was. I guess I was a little too delighted to be better than you at something."

"Hearing you talk about it..." I shook my head. "It really is like some sort of fairy story—a childhood totally different from the one I remember. Father really never told you about power mages or about my ability? He didn't leave any hints as to how, exactly, I was going to save Calista?"

"No. He told me about abilities, but not about the power affinity or about your seed. I was so confused when you were first tested, and they said your ability would be weak. It didn't make any sense. I think...I think I wasn't the only one who got used to keeping secrets. I think Father didn't know how to fully trust either of us. He certainly thought that if you knew the truth about seeds and abilities and your own strength, that you would run away at the first opportunity and get the first person you could find to activate you."

"I did used to be the adventurous one," I said with a sigh. "It seems like a long time ago."

"Do you want to go back to being that person?" she asked me.

I frowned, considering the matter. Did I?

"Yes and no?" I sighed. "I guess I don't know myself, fully. I like being useful and helping people, but I'll admit I'm relieved to have you back. I suppose..." I looked at her sideways.

"You want to go to the nomad lands with Zeke, don't you?" she said in a quiet voice.

"I'm not going to leave you," I said quickly. "I only just got you back. And what sort of sister would I be to dump all that responsibility on you after I hated having to carry it by myself for so long?"

"I'm not saying I want you to go tomorrow," she said slowly, "but you can't stay here forever just because of me. If you want to travel and explore, I want that for you, too. And you need a chance to learn how to use your ability properly. Can you do that here?"

I frowned. "I'm not sure I can do that in the nomad lands either. Renley might actually be my best hope. I know he's not activated yet, but he must have learned something from his parents and friends." I looked at her. "But what about you, Airlie? I spent a week traveling along the coast, you know. When do you get to see the ocean?"

Something flashed across her face too fast for me to catch before she shrugged.

"I'm sure I'll get my chance. In truth, I'm ready to be settled here for a while. I'm not certain you need me anymore—not like you used to—and that's not as freeing as I expected it would be. I guess I don't want to be released from all responsibility like I thought I did."

I slipped an arm around her shoulders. "No, you just need

the freedom to decide for yourself which responsibilities you want to take on, instead of having them forced on you."

She looked at me in surprise. "Yes. That's exactly it. When did you get so wise?"

I grinned. "It was while you were gone, and I was pretending to be you. So I guess you're right, and the pretending does work."

She slipped her arm around me as well. "All this thinking about the future, but the first thing we're doing tomorrow morning is visiting Hayes. I don't care what we tell him, but he's examining you and fixing up anything he can. Surely it's possible to heal whatever damage has already been done."

"Yes, Airlie," I said meekly, making her chuckle.

"Thank you again for rescuing me," she said. "Even if that was history's most foolish rescue attempt."

I snorted, unable to dispute the point. Without Airlie's assistance, the whole thing would have been worse than a disaster.

"You must be so relieved to be free," I said.

"I'm more relieved to have my ability back. I feel like I've been blind or deaf this whole time, missing a crucial sense I'd come to rely on."

I shuddered. "I can't imagine life without my ability these days."

She nodded, but her mind seemed to be elsewhere. After a moment she asked, "What do you think King Marius is going to do about the raiders?"

"Zeke thinks he'll set up ambushes anywhere they're likely to come across the border. It will be a siege of sorts."

"I suppose the Tartorans can't safely get a force across into Calista," she said slowly. "The king doesn't have anyone with a power affinity except you—and he probably doesn't even know that's what he needs to be safe, let alone that you're a power mage."

"Are you worried about Renley's family?" I asked, thinking how strange it was that we each now had a host of new acquaintances unfamiliar to the other.

"I am," she admitted.

"We'll find a way to help them." I took a seat at the table. "Maybe we can get them out."

"Maybe." She sounded less sure.

"What I want to know is how the neutralizers work," I said. "I don't understand how they could possibly store power like that. I keep thinking maybe it somehow relates to the stories about the Calistan king storing power."

Airlie looked as if she was going to speak, but she only shook her head slightly. Did she know something more than she was saying on the topic? I narrowed my eyes at her before sighing and letting it go. I was being paranoid again. She was probably just trying to hide the extent of her worry for the Calistan settlement.

Was it heartless that I wasn't more concerned myself? Even after Airlie's stories, I just couldn't consider them entirely blameless in the General's actions.

But Renley had helped us escape, and he seemed dedicated to bringing the raiders down. So maybe I was wrong about that.

The door slammed open, and I jumped up as people poured into the room. Airlie and I exchanged a surprised look as Zeke, Gia, Nikolas, and Evermund all joined us. We hadn't been expecting to see them any time soon.

I crossed over to Zeke, fitting myself under his arm.

"What's happened?" Airlie looked to Evermund. "Was the king very angry?"

"I thought for sure you'd be locked in a tower somewhere," I said to Gia with a grin.

"Ha! That was probably his plan," Gia said. "Along with all kinds of dire punishments. Except just after you left a messenger arrived from the nomads, and now his hands are tied. I'm sure he's even more furious than ever, but he can't do anything about it."

"For now," Nikolas said ominously.

I looked up at Zeke, trying to interpret the suppressed intensity lurking beneath his calm expression.

"What did the message say?" Airlie asked.

"King Fenix has died," Nikolas said, not bothering to mince words. "The nomad delegations are leaving as we speak to hurry back to the Hidden City to be part of voting for the next monarch."

My eyes leaped to Zeke's, fear seizing me. "Does that mean...?"

"I'm sorry, Cadie," he said softly. "I just came to say goodbye."

My arm tightened around him, although I knew I couldn't hold him tightly enough to make him stay.

"I understand," I forced myself to say. "You have to be there to support your mother."

"I do," he agreed. "But that doesn't mean I want to be apart from you. Which is why—"

"We're going, too!" Gia cried, unable to contain herself.

My eyes flew from her back to Zeke. "What?"

He rolled his eyes at Gia, but he couldn't keep the smile from his face.

"I asked permission from Tribe Patrin to invite you to come and witness the vote and coronation. And since I know you've been reluctant about coming to my kingdom, I asked for the twins and Airlie as well."

"But outsiders are never allowed in the Hidden City! Even its location is a secret." I couldn't wrap my mind around the news.

"These are new times, and new cooperation is going to be needed. My mother threw her weight behind the request, so they agreed." His eyes pleaded with me. "Will you come?"

"Of course she will!" Airlie said. "She's just been moping at me because what she really wants to do is visit the nomad lands with you."

"Airlie!" I glared at her.

"What?" She gave me a smug grin. "You know it's true. And this is perfect. Now you can go visit without having to leave me behind."

"What about the raiders?" I asked uneasily. "If both of us are gone…"

"We're the ones they want, remember? The Tartorans should be safe enough in our absence."

"You can't possibly say no, Cadence," Gia said reprovingly. "Think what an insult that would be to the nomads!"

"Since when do you care about that?" Nikolas muttered. "You just want the chance to go to the Hidden City. And to escape Father's wrath over our foolish visit to the raiders."

"I'm sorry," Zeke murmured to me, ignoring the rest of them. "I didn't mean to force your hand. I just panicked when Mother said we had to leave immediately."

I wrapped my free arm around him and squeezed tight. "Don't be silly. This is an amazing opportunity. Thank you."

He exhaled a sigh of relief and dropped a kiss in my hair. "Unfortunately, I really do have to go. Mother won't be happy if they have to wait for me."

I gave him a final, lingering squeeze, forcing myself to let go with a sigh. He cupped my face in both hands, looking into my eyes.

"Come as fast as you can," he whispered.

"I will."

His lips pressed against mine, feather soft and gone too soon, and then he disappeared out the door.

I turned back to the room, still in shock, to find everyone looking at me. I flushed under their various gazes—Airlie slightly shocked, Gia openly laughing, and Nikolas disgusted.

But it was Evermund who spoke, a serious note in his voice. "You all know *new times* isn't the real reason you received this invitation, don't you?" He looked around at each of us.

Airlie sucked in a breath, grasping his meaning instantly.

"They want Cadence." She looked from me to Evermund, her eyes filled with concern.

Evermund nodded. "King Marius might not understand it, but it's the only possible reason the nomads would bend their rule of refusing entry to outsiders." He fixed his eyes on me. "They must want you very much if they're willing to include the rest of us."

"Are you coming too?" I asked, feeling a measure of relief.

He nodded. "When the king was unable to convince the nomads to allow him to send an alternate delegation, he argued that three of you are Guild apprentices and can only travel under the authority of a plants and elements master."

"Master Augusta is to come as well," Gia interjected.

"The fact that they agreed tells us just how committed they are to having you there, Cadence. And while I'll do my best to protect you all—as will Augusta—I have no idea what we might encounter in the Hidden City. Are you sure you want to go?"

I frowned, considering his words. I couldn't deny they made me anxious, but when I tried to picture not going, I couldn't imagine abandoning Zeke.

"What about all of you?" I asked hesitantly. "Do you think we should refuse?"

"Of course we can't refuse!" Gia said. "It would be a horrible insult to the nomads at this point—which is the only reason Father has most reluctantly deferred our punishment. No Tartoran has *ever* visited the Hidden City, and they're allowing two members of the royal family in! With Evermund and Augusta along, as well as any number of guards, I'm sure, it's become an official delegation. This is a diplomatic opportunity

Father can't refuse. Especially when the wild power is encroaching more and more across the border. We might need the help of the nomads before this is all over."

"I have to admit I'm curious to see the Hidden City," Airlie said. "It would be hard not to be. But I don't want to put Cadence—or anyone—in danger." She looked at Evermund with a question in her eyes.

"I agree with Gia, which is why I consented to go," he said. "We can't pass up the opportunity. I just want everyone on their guard." He hesitated. "As long as you don't mind leaving so soon, Airlie. We have to depart in the morning if we're going to make it in time, and you've just been through an extended ordeal."

I looked at Airlie, concern filling me. She'd been telling me about how she wanted to stay put for a while. I should have thought of her straight away.

But the smile on her face was genuine enough to put my fears to rest.

"I always wanted to travel, so I'm not going to say no to this, regardless of the timing. With Gia and Nik along, they can hardly decide to keep us prisoner—which I'm sure is why Zeke thought to relieve our minds by including them. I'm inclined to view this as an exciting opportunity. Especially since it means Cadence can follow Zeke, and the two of us can also stay together." Her eyes dipped down, away from Evermund. "We can all stay together. That's what I care about the most."

I hurried over to put an arm around her shoulders. "Maybe we can even work out my ability while we're with the nomads." I looked around the others. "Surely if we all work together, we can figure it out."

"And once we do," Airlie said, "we convince the nomads to join forces with the Tartorans, and we take down the General."

I looked at her with raised eyebrows. "I thought you wanted us all to stay safe?"

A determined look came over her face. "I do. You asked me what I want, and this is it. I want *all* my friends and family to be safe. So first we grow strong, then we gain allies, and then we take him down. We might not be able to retake Calista, but we can save the remaining Calistans." She met my eyes. "Will you help me?"

I nodded. "Of course."

She looked around at the others, her gaze finishing on Evermund. She tilted her chin defiantly. "Does anyone else have anything to say?"

"Just that it sounds like an excellent plan," he said mildly. "Count me in."

"And us, of course," Gia said. "Because what else are friends for? Besides, it sounds like fun."

Note from the Author

Find out what happens in the nomad lands in book three, Thorns of Hope and Betrayal.

Or for more fantasy, romance, adventure, and intrigue, try my completed Spoken Mage series—where a world of written magic is upended by the first spoken mage—starting with Voice of Power.

To be informed of future releases, as well as A Mage's Influence bonus shorts, please sign up to my mailing list at www.melaniecellier.com.

And if you enjoyed Vines of Promise and Deceit, please spread the word and help other readers find it! You could start by leaving a review on Amazon or Goodreads or Facebook or any other social media site. Your review would be very much appreciated and would make a big difference!

HIDDEN CITY
NOMAD LANDS
KINGDOM of CALISTA
CALINARA
LAKE ATERRA
CADENCE'S HOUSE
HUNTING LODGE
KINGDOM of TARTORA
TARONA
NOMAD LANDS
CELADON RIVER
CELADON RIVER
VIRIDIAN RIVER
VIRIDIAN RIVER
N
S
E
W

Acknowledgments

Writing this book proved more challenging than I anticipated, so I am full of thanks for my team who enabled it to be published as scheduled despite my being my own biggest impediment.

I am constantly full of wonder that I'm so fortunate as to have such a fantastic group of loyal friends as my beta readers. Rachel, Greg, Katie, Priya, and Ber, I hope you know how appreciated you are!

And I would be completely lost without my awesome editors who support me through both the ups and downs of the publishing journey—Mary, Deborah, and Dad, you guys are the best.

Thank you to Karri for the beautiful cover and Rebecca for the map which now has pride of place on my office wall.

To my amazing husband, thank you. To my patient, sweet children—I've now finished and we can have all the snuggles you want!

And thank You, God, for everything, always.

About the Author

Melanie Cellier grew up on a staple diet of books, books and more books. And although she got older, she never stopped loving children's and young adult novels.

She always wanted to write one herself, but it took three careers and three different continents before she actually managed it.

She now feels incredibly fortunate to spend her time writing from her home in Adelaide, Australia where she keeps an eye out for koalas in her backyard. Her staple diet hasn't changed much, although she's added choc mint Rooibos tea and Chicken Crimpies to the list.

She writes young adult fantasy including books in her *Spoken Mage* world, her *Mage's Influence* world, and her various *Four Kingdoms* and *Kingdoms of Legacy* series that are made up of linked stand-alone stories that retell classic fairy tales.